King and Kingdom

Danielle Bourdon

Published by Wildbloom Press
Copyright © 2013

*For Sandy Bourdon, who had more of an
influence on my life than she will ever know.
Thank you.*

Chapter One

Chey stared at the door to the Queen's private parlor with trepidation and a niggle of fear. Was she about to get fired? Kicked out of the castle? Any number of things might happen, none of them good. Three days had passed since the attempt on Chey's life. Three days since she had decided to remain in Latvala and allow the heir of the throne to court her. The decision was not without risk and consequence, the latter of which she was about to become intimately familiar. For the Queen surely summoned her here to lambast her for the treachery she was foisting upon the Royal family.

Who knew dating could be so hazardous to one's health?

Smoothing her palms over her outfit, Chey glanced down at the pale pink pencil skirt and modest short coat. It was fashionable, sensible, and suitable for a meeting with Royalty. The three inch nude heels she wore with it were understated and plain.

Just then, she wished it was a suit of armor, capable of deflecting the Queen's scathing looks and viper tongue.

But it wasn't, and so, taking a deep breath, Chey knocked on the door.

"Come," said a regal, bored sounding voice from inside.

She's just a woman, not a God. Don't let her scare you. Chey opened the door, stepped in, and closed it behind her. The latch caught with a quiet click. Resisting the urge to reach up and fix an escaped lock of dark hair, Chey turned around.

As ever, when she entered any private domain of the Royals, Chey was struck by the opulence. Light peach and cream was the color scheme, with gold accents on frames, furniture and chandeliers. Painted in the style of an old master, the middle of the ceiling sported a scene of an expansive sky and half draped humans in dramatic poses. Crown molding surrounded it, like one gigantic frame. It was nothing less than breathtaking.

The parlor itself was the size of a small house, with a roaring fireplace against one wall and a balcony accessible through one of four French doors.

Queen Helina Ahtissari sat in a

wingback chair with a drink in her hand. Cool and aloof, the woman with dark hair and equally dark eyes wore her middle age well; whether it was by nature or the edge of a blade was difficult to tell. A few defining wrinkles creased her forehead and the corners of her down-turned mouth. Crows feet added personality, rather than charm. The expensive gown of pale grey brought to mind myths from ancient Greece, with fine gold rope wrapping Helina's modest waist and hips.

"Your Highness." Chey decided to dip the Queen a curtsy, even if it went against her grain. She hadn't been raised to show subservience to people, only respect after it was earned. Still, she was in *their* house, in *their* country, and she gave the Queen her due.

Helina looked unimpressed. Using the wine glass, she gestured to a less grand chair positioned opposite her own. With a thick accent she said, "Have a seat."

Not please, or will you.

Chey stepped over to the seat and sat on the edge. She didn't want to recline and even try to get comfortable. Comfort in this woman's presence was impossible.

"Thank you," Chey said. She waited, maintaining eye contact with Helina.

The Queen took her time getting to the point. She studied Chey as if she was an insect that had just crawled out from under the carpet and was determining the most expedient process of eradication.

"Let me be frank and to the point," Helina said. "No matter how close you get with my son, Prince Dare, there will, and can *never* be, anything more between you than occasional lovers. If you have visions of crowns and thrones swimming around your young head, I suggest you banish them now."

Taken aback at the blunt assessment, Chey rested her palms on her knees and fought down a flash of anger. "I have no designs on a title. But I will not lie and say that I'll ignore Sander—Dare—for the duration of my contract. What happens between your son and myself is our business--"

"No, child, it is not *just* your business." Helina interrupted Chey without apology or remorse. "You understand nothing of Kingdoms and the Monarchy. We are centuries strong, this family, and one little hellion from America will not displace us from our course. We have signed the contract, true, and it is not our way to break our word. But I will do exactly that and send you back to your homeland if I so much as suspect that you're attempting to finagle your way deeper into Dare's life. Have your fling, your wild nights." Helina flicked her fingers dismissively. "Also understand a relationship as you know it will not happen."

The contract, which tethered Chey to the country of Latvala and the Royal family for four months, was a legally binding document. Chey had it checked before she'd departed the United States. Here to professionally photograph the Royals through the encroaching seasons, she was not due to depart Latvala until February. However, she also knew there was language contained within that the Royals could use under duress to release themselves from fulfilling their end of the deal.

"I am here first and foremost to work. That's my main focus," Chey said, deciding to side-step any mention of a relationship. She and Sander agreed she would see the contract through to the end and at the same time, see where their attraction led. Nothing more, nothing less.

Helina regarded her in silence for a full minute. She sat forward a few inches and cocked her chin just so. "Do you really believe that we would allow you, or our son for that matter, to make such a mistake? Not only the King and I, but the legislators, our counsel—and many, many others. Think on that before you let your heart get too involved."

Chey read a threat between the lines. A threat that if she did not do as Helina suggested, she might find herself at the bottom of a ditch or some dark, forgotten corner of the castle dungeon. It eerily reminded Chey of the threats she'd received from Elise, the maid who had been hired to kill her. Helina was telling Chey in no uncertain terms that an alliance between she and Dare *would not be allowed.* Period. By any means necessary.

A cold chill raced down Chey's spine.

Helina sat back, reclining once more. She sipped her wine while holding Chey's gaze.

Standing, Chey said, "Is that all?"

"I believe you have received my message as intended." Helina used her fingers to swish Chey away. A shooing motion.

Infuriated at the rude dismissal, Chey pivoted for the exit. Without another word, she departed the parlor, closing the door with a quiet click instead of a satisfying slam.

. . .

It was just these kinds of situations that influenced Chey to believe she never wanted to live this life style. This wasn't the first time her feathers had been ruffled over her lowly status, and it wouldn't be the last. Sander had warned her that her mettle would be tested, that they faced impossible odds in their desire to have something deeper than a few random dates. And *that* encouraged her to want to try harder no matter how annoyed she was with Helina. The contradiction did not escape her.

"What a hell of a position to be in," she muttered to herself as she marched down the hallway of the private wing of the castle. Guards stood at the end, providing protection for the entire floor. Barred from this area unless she was summoned, Chey retreated down the stairs to the second level, where she belonged. It galled her and at the same time, she understood there had to be rules. People could not be allowed to run roughshod through the castle. The Royals needed privacy like everyone else.

Still. It irked her to be constantly put 'in her place'.

Part of her discontent had to do with Sander's subsequent absence. Three evenings ago he'd prepared her a delicious dinner, danced with her, and charmed her for hours.

Then nothing. Since that night, she hadn't heard a word from him except a text that had read: *Under siege. You can guess why. Will see you when it's over.*

The King and Queen had likely subjected him to three times the torture she'd just endured. Chey could imagine King Aksel, Sander's father, rolling out demand after demand, using scrupulous means to achieve his end.

In her room, she closed the door and leaned back against it. Not just a bedroom, but an entire apartment that took up a corner of the castle. After the attempt on her life, Sander had moved her here so she wouldn't have to constantly face the fact that someone had died on her old bedroom floor. This sanctuary was more beautiful than the last, with a large living area, separate bedrooms and her own private balcony. Majestic architecture shaped the ceiling and two chandeliers cast sparks and flashes of light through hundreds of teardrop shaped crystals. Works of art decorated the walls and several potted plants added a touch of green.

If she lived here fifty years, she would never grow tired of the splendor. It dazzled her on a constant basis, sometimes bringing her to a dead stop in one hallway or another. Just yesterday, in the back bailey, she'd stared up at the immense castle like a child at Christmas, absorbing all the detail. She'd done so before, while photographing the structure for the Royals, yet every time she saw something new.

What would it be like to become a permanent resident? Any woman with half an imagination would find it as fascinating as she did.

Removing her heels, Chey bent down, picked them up, and padded across Persian carpets toward the bathroom. As large as her apartment back home, the bath had a jacuzzi tub, two sinks, an enormous shower and a walk in closet big enough to house thousands of outfits.

Sliding the heels into a cubby, she peeled out of the suit, glad to be rid of it. Pulling on a long sleeved sweater of faded peach, she donned jeans and was just tugging up the zipper when she heard a knock at her door. Having learned the hard way that it wasn't always who she wanted it to be on the other side, she adapted neutrality on her way through the apartment.

It wasn't Sander who stood in the hall, but Mattias. His brother. The man with hair black as a raven's wing and dark eyes that glittered with intelligence and confidence. He had a tumbler of amber liquid in one hand.

"Hey, Mattias. Come in." Chey had grown used to spending time in Mattias's company. She felt close to him in ways she didn't to anyone else except Sander. He listened when she needed an ear, supported her in the face of hostility, and was genuinely charming to be around. If there had been heat and chemistry between them when she'd first arrived, Chey's time with Sander obliterated all that.

"How did your meeting go?" he asked, passing inside. Tonight Mattias wore sleek black slacks and a steel gray shirt with the sleeves flipped back to his elbows. Casual elegance, which seemed to be Mattias's usual fare.

Chey closed the door but didn't engage the lock. Following him to the seating arrangement in the living room, she plopped unceremoniously down onto a divan and tucked one leg beneath her. That was the level of comfort she displayed for the second in line to the throne.

"As terrible as you can imagine. It makes me cringe to think what they might be saying or doing to Sander." She secretly hoped Mattias had news of his brother.

Mattias chose a plush chair to sink down into. Arranging his limbs for comfort, he drew a foot up to rest his ankle across the opposite knee. Taking a drink, he arched his brows in understanding. "I'm sorry to hear it. What did she say, specifically?"

Chey twirled a piece of hair around her finger, elbow resting on the arm of the sofa. "That a relationship wouldn't be allowed, at all, between us. I got the impression that if Sander and I attempted to make it more, someone would physically do something to stop it."

"The cabinet and top military brass do all the hard lifting, as it were, regarding things of this nature. They do what's best for the country following the ideals of the King. Most of them are old school hardliners and agree that marriages should be arranged for financial and political gain. You won't find any friends there and you're right—they *will* attempt to derail this relationship." Mattias sipped from his glass and maintained eye contact.

"So this will be an uphill battle all the way."

"Yes. But you knew that," Mattias said.

"Sander warned me." And she'd made the decision to stay. To try.

"It's up to you to decide whether he's worth it. Obviously you think so, or you would have been back home by now."

"Of course I think he's worth it." Chey released her hair and rubbed her forehead instead. "It's just—how many people have to start off a relationship this way? We only had a week together without all this other stress and strain. I don't want all the chemistry between us sucked out of our time together because we're both aware this will probably go nowhere."

"This is only the beginning, Chey.

Nothing, and I do mean nothing, is easy about this life. If I were you, I would concentrate on your time with Sander and try to forget the rest. You'll know when you can't take anymore."

"Yes, and by then, my heart will likely be in a hundred shattered pieces."

"It's a good possibility."

"You're not very reassuring, Mattias."

"It's not my job to reassure you. It's for your own benefit that I'm straight with you."

"If Sander would have been honest from the beginning..." Chey didn't finish the thought. There were times she harbored anger over his deception. If he'd just informed her that he was the heir to the throne, they might not be in this mess.

Then again, she wouldn't be dating Sander, either, and she wasn't willing to just throw in the towel because someone else told her to.

"Neither here nor there," Mattias correctly guessed. "You've forgiven him already, which is why you agreed to stay."

"I hate that you can read me so well." Chey quirked her mouth at Mattias.

He swirled the drink in his glass. "It pays to be aware around here."

"Apparently. So you think Sander and I should allow whatever relationship between us to develop, but not expect it to ever amount to anything. I'm surprised you condone that, to be honest." Chey expected Mattias to advise cut-and-run, before it was too late.

"Like I told you that day at lunch. This is rare. What you and Dare might build between you happens once every other lifetime. I think it's risky, and I think there's probably a lot of heartache in both of your futures, but sometimes you have to take risks to win a greater reward." He finished off his drink and set the tumbler on the side table. Mattias's expression changed little, giving no hints to what he was thinking inside.

Chey considered his words. *A lot of heartache in your future.* She knew he was right. It shocked her that she was willing to take the chance even though getting hurt was a distinct possibility.

"I guess time will tell," she said. "What happened to Viia?" Viia, Mattias's former fiance, had been the mastermind behind the attacks on Chey. Jealously and fear seemed to be her reasons for taking action.

Mattias glanced at the dark panes of

the windows. Night cloaked the land beyond the castle. "She swears she had nothing to do with any of it."

"Of course she would say that. I'm sure she doesn't want to go to jail." Chey fiddled with the seam of her jeans. She thought she saw indecision flicker across Mattias's features.

"Jail for someone like her is the least of her worries. What this will do to her reputation is the real punishment," he said.

"Why do I get the impression that you might have doubt she was behind the attacks?" Chey frowned. Did Mattias feel more for Viia than he let on?

"Because I do have doubt," he replied with quiet confidence.

"Tell me what's on your mind."

Bringing a hand up, Mattias curled his fingers next to his mouth, still staring at the windows. Finally, he glanced at Chey's eyes. "Viia is many things. Conniving, truculent, petty, a social climber. I never suspected her of arranging murder. If so, I would not have coddled my mother and dated her even for a day."

"If I'm honest, I had my own doubts that Viia was behind it as well," Chey confessed.

15

"Why?"

"Well. First, it seemed a stretch to me that someone like Elise, with her standing and position in the house, would risk it on someone who wasn't actually a part of the family yet. And...I don't know. Something just felt *off*. Convenient, maybe." Chey struggled to put the sensations and emotions into words.

"Yes, Viia was very convenient, given her attitude toward you." Mattias frowned, a faint flicker that came and went on his brow.

"But if it wasn't her, then that leaves...your sister." Chey hated to even bring it up. Natalia, the youngest member of the Royal siblings, had it out for Chey from day one. What was more, the woman made no bones with her threats and her discontent that Chey was still in residence. Bracing for backlash and anger from Mattias, Chey regarded him warily. To her surprise, he didn't surge off the couch in his sister's defense.

"Mm." He hummed a quiet note of consideration. There was a disturbance in his dark eyes and displeasure turned the corners of his mouth down.

"Is she capable of it?" Chey asked, pressing the issue. Just how many people would she have to fend off to date Sander?

Mattias fell to silence. It stretched thick in the room between them. Only the crack and hiss of the fire interrupted the pause. Finally, he said, "I suppose she is."

"You sound purposefully vague."

"There are many things I know that I cannot say." He leveled a knowing look on her.

Chey understood then that the Royal family did indeed have dark secrets, and only the immediate family and a few close advisers would ever have knowledge of them.

"I see," she said. "If I don't go home, then the terror may begin again."

"Natalia may not like you, but she won't simply crank out orders for your demise on a daily basis. Trust that she's been talked to about all this and knows she's being watched."

"I'm not sure if I feel better or worse."

"Sander has his own pull. She will only defy him so far, so perhaps, if she *did* know of Viia's plans or helped to suggest things, she will now let it drop." Mattias moved his foot from his knee back to the floor and sat forward in the chair. He stared across the space with a contemplative expression.

"Sander had a talk with her?" Chey, surprised to hear it, regarded Mattias curiously.

"Yes, as have the advisers. Many others have been questioned as well, to see if anyone else had been brought into the plans."

"And what did you find?" Chey braced herself for bad news.

"It does not appear that anyone else was involved. If there were others, they're not talking. We've snipped the tail from the snake. With any luck, we've also severed the head." He stood in a smooth, effortless motion. "I need to be going."

Chey stood when he did. "I hope you're right. Thanks for stopping by."

"Of course." He smiled and turned for the door.

Chey followed. When Mattias stepped into the hall, she posed one more question for him. "Mattias? Is it true that you were just using Viia to keep your mother from setting you up with other women?"

He swayed to a stop, looked down the hallway, then swiveled a glance back to Chey. There was no deception in his eyes or his voice. "Yes. I never made Viia any promises."

"I was just curious. You two were an ill fit from the beginning, as far as I could tell. At least I know all my instincts aren't off." Chey leaned against the door. "Have a good evening."

Mattias inclined his head, then started off down the hall.

Closing the door, Chey retreated into her apartment and snatched her phone off a side table, hoping for a text from Sander. She needed contact, a message. *Something.*

The screen gave her an unpleasant answer: *No new messages.*

Chapter Two

"How fast can you pack?"

Chey jumped when Sander spoke behind her, so close to her ear. In the kitchen—which was not off limits to her— she set down the butter knife and twitched a look back and up.

"You startled me. Pack for what? Hello." She squeezed in her questions and greetings all at the same time. Struck by how clear and blue Sander's eyes were, and by the sense of expectancy he exuded, she left the sandwich she'd been making on the counter and gave him her full attention.

He cut a fast smile and leaned in to kiss her right on the mouth.

None of the chefs or their aids elsewhere in the expansive kitchen said a word. No one bothered them at all.

"Hello. For a trip. I've cleared your schedule for the next four days."

A day had passed since her meeting with the Queen and Mattias's unexpected visit. Chey hadn't heard from Sander the entire time. She had half a mind to voice her ire over his silence; in the end, she was more interested in this proposed trip than she was wasting her breath on admonishment. At least for now.

"A trip where? I can pack very fast, trust me." If it meant time alone with Sander, Chey would make Speedy Gonzales resemble a snail. She tried to turn all the way around to face him, but he crowded her back, towering over her with his height and masculine scent.

"It's a surprise. Bring something comfortable and something dressy. I'll meet you in the courtyard in a half an hour."

"But is it here, or is it--"

"Shhh." He silenced her with another kiss.

Chey palmed his jaw, reaching across her body and over her shoulder. She lingered in the kiss, then smiled. "You're on. I'll be there in time."

He winked and receded like the tide.

Chey watched him go. She had to admit, he looked as good in his black slacks and black button down as he did in the more rugged gear he wore outdoors. The breadth of his shoulders was more pronounced in the tailored shirt as well as the leanness of his hips.

With quick motions, she cleaned up her mess from lunch, snagged her half tuna sandwich off the counter, and departed the kitchen at a brisk walk. Like the heathen some here thought her to be, she ate on the fly, holding a napkin under the bread to prevent crumbs from littering the polished floor.

By the time she reached her apartment, the sandwich was gone and the napkin rolled into a ball. Evening was encroaching once more, the landscape giving way to darkness. The snows that had gripped Latvala four days past had melted, the skies cleared of the storm.

In short order, Chey had a suitcase and overnight bag packed. She chose jeans and sweaters, a silk shirt or two, and several pieces of a more formal make for the trip. It would have helped if she'd known their destination. Regardless, she thought she'd covered the basic necessities at the very least. The jeans and red sweater she wore would have to do for travel.

Of course, she brought one of her cameras.

Excitement and anticipation gripped

her as she left the apartment with eight minutes to spare. A guard outside her door held a hand out for her suitcase; after reminding herself that this was expected of her, she passed it over. Keeping the overnight bag, she made her way down to the first level and across the immense foyer to the front doors. They opened just as she reached for a heavy, iron handle.

She suffered a surreal moment when she saw Sander standing next to a silver limousine, door open, his security detail spread out around the courtyard. Not a week ago, she'd witnessed Sander departing the castle in this very manner. Now she had a different view than one from a distance, behind the lens of her camera.

In the time since finding her in the kitchen and now, Sander had added a sport coat to go with his attire. All in black, he looked refined, decadent, yet somehow rakish. The length of his hair was loose instead of caught back into a tail and his jaw sported a layer of golden whiskers. He smiled, flashing a line of straight, white teeth. Then he tilted his head toward the waiting limousine, silently cajoling her to snap out of her stupor and get in.

That was when she realized she was standing half in and half out of the doorway, blocking anyone else from coming or going, and that the men surrounding the car were staring.

Galvanized into motion, wearing a sheepish grin, Chey crossed the porch and slid into the limousine. Setting her overnight bag on the floor at her feet, she tucked wayward strands of hair behind her ears and glanced over when Sander got in.

"Sorry. Sometimes all this doesn't seem real."

"Don't apologize. Your deer in the headlight look is amusing." He closed his door and immediately slung an arm up behind her along the back of the seat, grinning like the devil himself.

"Stop being so smug." She pinched his ribs.

Laughing, he curved his body away and set his hand on the armrest, where several buttons sat at his disposal. He depressed one that raised the privacy divider between the back of the car and the front.

Chey noted that this limousine was more lavish than the previous ones she'd ridden in. The seats were ivory leather, with steel gray carpeting on the floor and lighter gray around the rest of the interior. Thin strips of gold added accent around the small bar and the base of the seats. The family crest was present in gold as well on each door.

With an SUV in front and one following behind, the limousine pulled away from the castle and cruised through the tunnel toward the gate.

"What do you think?" he asked, settling in. Sander draped himself comfortably on the seat, knees tipped out, jacket open down the front.

Chey sought to get as comfortable as Sander looked. Resting her hands on her lap, she glanced out the windows, then across the seat.

"I won't lie. A part of me misses the cabin days," she said. When Sander had been just the head of security and she had just been the photographer. Which she still was—and yet not. Everything had changed as she knew it. "The other part of me doesn't know what to do with all...this." She gestured toward the interior of the limousine, indicating his lifestyle in general.

"There will always be cabin days. We

can go back any time you want." Sander tipped his gaze over the interior of the vehicle in the way a man did when he was immune to the luxury. "I suppose it is a little overwhelming."

"A *little?*" Chey puffed a quiet laugh. "It's more than overwhelming. I'm just not used to it. I keep forgetting that someone else gets the door, and brings breakfast, and takes the luggage."

"I have no problem with you carrying your own things. Except in the presence of foreign dignitaries or other people of importance. You'll be expected to accept it." He studied her with an amused look.

The limousine cruised along the open road, picking up speed. On her left, the ocean glimmered like liquid satin under the moon. To the right, the meadows of Ahtissari land stretched into the darkness.

"And I'm guessing that's common. Meeting up with important people." Chey was still trying to wrap her head around the reality of it all.

"Yes. Balls, formal dinners, soirees, luncheons, honorary ceremonies—you name it. It slows down in winter, but doesn't come to a complete stop. Then it gets crazy in spring and summer. I'll tell you a little secret though. I slip out often, like the Sander you got to know in the woods, and go among the people. Visit pastry shops, buy a paper, stop and talk. It makes security crazy because I insist they can't go with me. But the citizens of Latvala love it. I think they've come to expect my visits without all the guards. I was thinking maybe one day you'd like to go with me."

Chey could see Sander doing exactly that. Dressing down, wandering from one shop to another, being normal like everyone else. It was one more thing that endeared him to her. "I'd really like that, yes."

"Excellent," he said, sounding genuinely pleased at her reply.

Considering all that, she looked out the windows. She wasn't sure, exactly, but she thought they were heading toward the private landing strip. Interesting. Where was he taking her? Getting back to the topic of soirees, she said, "The party I attended with Mattias was interesting. The little I got to see of it, anyway. Oh— who was that guy? Prince Severian or something?"

Sander's silence drew Chey's attention back across the car.

A pensive expression crossed his features. "He's third in line to the throne on Weithan Isle. Brother to the woman I'm supposed to marry."

. . .

The transition from limo to private plane disrupted any retort Chey might have made about 'the woman I'm supposed to marry'. At least until they were ensconced in the familiar, plush seats, buckled in, and taxiing down the runway. This was another luxury she would never get used to: simply flying wherever on a whim, with no bother about reservations, long lines or busy terminals.

Finally, she pinned a look on Sander after the stewardess delivered a bottle of chilled water for her and a glass of some sort of liquor or another for him.

He eyed her like he knew what was coming and had his first drink.

"Just how serious is it?" she asked.

"How serious am I about her, or how serious is the situation regarding the marriage itself? I have no plans to walk down the aisle with her, but the King and Queen, along with their advisers and council members, have begun making private arrangements."

Chey felt a stirring of anger. She straightened the leather piece over the arm of her chair, then straightened it again. Fidgeting. "And there is nothing you can do about that? I mean, if you say no, that should mean no, right?"

"They're making political arrangements, not wedding arrangements. One eventually leads to the other, however, and it won't be long until they apply pressure for a commitment." He had another drink.

"It all seems very pointless to me. You won't do it, yet they're going ahead anyway. Why bother if they know you won't agree?" Chey didn't understand. She needed him to spell it out for her.

"Because they think I'll eventually change my mind. There have been," he paused, then continued, "persuasions put in place."

"What kind of persuasions?"

"The kind that remove me from my position in line to the throne."

Chey gasped. "What? You can't be serious."

"I'm absolutely serious. Valentina Novak is second in line to the throne in her country, quite powerful in her own right, and is well appointed in Royal circles. She's made all the right connections and knows how to use them. In short, she's a force to be reckoned with."

"I suppose she supports this whole arranged marriage idea, too." Chey couldn't see many women in their right mind turning down Sander for anything.

"She does."

"How long have they been attempting to foist her off on you?"

"Mm...three years now, I guess?"

"*Three* years? I thought this was something relatively new." Incredulous, Chey stared hard at Sander's profile. The blazer spread open wider when he raked a hand back through his hair and she had a difficult time not looking at his chest.

"No. I have resisted making anything serious, although I have spent time in her company."

A spike of white-hot jealousy raged through Chey. What an unusual sensation. She wasn't used to feeling it. "Really."

He glanced at her eyes. "Yes. Several

times, I was duped into meeting her. Meaning the King's people made plans with her people and I arrived at a place thinking I was doing one thing, when in reality, I was doing another."

"That's unbelievably forward," she pointed out.

He laughed. "This is the way of it, Chey. I'm sorry if it sounds cold, but this is minor compared to some of the things that go on. Get used to it." With an indifferent arch of his brows, he finished off his drink.

Chey leaned sideways in her seat, peering at his eyes.

He frowned. "What are you doing?"

"Looking for the Sander that tackled me off a horse. Because you must be an impostor. The Sander I got to know canoeing and in the old ruin of a castle wouldn't put up with tactics like that."

"I never said I *stayed.* Why do you think they keep setting up meetings? Once I know what's going on, I usually take my leave."

"Usually?"

"Every once in a while, I'm not in a position to depart."

"What kind of position would that be?"

"Did you take classes on

interrogation?" he asked with a laugh.

Relenting in the face of his humor—it was difficult to stay annoyed with him for long—Chey took a drink from her bottle. Then she said, "I'm waiting."

"I can see that."

Silence.

"The kind of position where other, important people were present and to simply walk away would have painted me in a bad light. Things I do in public will be remembered."

"So really, she's a perfect match for you. Politically speaking." Chey reclined into her seat once more. It bothered her on many levels to know that others in the Royal family wanted this match badly enough to resort to clandestine machinations.

"Politically speaking."

Chey considered his tone. The implication was that although Valentina might be a good match politically, he wasn't interested on a personal level. She supposed she could take heart that Sander wasn't intent on seeing the charade through. He wasn't like Mattias, who would follow his orders regardless of his own personal feelings.

Or would he?

"And if they remove your right to ascend the throne?" She fiddled with the cap on the bottle then set it in the holder to the side of the chair.

"That's where it gets tricky. Right now, it's all just threats. The people of Latvala want me as their eventual King, and their voice is strong. Never mind it has been centuries since one heir was skipped to put another in his place."

"But it *has* been done."

"Yes." He lidded his eyes and accepted a refreshed glass from the stewardess.

Chey watched him take a drink. The muscles of his throat contracted as he swallowed, bringing to mind several times when she'd had her mouth there.

"What?" he asked, before meeting her gaze. Like he'd felt her staring.

"Nothing. It's all very complicated and confusing for someone like me who isn't used to how this all works." After giving him a small smile, she looked out the oval window at her shoulder. There wasn't anything to see, not even a glimmer of lights far below. Maybe they were still over water.

"I know it is. But you're handling it well so far."

The warm praise turned Chey's

attention back to Sander. "Really? Because I feel completely out of my depth here."

"Of course you do. But back to a moment ago—you weren't thinking about complications. You were looking at my throat."

"Yes. Yes, I was." Why deny it? Sander knew her well.

"I bet I know what you were thinking, too." His tone took a devilish turn.

Chey contained a smile with effort, but she knew her eyes were gleaming with intrigue and interest. "I bet you don't."

He tilted his shoulders closer and mock whispered. "Come with me, and I'll tell you in private."

"In private?" She couldn't see over the high back of the seat, but Chey had seen a short hall at the back of the plane and several doors.

"Yes." He set his glass down and stood. Holding a hand out for her to take, he watched her eyes.

There was just no way she would pass this up. Removing her buckle, she took his hand and let him lead her through the plane. It was situated more like a luxury living room than not, with sofas facing each other, leather chairs at angles to one another, and a television screen tacked to a wall. She thought forty people could comfortably reside in the available seating. Passing a smaller door that proved to be a bathroom as well as the galley, Sander led her straight back and into a decadent bedroom that boasted a king sized bed, two dressers, one thick chair and two small closets. The color scheme matched the rest of the plane, lavish and expensive.

The door closed with a decisive click.

"But the stewardess will know--" Chey didn't get far with her surprised protest.

Sander stepped close and cupped her jaw in his hands. "Of course she'll know. It's hard to hide on a plane. So let me tell you what you were thinking, and then I'll open the door."

Chey wasn't sure she wanted him to open the door. She all but melted in his hands, face tipped up to his. Another one of those surreal moments hit her broadside; she couldn't believe she was on a plane, in a Prince's arms, on the way to some exotic locale. "Okay. Tell me."

"You were thinking about those times in bed when you almost left marks on my neck. And you weren't just thinking about leaving the marks, but the rest of it, too."

He cut her a knowing grin.

Chey rested her hands on his hips and basked in his attention. "I won't lie. That's exactly what I was thinking about. Good thing we didn't bet for real."

Without warning, he kissed her. Hard and full, tongue searching out all the secret places of her mouth. Arching into him, she slid her hands around his back under the coat, following the shape of the muscle along his spine. He was built solid and sturdy, shoulders temporarily blocking out the room. The kiss changed angles and depth and became something more serious when she slipped a groan past his lips. Then it was a matter of shedding clothes along with her modesty; there would be no hiding what they'd done when they returned to their seats.

He laid her down on the bed less like she was fragile and more like he meant to claim her. It was the way he loved her, too, relentless and confident and primal. He whispered her name twice, once to drive her toward the edge, and again in the aftermath of ecstasy. The intensity of it left Chey dizzy and disoriented. In these most private moments, she opened her heart to him, let him hear and see and feel just how much he moved her.

In return he engulfed her in his arms, shielding her with his body, as if he meant to never let anything hurt her again.

Chapter Three

The city of Monte Carlo sparkled in the waning hours of the night. Chey stared at the glittery buildings out the window of a limousine that ferried them along an avenue next to the harbor. Even this late, people were everywhere. On the docks, partying on yachts, crossing from one lavish hotel casino to another. The playground for the ultra rich teemed with life and the promise of a good time.

Tucked against Sander's side, one hand resting on his chest, she watched as the avenue cut away for a drive leading into an expansive, beautiful hotel right on the water. A simple yet elegant sign identified the structure as *The Trident.* Tall and majestic, the hotel sprawled over the ground with its stunning mediterranean architecture on prominent display. Ivory columns supported an arched overhang that protected doors leading in.

It wasn't this more obvious front

entrance that the limousine navigated to, but a private VIP area replete with a breezeway for easy unloading and loading. Security was thicker here, with uniformed men guarding all three sides of the breezeway as well as the drive. Sander's personal security, in two separate SUVs, parked ahead and behind and kept watch while they disembarked.

Still reeling from their tryst on the plane, Chey got her feet on the ground and accepted the elbow Sander elegantly offered her.

"Thanks. This place is amazing," she said, trying not to gawk. Chey, distantly aware of the difference between Sander's regal authority and her childlike wonder, attempted to act more like she'd done this before. It wasn't easy. She'd never moved in the circles of people who *expected* this kind of treatment.

"It's the nicest hotel in Monte Carlo," he whispered near her ear. He winked on the sly, then headed toward the double smoked glass doors. One was held open by a doorman.

"Your Highness, it's good to have you stay with us again," another man said, obviously a manager by the cut and cloth of his suit. He smiled and inclined his head. "Would you like anything sent up to your room straight away?"

"Robert, nice to see you," Sander replied. There was a briskness to the edges of his accent that hadn't been there before. "Only the things I asked for when I made the reservation."

"Everything is accounted for." The manager escorted them inside and into a hallway immediately to the left. It ran along the the back of the hotel and had adequate security guarding the entrance.

Sander's men swarmed by and cleared the way. Others lingered behind, bringing up the rear.

"Excellent." Sander said no more.

Chey had the sensation of watching this from a distant perspective, as if she wasn't the woman on Sander's arm. The edges of the picture were fuzzy, distorted. Ferried along toward a waiting elevator, Chey tried to clear her head, tried to get a grip on the here and now. It was all so foreign, the way people treated Sander—and herself. From the discreet glances, to the reverence in their actions, to the way people anticipated what Sander wanted before he asked.

Escorted into a lavish elevator, Chey stood next to Sander with her fingers clutching his arm harder than she meant to. As if he understood, he reached across with his other hand and laid his fingers over her own. His skin was warm, the weight firm and sturdy.

Pushing a button, the manager, who rode in the carriage with them along with several security members, watched the numbers light up and did not make small talk. When a *ding* announced their arrival on the correct floor, the manager stepped aside so the security could proceed him out into the hallway.

Once the all clear came, Sander led Chey into an area that resembled a foyer, the décor luxurious and expensive. A divan, small table, and one wingback chair sat against the far wall. To the right, a short hall was the only access to a pair of elaborate doors that the manager set a brisk pace for.

Chey took it all in with growing excitement. That strange sense of distance evaporated the second the manager opened one of the doors and gestured inside. The penthouse Sander accompanied her into after his security swept through was a study in cream walls, white crown molding, glittery chandeliers and ritzy furniture fanned out over a shockingly large area. Doors to several bedrooms led off the main room, which was equipped with a kitchen, dining room, and floor to ceiling windows with a view of the ocean. A long balcony could be seen thanks to small lights set every few feet along a waist high wall. Flowers of all colors, sizes and shapes had been set about in vases that accentuated the rich setting.

She wasn't sure where to look first. Sander led her further in while one of the security passed the manager a healthy tip.

"Will everything suit, Your Highness?" the manager asked, discreetly thanking the security for the envelope before he tucked it inside his coat pocket.

"For now, yes. Thank you, Robert." Sander smiled with cordial finality.

"Very good. Ring for anything you need," Robert said, before departing the room.

After the following security members brought in the luggage and closed the door on their way out, Sander glanced at Chey. "What do you think?"

"It's staggering. So much space for two people." Releasing his elbow, she headed to a table where a Welcome basket had been left by the hotel staff. Fruit, cheeses and two unopened bottles of wine sat ready for consumption. Two more bottles of wine in silver buckets flanked one of the vases of flowers. Real flowers, Chey noted, not fake ones.

"With a fantastic view, too, which you'll be able to see a lot better by morning. Do you want something to drink and open a few presents, or do you want to go straight down to the casino?" Sander strolled to the balcony doors and opened one. The lights from the harbor framed his masculine silhouette, outlining his broad shoulders and narrow hips.

Chey explored the living room, then glanced at Sander. She spent a few moments just appreciating how regal he looked in his suit and how different he seemed from the khaki wearing canoe guide who had heckled her over a game of Scrabble. He distracted her from all that with one particular word: "Presents?"

"Look in the master suite," he said with an amused glance over his shoulder.

Chey found the double doors leading into the main suite and paused just past the threshold. The room, as luxurious as the rest of the penthouse, sported an enormous bed situated against the far wall. Spread out over the pale blue and gold accented covers, several elegant gift boxes waited to be opened. Always a sucker for surprises, she forced herself to forgo the pleasure of opening them in favor of sight seeing.

"I think I'll wait. It can wait, right?" Backtracking, Chey advanced on Sander until she stood right behind him. Helping herself to his person, she wrapped her arms around his middle. He was tall enough that when she pressed her cheek against his back, her head only reached the spot between his shoulder blades.

"Yes, it can wait. But I'm changing before we go down." Arching an arm back, he half hugged her, then turned in her grasp until he was facing her. "Give me a few minutes. I'll be quick."

She got on her tiptoes to kiss his mouth. "Are you crazy? I'm coming to watch."

He kissed her around a laugh. "All right then."

After a squeeze, she released him.

He brought some of their luggage into the bedroom and unpacked jeans, a steel gray sweater and boots. As promised, it only took him a few minutes to do the deed. Chey watched from her lean against the doorway, arms crossed over her chest. Without shame, she admired his chest, the ripple of muscle in his stomach, and the thickness of his thighs. Catching his gaze when he glanced up once or twice, she smiled.

The smile he gave her in return was rife with deviant intent.

"Now that's the Sander I met in the woods," she said.

"Is that an invitation to tackle you to the ground?" He surged up off the edge of the bed.

Chey laughed and held out a palm. "No!"

"Are you sure? I think you want to be tackled. You're just too shy to ask." He stalked her, resplendent even in simple clothes.

Chey backed out of the doorway, stricken by a bout of laughter. "Sander, I will *hurt* you if you tackle me."

"That's not really a threat." He bent suddenly when he was within range and scooped her up by the hips. Over his shoulder she went. The sound of an obnoxious crack against her backside wrought a startled yelp out of her.

"Sander!" She pinched his back to no avail. "This is so not Royal-like."

"Exactly. Now, the only thing I have to decide is whether or not to carry you all the way to the casino like this."

. . .

Rows upon rows of slot machines, poker tables, craps, keno—none of it kept her attention like watching Sander in a crowd. With his security forming a loose circle around them, they made their way through the expansive gambling area, discussing what to play. As if people knew (and perhaps some of them did) that he was someone of note, men and women both whispered behind their hands, staring until he was out of sight. Even a few of the hotel employees loitered nearby, though Chey suspected it was more out of a desire to serve him and receive a hefty tip than to get his autograph or have their picture taken with Royalty.

Sander, exuding supreme confidence and sexy nonchalance, escorted her with a hand either at her back or with his elbow. He paused once or twice to point something out, yet Chey had trouble following his gestures. Drawn to his power, his masculine grace, she murmured incoherent replies until finally, he glanced down straight into her eyes. A flicker of amusement moved through his own.

"I'm not a rockstar. Quit looking at me like that."

"But that's what you seem like. So many people know who you are." She whispered so that no one would accidentally overhear.

"Not all of them. It's the security detail, too. Kind of gives it away." He winked. "What do you want to play?"

"Roulette."

"Oh? Is that your favorite?" He arched a brow.

"Yes, actually. My parents and I visited Vegas a few times, and I went with some of my friends." She broke eye contact and brought a hand up to whisk a strand of hair from her cheek. Chey wondered if things would always feel this surreal. Any second, she expected to wake up back in Seattle, with all of this nothing more than a very pleasant dream.

"Then Roulette it is." He changed direction, guiding her past several banks of five dollar slots, until they came to the roulette tables. The floor manager gestured to another table cordoned off by red rope. Sander declined with a cordial smile.

"What was that about? Do they have separate tables for people like you?" Chey asked, glancing between the floor manager and Sander.

"Yes, and even more in rooms off this one. Strictly catering to high rollers. I thought it might be more fun, for now anyway, to just blend in." He gestured to an empty seat at a general roulette table with two other people filling the chairs.

Chey slid onto the leather cushion and realized belatedly that she'd left her purse up in the hotel room. It was in her luggage, of all things, still unpacked.

Sander sat next to her, returning a nod with the dealer and the other occupants at the table who quickly realized they were in the presence of a high profile guest.

"This is good for me," Chey said, relaxing her spine into an arch over the lip of the table. She was about to admit that she'd left her purse in the room, and that they had to go back for it, when she caught sight of the Buy-In placard just past Sander's arm. *$5,000.* The minimum bet was fifty dollars, the maximum five hundred. Chey almost fell off her chair. She knew roulette well enough to understand bets placed outside the inner grid of numbers could be higher than the five hundred dollar 'inside' bet.

She wouldn't have been able to afford this table even if she *did* have her purse. It made her stomach roll and clench to think of betting five hundred at a time on one spin of the wheel. How much were the Buy-Ins at the tables she *couldn't* see? Fifty thousand, a hundred? Glancing aside, she tried to assess whether this was a step down for Sander, gambling wise. He'd sought this table in a more 'normal' area, and though it was high stakes in Chey's world, he was probably used to the back rooms with much higher minimums.

Just when she thought she had her first real taste of the difference between the ultra rich and herself, Sander signed off a marker for the floor manager and the dealer pushed stacks of one hundred and five hundred dollar chips her direction. There wasn't one fifty dollar chip in sight. There were a lot of stacks, high stacks, and though she wasn't a math wizard, she knew there was at least twenty thousand dollars sitting in front of her.

The dealer pushed a similar stack in front of Sander.

Chey stared at the chips with guilt flushing hot under her cheeks. Just a little more than a week and a half ago, she'd been fretting over paying the rent on a moderate apartment in Seattle. Her bank account balance at that time had been laughingly low, and now here she was, about ready to place hundred dollar bets on the whim of a roulette wheel.

She felt...conspicuous. Like someone might march up behind her and start ranting about starving children in foreign countries.

"You want something to drink?" Sander asked, voice quiet between them. Then he glanced at her face. "What's wrong?"

Chey met his eyes. She couldn't very well explain herself, because even if she spoke quietly, the dealer, if not the other gamblers, would hear. But trust Sander to guess her thoughts. He smiled without warning and jutted his chin toward the chips.

"Come on, Slinky. I know you must have favorite numbers." He picked up a few chips and began placing them over the board. All red, no black.

"Slinky? When and where did I pick up

that nickname?

"When you sidled up onto your chair a few minutes ago. Slinky." He wagged his brows with ridiculous exaggeration.

That's when Chey understood he was attempting to distract her, make her think about something else than the high number staring back at her on the chips. She laughed, nudged him with an elbow, and passed him a drink order.

Then she got down to the business of trying to at least break even on her bets, so she wouldn't lie awake later, fretting about how many thousands she'd lost.

. . .

Roulette was a smashing hit. Chey got lucky several times, winding up with fifteen thousand dollars more than she started. Which was a good thing, since Sander couldn't buy his luck. When she tried to give him the winnings, he stoutly refused and escorted her to the slot machines next.

Between a few drinks, Sander's easy going manner and laughter, Chey's misgivings about the money disappeared.

They played slots, blackjack, and craps. Sander drew a bigger and bigger crowd as the evening wore on, forced several times to stop for pictures with people from all around the world. He was amiable about it and good natured, always keeping Chey at his side.

It startled Chey to realize how many strangers knew who he was, when she'd never heard his family name before the initial contact for pictures. She really needed to read more about foreign goings-on. This gave her a glimpse of his world outside Latvala, as well, and he impressed her with his knowledge of several other languages when addressing admirers.

Even later in the evening, he took her to one of the hotel's bars and danced slow and close, towering above her with his intense eyes and natural charisma. His raspy, intimate laughter did strange things to her heart.

Well beyond midnight, back in the hotel room, after she'd opened her gifts of beautiful dresses, matching shoes and other, more casual articles fit for Monte Carlo, he took her to bed and reminded her what it felt like to be claimed as well as cherished. He left bruises on her hips and she left furrows down his back.

In the morning they ordered room service, languished in the shower, and got dressed for a sight seeing day. He took her to all the hotspots and she captured it all on camera. The moderate weather cooperated, sun shining down, a few clouds scuttling across a pristine blue sky. They lunched on a yacht, bought souvenirs, and flirted like the new couple they were. Sander treated her with charm and chivalry that did not come across as contrived. Everything he did, from carrying her shopping bags to opening doors was natural and easy. Together, they had an alluring rapport that often ended in either witty banter, outrageous come-ons or stolen kisses.

The longer she spent in his company, the more smitten Chey became. She could feel herself falling deeper with every roguish smile, every act of kindness, every lingering glance.

Back in the room, after an order-in dinner, Sander had some surprising news.

"We have an engagement tonight at nine," he said, finishing off the last of his wine.

Chey glanced up from the balcony chair, reclining now that she'd had her fill of the meal. "An engagement? What kind of engagement?"

"You'll see. Wear that long dress I got you, all right?" He set down his glass and rose from his chair.

"Sure. Why are you being so secretive?" She pretended to scrutinize him, but the playful gleam in her eyes gave the game away. When he rose, she did the same.

He flashed her a devious smile. "Because if you knew, then you probably wouldn't want to go with me."

"Now you have to tell me."

"No I don't." He winked. "I'll use the shower in the guest bedroom after making a few phone calls so you can have plenty of time to do that girly thing you do."

"I really hate when you do that. Tease." She didn't really hate it, she just liked to harass him.

"It's one of my many charms." He retreated to one of the bedrooms he was using as a temporary office with a smile still in place.

Chey followed him inside, content to absorb the ambiance of the suite and the lingering effect of his presence for another few minutes. Habitually, she readjusted the bottle of wine in the bucket so that it sat better in the ice. Next she turned the thin but pretty vase of flowers in the middle of the table so that its best side faced the front of the room. All these little tics pointed to growing nerves about the 'engagement' coming up this evening. What could it be? Would she fit in, or feel awkward because she wasn't of Royal ilk?

Thoughtful, she finally vacated the main room for the bathroom and a shower. She took her time getting ready, taking care to put rollers in her dark hair and to apply her make up a little more dramatically. The smudges of kohl made the blue of her eyes stand out. Removing the ankle length gown from the hanger, Chey appreciated the fine style and elegant cut. Pale peach in color, it had a tight bodice with a piece that angled toward her neck, ending with a band around her throat. It left her shoulders and arms totally bare, as well as her back. Swooping low around the base of her spine, it conformed to her hips and flared out halfway down her thighs. The dreamy hem floated around her feet, whimsical and feminine. Tiny crystals had been sewn into the material in swirls and flourishes, adding sparkle and shine.

Sander had chosen the color and design well.

Drawing on a pair of white, elbow length kid gloves, she slipped her feet into delicate heels and transferred what few things she needed into a matching clutch.

When she stepped into the living area, she found the remains of their dinner already removed and Sander pacing near a couch with a phone to his ear. He looked striking in a steel gray gabardine suit that accentuated the golden color of his hair and skin. The layers beneath the jacket were darker gray, white and silver, with a tie that fit snug against his throat. Freshly shaven, hair pulled back into a low tail, he presented himself as a man of money and power.

The longer she stared at him, the more she felt that peculiar pang in her heart. It was a combination of things that put it there: the trip to a new and exciting place, getting a glimpse of Sander in this element, how people reacted around him and all the time they had to themselves with the strain of his family bearing down on them. Not just that, but the growing affection that often left her smiling or blushing.

He met her eyes across the room and ended his call. Pushing the cell phone into his pocket, he stood with his feet braced apart, assessing her with obvious masculine appreciation.

Nervous, she smoothed a gloved hand down the outside of her hip and waited to see if she met his approval. Which was new and different in itself. On other dates, with other men, she never worried about meeting expectations. She was just Chey, take it or leave it, and that was the attitude with which she approached most things.

Tonight, it mattered that she passed muster.

Prowling around the edge of a sofa, he paused to pick up a velvet box on an end table and continued toward her.

"You look stunningly beautiful," he said. Coming to a stop just before her, he searched her face, her eyes.

"Really? Thanks. Did you pick this out, or did you have someone else do it?" Chey realized belatedly that Sander might have had one of his assistants go shopping for him. She glanced at the box, then at his face.

"I picked all of it out. As well as these to go with it." He opened the black velvet box that was longer than it was wide. Nestled on more velvet inside was a glittering tennis bracelet and diamond drop earrings.

"Oh, Sander. Those are beautiful." She was afraid to touch them. As with Mattias's gift, she thought these might be on loan from a jeweler. With her luck, one of the diamonds would fall out or she would lose an earring.

"I'm glad you like them. There's a matching necklace, but I knew you couldn't wear it with that high neckline. Here, let me get the bracelet." He set the box down on the arm of a nearby wingback, pulling the bracelet free. Turning around, he wrapped it around her extended wrist and fastened the clasp.

"A necklace, too? I'm not sure what to say." Overwhelmed, she adjusted her wrist, diamonds sparkling against the gloves.

"You don't need to say anything. Your expression is doing a fine job for you. Want me to put the earrings in, too? Might be difficult to do it with your gloves on." He pulled both earrings out of their holders.

She laughed, a quiet sound in the spacious penthouse. "I hope I don't lose an earring or something." Lowering her hand, she debated him putting the earrings in. "All right, go ahead."

"Don't worry, it's insured." He stepped to one side and with deft fingers, poked the stem of the earring through the hole in her lobe and pushed the back into place. Moving around the other side, he repeated with the other ear.

"Insured? These aren't...borrowed?" she asked, taking a deep breath of his masculine cologne.

"No. They're yours. If you lose a diamond or knock the setting, just let me know and we'll get it fixed." He stepped back and eyed her with the addition of diamonds.

Lifting a hand, she touched the dangling diamond on the end of the earring. "Thank you."

"You're welcome. Now, are you ready to go, or are you going to stand there looking at me like I'm wearing armor and just hopped off a white horse?" He quirked an amused smile.

She laughed in delight at his wry quip. "Keep sassing me, and I might make you kiss me to round out the fairy tale."

"Oh, now there's a hardship," he retorted. Taking a step closer, he stared down into her eyes, one finger trailing along the edge of her jaw.

Chey's mouth went dry. Holding his

gaze, she watched him bend his head to kiss the spot just outside the corner of her mouth.

"Lipstick," he whispered, explaining why he'd not kissed her lips.

"Shame. I think the plum shade would suit you."

He laughed. "Now who's sassing who?"

Chapter Four

The hotel the limousine pulled up to was a sprawling structure less than half a mile from *The Trident.* Security fanned out around the car as they disembarked at the entrance, a barrier between the Royal heir and a small collection of photographers. Somehow, they'd gotten wind of the event.

Sander escorted her through double doors opened by a valet, stride tempered to match her own so he didn't leave her behind. Chey appreciated that he didn't hurry her along. The heels she'd worn were higher and more precarious than she preferred.

Crossing a large, impressive foyer, following a red carpet lining the floor, they approached another set of doors that opened onto an opulent ballroom done in colors of peach and cream. Crystal glittered on linen covered tables and chandeliers shined over the heads of the gathered. People were everywhere;

dancing, talking in groups, standing near the champagne fountain. It wasn't quite a black tie affair, but it was most definitely formal, with the women in long gowns and the men in elegant suits.

Chey took a breath and braced herself. She couldn't have felt more out of place if she'd walked in buck naked. The most elaborate party she'd ever attended, barring the one Mattias took her to, had been a wedding reception for a co-worker. Chey used the analogy of cars to make a comparison: that party had been a Pinto, this was a Rolls Royce.

"What's on your mind?" Sander asked, as if he'd felt her inner discord.

"Rolls Royces," she said under her breath.

"...what?" He frowned.

"I was thinking that the most upscale party I've ever attended was a Pinto. This is a Rolls Royce." Well, he'd asked. And Sander knew her penchant for blurting the truth. His body shook with silent laughter.

"I dread to think you compare me to any of your old boyfriends like that," he said, leading her deeper into the room. Sander smiled cordially at a few people as the crowd began to take note of the new arrivals. Two of his private security members branched out at their flank, discreet and covert.

"I kind of have. Do you want to hear the analogy?"

"Now that you mention it, maybe no--"

"They were The Breakfast Club. You're Pretty Woman."

Sander barked a laugh that drew several pairs of eyes. He tilted his head toward hers to keep his next remark between them. "Does that make you the whore?"

Chey gasped, mouth shaping an 'o' of shock. Eyes wide as saucers, she stared up at Sander. She was surely the only woman present expressing so much indecent animation. In Pretty Woman, the female lead had started out as a hooker to an austere, affluent businessman.

Sander tipped his head back and laughed the kind of laugh that drew half the room's attention. Rolling, rich and deep, it could almost be considered a guffaw. Almost.

Chey lost her battle to remain stern and trembled with amusement. One glance at the room assured her they had just become the topic of several people's conversation.

"You're a pest," Chey announced just loud enough for Sander to hear. "Look, they're staring."

He brought a fist to his mouth and cleared his throat, though his eyes gleamed with mirth. "Do you care?"

"No."

"Really?"

"...maybe just a little. I feel like we're under a microscope."

"That's because we are. Another thing to get used to."

"I'm not sure I'll ever get used to it." Chey smiled at a distinguished looking couple standing to the side of a dance floor that took up a good portion of the room.

"You're doing fine, don't worry. I'll let you know if you stumble." Sander paused to shake hands with several men and trade generic greetings.

A waitress came by with a tray filled with flutes of wine. Sander declined with a subtle shake of his head. Chey figured there was a reason, and followed suit. While he made small talk with the gentlemen, who had all inclined their heads to her and greeted her cordially, Chey tipped her attention to the room. She didn't recognize one person so far.

Not that she really expected to.

"Sander Ahtissari, you walked right by without even a hello," a feminine voice said behind them.

Chey glanced back to see a stunning woman in a white fitted gown with elegant layers of tulle from her waist to the floor. Gray eyed, lashes long and thick, she had flawless tawny skin and highlighted brown hair styled into a classic updo. Her features were delicate, refined, with a straight nose and full mouth.

Sander stilled, then turned he and Chey around to face the new arrival. It took a moment for a smile to hook onto the corners of his mouth.

"Princess Valentina, what a surprise to see you here," he said.

So this was the woman who the Queen wanted to become Sander's wife. And she was beautiful, there was no doubt about it. Cultured, statuesque, the Princess looked confident and capable. Her accent was different than Sander's, more clipped and defined.

"I could say the same about you." Valentina's attention switched to Chey, as if expecting an introduction. Her expression was curious, intrigued.

"Princess Valentina, may I introduce

Miss Chey Sinclair." Sander indulged the introductions while never taking his eyes off Valentina.

For a moment, Chey panicked. Was she required to bow? Curtsy? Shake hands? She wasn't sure what the protocol was in situations like these. She declined to extend a hand and only greeted Valentina verbally.

"Pleasure to meet you," Chey said.

"Likewise, Miss Sinclair," she replied. Valentina switched her attention back to the Prince. "I wasn't aware you were slated to attend this event, Prince Dare."

"It was a last minute invitation. The Ambassador was kind enough to contact my people when we arrived. If you'll ex--"

"How ironic," Valentina said, delicately interrupting as if she sensed he was about to beg off. "We were notified rather late ourselves. Your mother, the Queen, seemed to know you would be attending before you did, it appears."

Chey bit back irritation. So this was another finagling of the Queen. No wonder Sander had mentioned that sometimes, he wound up with Valentina by surprise.

"Isn't that something," Sander retorted, droll and unamused.

"Have you heard the news?" Valentina

inquired.

Chey decided that whatever Valentina had to say would change the course of their evening. Intuition this strong had never failed her yet.

"I'm sure I haven't," Sander said. He wore a mantle of polite indifference that sharpened at Valentina's leading question.

Valentina smiled, gaze traveling intimately over Sander's features. It might as well have been a lover's caress.

"My father said yes. Our wedding, yours and mine, will be in the spring."

. . .

Chey felt Sander tighten beside her. The news did not seem to sit well with the heir to the throne. Yet he tempered his response, a low roll of laughter filling the sudden silence.

"Not only have I not been notified of that event, I have not agreed, which means all the wedding planners and advisers will have to hold off. I'm sorry if you were led to believe it was set in stone."

Valentina arched her brows. "I didn't think it needed to be set in stone, Dare. We both know how long this has been volleyed back and forth between countries. Your people made the offer, ours agreed."

Chey cut a quick look aside to Sander. She recalled his words about their own relationship being an uphill battle, that they would have to stand firm against those whose job it was to orchestrate the affairs of the state. Once more, she wondered just how much choice Sander really had. Was he kidding himself, thinking he would marry who he wanted to? An uneasy knot began to take shape in her stomach. After the day just passed, and the easy way she and Sander had warmed to each other's company, Chey knew it would already hurt if she was forced out of his life by forces stronger than them both.

"This really isn't the time or the place," Sander said.

Valentina lifted her chin a fraction, as if she was fending off hurt of her own at his apparent wish not to take her to wife. "We have much to discuss. When you've come around, call me."

"Valentina--"

"You know this is the way, Dare. Call me." Valentina, too classy by far to be rude in public, dipped Chey a polite nod and turned to leave.

Sander escorted Chey the opposite direction, expression neutral.

Chey detected the tension in his body through the connection of her fingers on his arm.

"Dance?" he asked, glancing down to meet her eyes.

Chey inclined her head. "I might trip all over your feet, because I don't waltz well, but yes. Let's go."

"Just follow my lead. That's all you have to do." He seemed to be speaking of more than just the dance right then.

Sander led her onto the floor, swinging her into an easy, practiced twirl before finding more routine footing. He was expert at leading, graceful and smooth, and obviously skilled at the dance.

Chey stared up into his eyes, finding it effortless to match his rhythm. He made everything so easy. All the political schemes, confusion and conflict fell away during the three minute dance. It was just Chey and Sander, turning and twirling, gazing at each other no one else existed.

When the song ended, Sander brought them to a halt and inclined his head in chivalrous fashion. Bringing her hand to his mouth, he dusted a kiss across her glove covered knuckles.

"People are going to talk," she said, whispering.

"They're already talking."

"Well, then they're going to assume."

"They're already doing that, too," he said with a rakish gleam in his eyes.

After a brief look past his shoulders, Chey discovered he was right. Certain groups were watching their every move, some with their heads bent together. She even caught several glancing between her and Sander as well as Valentina, as if attempting to figure out what the game was and whether Chey was a serious contender for Sander's hand.

His loyalty to Chey was put to the test a moment later when a new song began, and a gentleman decked out in a black and white tux asked after Chey for a dance.

"She's taken," Sander said without preamble and a broad grin.

The gentleman arched his brows, lips ticking with amusement, then bowed out and approached someone else instead.

"You're assuming an awful lot, aren't you Prince Ahtissari?" Chey asked with a coy bat of her lashes.

Sander led her into another waltz, laughing low and quiet. "Am I?"

"I don't remember you asking me to be exclusive with you, which means I'm not taken in the way you're suggesting."

"Which in turn means you're available to dance with other men," Sander said, wearing an amused look on his handsome features.

"Exactly."

"Except you don't *want* to dance with other men." Sander dropped his voice to a stage whisper.

"I don't?" Chey tilted her head as if to better hear his explanation.

"Of course not."

"How do you know?"

"Because you're looking at me with an infatuated, doe-eyed stare and you couldn't be bothered to even glance at the other man when he asked for a dance."

"I'm not infatuated," she scoffed, laughing.

"Yes, you are. Don't make me prove it."

"And how would you do that?" she challenged, then decided a moment later she wasn't sure she wanted to know.

Sander was known for pulling tricks out of his hat that she never expected. "Wait...I don't think I want to know."

He set his shoulders back, chin lifting in triumph. "See?"

"You're incorrigible. I still don't agree that I'm infatuated, but I *am* smitten. How's that?"

"Smitten, infatuated, it's the same thing."

"It is not." She scoffed again, stepping into a turn, then out for a twirl. He caught her around the waist and brought her back close to his body. Chey got lost in the possessive hold of his hand low on her spine and the equally possessive look in his eyes. She wondered if anyone else noticed or if she was just seeing things she wanted to see. The way he focused on her, as if she was the only woman in the room, couldn't be her imagination.

The song wound to a conclusion, leaving Sander bowing elegantly over her knuckles once more. Chey smiled and feigned a curtsy, which brought a flicker of amusement to Sander's eyes.

"Pardon," Valentina said, appearing at their side. She turned an expectant look up to Sander. "May I have this dance?"

. . .

Chey watched Sander and Valentina from the side of the dance floor, a glass of champagne in her fingers. It wasn't like he could turn Valentina down when the Princess so blatantly put him on the spot. Half the room had been focused on Sander's answer and Chey chose to take the high road, demurring away from the couple with a specific look at Sander that said she didn't blame him and wouldn't hold it against him.

How could she?

People expected things from him. Tongues were wagging and even someone as inexperienced as Chey could see the schemes churning beneath the surface of society. It would have caused a minor uproar if Sander had refused Valentina out of hand.

Even so, it worked Chey's patience to see the Princess in Sander's arms. From this new, unique perspective, she saw just how commanding the heir to the throne was on the dance floor, how polished and smooth he took Valentina through the turns. He filled out his suit in a way that most other men did not, shoulders broad and strong, his coloring setting him apart from the rest.

No wonder Sander was considered one of the top ten bachelors in the world. He had everything going for him from position to money to looks.

She wasn't the only woman who noticed, either. Chey caught glimpses of other debutante types whispering behind their hands, watching Sander on the dance floor. Chey could just imagine what they were saying.

"They make a stunning pair, do they not?" a man said at her side.

Caught off guard daydreaming, Chey glanced over. Her new companion must have been someone of importance, considering his security team hovered not far behind. He was middle aged with distinctive, darker coloring and clothing that suggested mid-eastern descent.

"Yes, they do," Chey finally said, cautioning herself not to say too much. She glanced at the dance floor, back to Sander and Valentina, since they were the object of discussion.

"Rumor has it they will be married in the spring. A strategic move, if I say so myself." He took a drink from his glass, watching Chey rather than the Prince and Princess.

"As far as I know, it's just a rumor," Chey said, glancing back to the man.

"Really," he said, and it wasn't a question. "It seems the entire congregation thinks otherwise. What do you know that we don't, I wonder."

"Only that it's a rumor, rather than solid fact." Chey bristled at the thought Sander and Valentina's 'engagement' was already a done deal.

"Interesting," the man said. "That will change a few people's political affiliation with Weithan Isle if so. The connection with the Ahtissari family was an important factor in decisions on importing goods from an untried source."

Chey cursed under her breath. She was in way over her head and had no idea how to respond to such a claim. Why was this man even talking to her? Chey was just a guest, not a Princess or a Liaison or an Ambassador better suited to discussions like these.

He's using your naivety to see if there is weight to the wedding rumors.

"I really wouldn't know anything about that," Chey said, and at least it wasn't a lie.

"No, I suppose you would not," the man said with a thin smile and a glance that suggested he thought her purpose a much more tactile one with the Prince.

Before Chey could think of a suitable reply, he turned on a heel and strolled away, causal as you please.

Had she just given him the wrong ammunition? Would it really damage Weithan Isle politically, that small exchange? Chey couldn't be sure. It was ridiculous to think someone of such obvious importance would put too much stock in what she had to say. Yet perhaps this was part of Valentina's insistence this evening that their engagement come to light. Maybe there *were* heavy political implications lurking at the fringe.

It serves Valentina right for jumping the gun, Chey thought. The woman should have never just assumed Sander would agree without talking to him first.

Once again, Chey felt out of her element. Way out of her league. Tipping the champagne up, she finished off what remained.

"This must be your first time at a function like this," a masculine voice said at her side.

Chey glanced from Sander and

Valentina to her newest companion. The Chey of three months ago would have melted on the spot at the handsome lines of his face and linebacker type build. Dark haired, with a rakish dimple in his tanned cheek, he was the epitome of charismatic charm and devilish allure.

The Chey of today, smitten with a certain Prince, barely noticed the man's ample attributes.

"My second, actually," she replied, and wished she had another glass of champagne to help her relax.

As if he'd anticipated her need, the dark haired man presented her with a sparkling flute, exchanging it with the old.

"Thanks," Chey said, bringing the flute up for a quick sip. It was chilled, bubbly and smooth on the tongue.

"Of course." The man passed off the empty flute and slid his hands into the pockets of his coat. "So, your second event. What do you think, then?"

The way he kicked his chin toward the dance floor could have been construed to mean Sander and Valentina.

Either that, Chey thought, or she was reading too much into things.

"It's very interesting," she finally said, again reminding herself to be cautious.

He could be another like the last, pumping her for information.

"Indeed. What do you find most interesting about it? The location or the collection of the world's elite?"

Chey let her gaze skim back to Sander and Valentina. The Princess was stroking her fingers through the end's of Sander's hair at the nape as if she had a right to. It was a small sign of affection, but one that put Chey on edge. Resisting the urge to deliver a blunt retort to the man at her side, she took another sip from the champagne and offered up something less inflammatory.

"The mystery of who everyone is," Chey said. "I don't really recognize anyone, yet it's obvious there are some very big players here."

"An understatement," he said with a raspy laugh. "I could point them all out, but that's boring. I'd rather dance, if you would do me the honor."

"Absolutely, thank you." Chey drained another swallow of the champagne and let the man take the flute from her fingers. Why not dance? It would put her closer to Sander and Valentina so that she might overhear whatever conversation had put that disgruntled look on Sander's face.

The devilish man swung Chey out onto the floor with a chivalrous flourish and settled into a gliding waltz. Skilled and efficient, Chey found she didn't have to concentrate hard on the steps to keep up with him. She caught Sander's eyes when they spun close to him and Valentina; he glared at Chey's dancing partner with something like irritation.

Chey attempted to convey that Sander had nothing to be irritated about, but found it difficult to shape the right expression. She bubbled an unexpected laugh as her partner led her into another turn.

"Having a good time?" the man asked.

Chey realized she didn't even know his name. His face swam above her when she sought his gaze. "Yes. Dancing was a good idea."

"It was. You dance well."

"Thank you." She swallowed once, then asked, "What's your name?"

"Damon."

"Just Damon? No Prince or anything in front of it?" Chey wished she could stifle the urge to laugh. Everything was suddenly funny.

He chuckled. "No, sorry. Just Damon. And you're Miss Sinclair. The gossips made that clear even before I got my hands on my first drink."

"Yes. You can call me Chey though." The room felt so light, so bubbly—like the champagne. The drink must really be going to her head.

"Chey, then. Careful there," he said, when she missed a step and stumbled.

"Sorry. I guess it was that second drink." A small laugh tittered free.

"Did you eat? Sometimes if you drink without dinner, it goes to your head faster."

Chey couldn't remember if they'd eaten or not. "I...don't know."

"No worries, Miss Sinclair. You're in good hands with me. I'll make sure you don't trip or bump into anyone else," Damon said, tilting his head closer to her own.

Faces swirled at the edge of the dance floor, blurring into each other. For one startling moment, a sharp pair of ice blue eyes stood out among the other dancers. Sander. Chey realized it was Sander only after he'd turned out of sight. Well, now he knew what it felt like to watch her dance with someone else. What was good for the goose was good for the gander, right?

"Thank you, Mister Damon." Chey, lightheaded, stifled another laugh against his shoulder. She felt his chest shake with humor under her cheek.

"You're welcome." He guided her through another set of steps as the music's tempo increased.

Chey found it harder and harder to keep up now, as if her feet didn't want to listen to the commands of her brain. It was only mildly disconcerting. Mostly, she just didn't care.

"It's really hot in here," she said a few minutes later, after catching another particularly bold stare from Sander. He wore an intense, unhappy look that Chey barely caught between one twirl and the next.

"It's all the people on the floor. We can step out onto the balcony, get some fresh air, and come back in if you'd like," Damon said, already guiding her that way.

Chey thought fresh air sounded fantastic. She followed his lead, allowing him to escort her past a pair of open double doors to the broad balcony overlooking the bay. Salty ocean air gusted against her skin and threatened to make a mess of her carefully coiffed hair.

Damon led her to a shadowy niche in the wall surrounded by climbing ivy and little pink flowers.

"This should help," Chey said, gulping down oxygen as if it were wine. She couldn't get her bearings, couldn't focus on anything longer than a minute or two. Somewhere in the recesses of her mind, warning bells were clanging, though over what, she couldn't be sure.

"Yes, it should," Damon said, crowding her into the niche.

He obliterated the moonlight, the bay— everything. Chey couldn't see past his shoulders for the way he loomed closer. She brought her hands up to his chest with the intent to ward him off, to put some breathing distance between them. What was he doing?

What was *she* doing? She didn't want to be out here with him. The warning bells clanged louder. Chey wished she could concentrate on what they meant, on what she needed to do. Something was wrong. Her tongue felt numb, like her brain.

Damon claimed her mouth, hands on her hips, body pressing hers into the ivy.

Chey mewled protest, pushed harder at his chest. The slight weight was ineffectual against his strength. She wasn't even sure he noticed.

This was all wrong.

Damon, wrenched back by someone gripping his shoulder, reeled away from Chey. She saw fists fly and Damon sprawl backward on the balcony.

"Some women really are title chasers," Damon said with a smug, bloody smile. "I don't think she cared *which* Royal she had, as long as she had one. Right, darling?"

Sander, with fury on his face and in his eyes, growled what sounded like a threat in his mother tongue. Then he said, "I know better."

"Do you? Because she was all but begging me to have her. Something about what did it matter now that the mighty Heir to the throne was engaged to the alluring Princess Valentina. Got to hand it to her," Damon said with a rude gesture at Chey. "She didn't waste any time."

"What? No." Chey sought to deny the horrible things Damon was saying. She looked from the sprawled man on the ground to Sander, who glared down into her face. There was a gleam of uncertainty in his eyes, as if he didn't want to believe what he was hearing. Catching her pressed into a shady nook with a handsome stranger couldn't have encouraged his trust in her. Chey staggered away from the niche, panic trying to sear a path through the haze.

"Sander..." Chey's protests got cut off by a sudden influx of security. The balcony, empty of all but three bodies a moment ago, became flooded with men in black suits.

"Prince Dare, there's been a security breach."

"This way, this way," another said as the quartet surrounded Sander.

"Get her out of here," Sander barked as his men smothered themselves around him. "Take her home."

"We're on it, Sir."

Dizzy and disoriented, Chey found herself in the escort of Sander's security. She caught a glimpse of Damon in the flurry of bodies, something knowing and sly in his gaze. He looked pleased with the incident and gave no resistance as his own team hustled him off the balcony down a side set of stairs.

Everything after that happened so fast she couldn't keep track. One moment she was being guided into a sedan, the next she was back in the parking lot at *The Trident*. There was no time to organize her scattered thoughts, no chance to recover from the shock of Sander catching her with another man. Guards collected her things with speed and efficiency while she sat in the idling car. They loaded suitcases into the trunk within minutes. People moved around her in a blur, much like the faces around the dance floor had. The sedan pulled out of the lot and onto the street, Sander no where in sight.

Chey's weak protests and questions went unanswered. The security members weren't talking when it came to Sander's whereabouts or safety. Fear and panic clamored for dominance, though neither could pierce the strange daze Chey currently saw the world through.

Before long she was on the private jet and helped into a seat. Her body felt like a limp noodle, unable to hold itself upright. She consoled herself with the thought that she would straighten everything out with Sander as soon as they landed in Latvala. Between now and then, she would sleep off the effects of the champagne and allow Sander's temper to cool.

The abyss rose up to claim her before the jet ever left the tarmac.

Chapter Five

"Miss Sinclair, we're here," a guard said with a gentle shake of her shoulder.

Chey stirred, but didn't open her eyes right away.

"Miss Sinclair?"

"Mm?"

"We're here. Open your eyes." The security member gave her shoulder another gentle shake.

Chey slit her lashes open, wondering why her ears needed to pop. The luxurious interior of the jet reminded her she was on a plane, but she couldn't figure out for the life of her *why.*

"We can disembark as soon as you're ready," he said.

Yawning, Chey sat up in her chair. The plane...*oh.* She glanced across toward the other seats and the sofas for Sander. He wasn't anywhere to be seen. Perhaps he'd crashed in the bedroom in the back.

Suffering a wild headache, she got up and stretched with a groan of pain.

"Where's Sander?" she asked, stepping free of the seats. She was still in the gown she'd worn to the party at the hotel. Distantly, alarms sounded in her head, vying with the headache that seemed far too sharp and acute to be born from champagne.

Little by little, snippets of the evening came back to her. She fought off a bout of panic that wanted to lodge itself in her stomach.

"He's away, Miss Sinclair," the guard said. "All your luggage is here. Do you feel up to leaving the plane?"

"Yes, yes, I think so. Is Sander at the castle?" she asked, wobbling her way toward the now open door. Faint strains of twilight sought to pierce an overcast, still dark sky.

"I'm not sure, Miss Sinclair. Perhaps." The guard provided her a helping hand down the stairs to the tarmac. Another man came behind with her luggage.

Finding it strange that the guard wasn't sure where Sander went, she made it to the ground and murmured her thanks for his help toward the waiting limousine. Groggy and still unable to fully get her mind to function right, she got into the vehicle while the men stored her luggage in the trunk.

She had a lot of explaining to do with Sander. Recalling the man who'd pressed her into the niche—what *had* she been thinking—Chey cringed. The details were muzzy and unclear, as if she couldn't quite pull everything to the surface. Sander's uncertainty pried at her memory until his face swam behind her eyes. He'd looked so disbelieving, so...not quite accusing, but certainly not happy. And why should he? That Damon had lied his pants off.

Just why *had* he lied his pants off, anyway? What had been the point of driving a wedge between her and Sander?

Disgruntled, Chey rubbed her fingers over her forehead. At some point during the flight, someone had peeled the gloves off her hands. Thankful for that, at least, she slouched into the plush seat of the limousine and concentrated on what she was going to say to Sander when she got back to the castle.

Obviously, someone had slipped something into her champagne. That knowledge presented itself as her mind began to clear away the cobwebs of sleep. Had it been Damon? He'd been the one to offer her the glass before sweeping her onto the dance floor. Up until his traitorous lies at the end, after Sander caught them together, he'd been courteous and polite. Surely he'd had no other ulterior motives. He didn't even know her, what could his agenda have possibly been? Not to pursue her hand— there were much less drastic ways of getting her attention. And he'd ensured at the end that no woman in her right mind would want him after lying so blatantly about what happened.

Her gaze fixed on the gloomy landscape beyond the window. She didn't really see the terrain, it was only a backdrop for the inner film rolling through her mind's eye. Nothing made sense. The entire evening had been fraught with tension ever since she and Sander had arrived, from Valentina's little wedding announcement to the sudden declaration that security had been breached at the hotel.

Or something to that effect. Diplomats and Royalty alike had been scattered away from possible danger.

It wasn't for another half hour, until Chey caught a glimpse of sparkling lights of the approaching cityscape, that she realized something was wrong.

There shouldn't be any cityscape

against the skyline.

The Ahtissari family seat sat amidst acres upon acres of wild, untouched land.

Sitting up straighter, Chey peered out the window to see if it was Kalev, the main city of Latvala, they were entering. To her shock and dismay, she realized a few minutes later that they weren't in Kalev at all. Not in *Latvala* at all.

She stared at the outline of Seattle in disbelief.

"Wait, why are we in Seattle? Where's Sander?" Chey blurted out her questions to either of two guards sitting in the limousine further up near the dividing window. One turned his head to glance her way. Fair haired, blue eyed, he was not a guard Chey was intimately familiar with.

"Miss Sinclair, Prince Dare ordered us to bring you back here. He regrets things did not work out as planned, and hopes you understand that this was for the best regarding both of your futures."

Chey stared at the guard as if he'd grown a second head. Sander had done this? Was he so upset, then, that he'd dismissed their relationship completely? He'd given her no indication last night that this would be the end result. Didn't they at least owe it to each other to discuss things? Or had seeing her with another man, along with Damon's damning words, been enough?

After all, Sander could have his choice of women. He didn't need one that cheated on him at the first sign of trouble.

"No, I don't really understand," she said, upset at the tremor in her voice. "He wouldn't have just dismissed me like this."

The guard's mouth quirked to the side. It seemed he struggled to find a diplomatic way to answer, instead of coming off with *Well he just did, didn't he?*

"Prince Dare was very certain of his actions, Miss Sinclair. There was no doubt, no question. I'm sorry." The guard turned his attention back to his companion.

"So this is it? What about my contact with the Royal family?" Nausea hit Chey like a ton of bricks. Not only had she lost Sander, but now she would be required to pay back money she'd already spent. One of her worst fears.

"Prince Dare has kindly covered the money you were advanced before your arrival. The rest will simply not be paid, since you won't be continuing with your photography of the family," he said.

Kindly covered your advance. Chey wanted to chew nails at how that grated on her nerves. On the one hand, she should be grateful that she didn't have to sell her soul to pay these people back. On the other—it galled her to know that Sander cavalierly sent her home and paid her advance as if buying her off.

Spending the rest of the ride in silence, Chey alternated between seething anger and crushing remorse. Just twenty-four hours ago, she and Sander had been flirting and happy and making plans for their immediate future.

Now she was ten minutes from her old stomping grounds, stripped of a relationship and a man she'd grown terribly fond of.

When the limousine pulled into her complex, a sense of the surreal hit Chey on an entirely different level than it usually did. She couldn't believe she was back here again.

Rolling to a stop in front of her building, the driver put the limousine in park and popped the trunk before coming around to open her door. Chey got out on her own, feeling ridiculous in her expensive gown. The guards followed, one collecting her luggage from the back. It felt a lot like a gallows march toward the stairs leading up to her door, and it took her several long minutes to fish her keys out from her belongings. Someone had tucked her clutch in among the other things.

"Again, we extend Prince Dare's sincere apologies. Be well," one guard said, before they turned on a heel and descended the stairs to the parking lot.

Chey watched them go. There was nothing left to say.

Turning the key in the lock, she opened her door and pulled her luggage inside. Today, she didn't care if it sat haphazardly against the wall instead of her usual preference to line it up behind the couch. Closing the door with her hip, she stood there and stared at the small, rather plain apartment. Her head buzzed with disbelief. It wasn't the luxury of the castle she missed, or the expansive space of her suite of rooms on the second floor.

It was the gaping hole Sander left in her life. His presence had filled every waking second, and even some of her dreams. He was all consuming, a vivid persona that had engaged her imagination, her laughter, her fears.

Now he was gone and it hit her as hard as his death might have, leaving her wallowing in bleak despair.

Burying her face in her hands, she cried.

. . .

Twenty-four hours later, sitting amidst a pile of used tissues, Chey felt no better. Sleep had eluded her all night. The morning found her sitting lotus style on the couch, the television buzzing white static instead of a show, her cell phone parked next to her knee. It wasn't the same phone the Royals had given her to use, but the one she'd left Seattle with. Chey realized after searching for her cell that the other one had been removed from her belongings.

Any direct contact to Sander was gone.

A half hour before, in desperation, she'd called her best friend Wynn. They'd met in seventh grade and had been inseparable ever since. In her rush to depart Seattle, Chey hadn't had time to call Wynn and tell her what was going on.

She'd meant to correct that oversight once in Latvala until her life had been threatened and put in jeopardy. Now Wynn had no clue why Chey was heartbroken and sobbing, though she'd promised to come over right away.

Without knocking, using a key Chey had given her months before, Wynn let herself in. Slim as a willow reed, she slipped past the door and closed it resolutely behind her. For her height, an unimpressive five-foot-three, Wynn nevertheless cast off a sturdy, capable air. This was a girl who got things done. Without fuss, without muss, and with enviable efficiency. Doe-like dark eyes, framed by indecently long lashes, peered out from the fragile bones of her oval shaped face. Silky black hair cut into a bob brushed the top of her shoulders, a more modern cut that went with the red lipstick painting her bow shaped mouth. A blue and green argyle sweater with a white collar peeking above the neckline at the throat topped a pleated skirt the same navy color in the sweater. Long leggings disappeared under the modest hem, her shoes patent leather with a strap across the arch.

"What's all this?" Wynn said, stalking

through the apartment like the force of nature she could sometimes be. Tossing down her keys on the table near the wall, Wynn dropped her purse on the floor and stared at the luggage—as well as the elegant dress Chey had changed out of in favor of candy-cane decorated pajamas—with no small amount of confusion. The luggage remained unpacked and the dress had been tossed over the back of the other couch. Very unChey-like.

Blowing her nose for the hundredth time, Chey made a wayward gesture with her hand. "I have a lot to tell you."

"You bet your hiney you do. What in the world is going on? Chey Sinclair, *crying?* Did the apocalypse happen when I wasn't looking? Look at all those tissues! You've been at this for hours." Apparently appalled, Wynn crossed the room and threw herself down among the layers of balled up tissues and stared at Chey.

"You're not going to believe this," Chey said, warning her friend of the impending story that she hardly believed herself.

"Try me." Wynn looped an arm behind Chey's shoulders and smoothed a palm reassuringly across her back.

And so Chey began at the beginning. From the first visit of Allar and Hendrik and their offer to come photograph the Royal family. She explained in halting detail her flight over, the grand castle, and all the meetings with different members of the Ahtissari family. She didn't forget Natalia's spite, her mug throwing, or Viia's plot to have Chey removed from castle life.

Wynn listened, sometimes gasping, other times struck for words. She blurted out questions when she wanted more detail and expressed shock at the attack in the old castle when Sander had come to Chey's rescue.

Chey left nothing out. Not the nights she'd spent with Sander, nor their agreement to try and date despite the knowledge the King and Queen disapproved (to put it mildly).

Wynn grew more wide-eyed as the story unfolded, until Chey reached the event of the day just past, when Sander had caught her with another man and sent her packing.

Outraged, Wynn made her displeasure known. "What? Why would he have gone to that extreme? Sending you home without even a chance to explain?"

"I guess finding me kissing that devil-man was too much. I mean, *I* wasn't kissing Damon, he was kissing me, but that doesn't matter. It's what it looked like that matters," Chey said. She tossed another spent tissue onto the growing pile.

"It just doesn't seem *right*. Are you positive that someone put something in your champagne?" Wynn asked, pressing the issue.

"Pretty sure. I've never had any alcohol hit me like that. I was woozy, dizzy. It just sounds like a petty excuse, though. I have no proof."

"Do you really need proof after someone tried to take you out at the castle and the King and Queen's obvious disapproval of the relationship? Sounds to me like you were set up, especially if that guy gave you a *look* while you were being led away. What did that mean, anyway, if he hadn't been sent as a distraction?" Wynn crossed her arms over her thin chest.

"That seems so far fetched, though. You know? Like I'm reaching for excuses." Except Chey *knew* something had been in her drink. All these hours later, the signs were more recognizable. She sniffed and dabbed at her eyes with another tissue.

"Honey, all of it seems far fetched.

Being whisked off to a far-away castle, meeting a Prince you thought was someone else. Think about it. It's like a modern day fairy-tale—except not."

"Yeah, it can't be a fairy-tale with an ending like this."

"The story isn't over yet," Wynn insisted.

"According to the King and Queen it is." Chey shoved some of the tissues onto the floor. She just didn't care about the mess right now.

"The Chey I know wouldn't sit back and take it. She would call this Sander fellow and explain. He owes you that and you know it."

"I can't just call him. They took my phone. The one--"

"I know the one you mean. But I also know you, and you memorized his number the first night you had it." Wynn smiled knowingly.

Chey had to laugh. Wynn *did* know her well. "Okay, I memorized it."

"That means you can call him. Right to his phone, too. No one to route you around and give you excuses." Wynn gestured to Chey's cell phone with an impatient gesture.

"I can't just call right now," Chey said,

protesting. If she was honest, her nerves were shot. She didn't know what she would say first.

"The sooner the better. They have these old sayings for a reason. Now call while I'm here to be your shoulder for support."

Chey rolled her eyes and picked up her cell phone. Would she really be able to get through? She thought ahead to the time difference and what Sander might be doing later in the day.

"Go on. Give him a ring."

"Okay, okay. Pushy. Give me a minute." Chey blew her nose twice more and took a drink from the tepid bottle of water sitting on the end table.

Wynn watched her like a hawk.

"I'm calling," Chey said, picking her cell up off her leg.

"I know. I'm waiting."

"I can feel you staring at me."

"If I don't, then you'll chicken out and wait until tomorrow, and then tomorrow you'll talk yourself out of it again because of the time difference or--"

"Oh my God. *I'm calling.*" Chey tapped the phone to life and brought up the keypad screen. With her thumb, she pressed in Sander's private number. What was she going to say when he answered?

Hi, I think my champagne was drugged sounded melodramatic and desperate. Even if she thought it was true.

A click on the other end made Chey catch and hold her breath. She didn't realize how much she wanted to hear Sander's voice until the click.

"*You have reached a number that has been disconnected and is no longer in service. If you have reached this number in error--*" Chey hung up before the automatic message could finish.

"What was that?" Wynn asked, frowning.

"They changed his number."

"Already?"

"It appears that way." Chey stared down at her phone. She should have known it wouldn't be that easy.

"Did you memorize anyone else's?"

"I didn't. I figured it wouldn't matter if I memorized Mattias's number or not." They might have changed his, too, just so she wouldn't have access to anyone.

Wynn leaned back against the seat and withdrew her arm from around Chey. "You can't let that stop you."

"What do you mean?" Chey glanced aside at Wynn. The girl had that determined gleam in her eye that Chey usually wore. It was one reason they'd gotten along so well through the years. Each was as stubborn and bull-headed as the other. Today, Chey just felt like a wet rag and wasn't up to her old stubborn antics.

"I mean you need to take action. Let's go to Latvala. Don't let him get away without trying to save your relationship."

Chey gasped. "Are you crazy?"

"It's the same thing *you* would tell me to do if the situation was reversed," Wynn said with a wry twist of her lips.

Chey realized she was right. It was exactly what Chey would tell Wynn to do. In fact, it was probably what Chey would have considered after another day or two of feeling sorry for herself and her circumstance.

"We can't just pick up and go to Latvala," Chey said with a dubious expression. Yet the seed had been planted.

"Yes we can. I have a passport. As long as you have one, and I suspect you do if you've already been over there, then we just need a flight." Wynn surged up off the couch and clapped her hands like a drill sergeant. "C'mon, c'mon, c'mon. Let's go, let's move!"

"They probably took that along with my private phone." Chey wouldn't doubt it. She got up off the couch however, more tissues spilling onto the floor, and crossed to the small purse that sat next to her luggage. Picking it up, she rooted through, expecting to find the passport long gone.

Much to her surprise, it was there with her lipstick and other minor belongings.

"It's here. I'm shocked they didn't take it," Chey said.

"They probably knew you'd need it going through customs, even if they do it privately or whatever for the Royals." Wynn brought a trash bag from the kitchen and began to scoop piles of tissues in.

"I can get that," Chey said. Wynn knew her well; Chey wouldn't be able to depart with her apartment in its current state. She needed to hang the dress up and straighten the cushions on the couch as well as clean the mess from her crying jag. Wynn was already on it.

"You go do whatever else you have to. Call and get flights. Use my credit card." Wynn paused to point toward her purse on the floor.

"No, don't worry, I've got this one. If

you're coming with me, the least I can do is get the flight. Besides, the Royals can pay for it." Technically, although Chey shouldn't be spending the money in the bank. There was only so much left after paying her rent so far in advance. Still. Right now, she didn't care.

Gathering the dress off the couch, she hauled it into her bedroom and hung it up in the closet.

Then, she took the bull by the proverbial horns and made flight arrangements to Latvala.

Chapter Six

"What am I doing? Is this even the right decision? Sander told the men to tell me that this was best, that it was over. Are we wasting a whole trip for nothing?" Chey suffered a panic attack about returning to Latvala as they settled into the seats of the Boeing 747 two days later. Stowing her overnight bag beneath her feet, she buckled in and exhaled.

"Yes, it's the right thing to do. Look, if you don't at least clear the air, and get the answers you need, you'll regret it for the rest of your life. Can you imagine trying to move on after this? You'll question everything and it might ruin whatever relationship you try to get into from here." Wynn clipped her buckle with a smart snap and laced her hands in her lap.

"You make a good point." Chey knew Wynn was right. It was nerve wracking, however, to take matters into her own hands and chase down a Prince of all things in a foreign country she'd only visited once. Maybe what she was really afraid of was that Sander would tell her to her face that he didn't want anything to do with her. That they were finished. It would break her heart.

At least she would know.

The flight to Latvala went without mishap. It was long and arduous, with two stop overs and plane changes. Wynn was, as ever, great company. Upbeat and enthusiastic, she insisted on taking pictures with Chey in front of terminals and iconic signs as they passed from one country to another. The closer they got to Latvala, the more Chey felt like it was coming home.

Landing in Kalev that evening, Chey was both excited and nervous. After waiting an hour to get their luggage, the girls departed the terminal and took a taxi to one of the hotels near the shore. It wasn't the same one she'd walked through with Mattias once upon a time, but a smaller, quaint business a block from the waterfront.

Their rooms were on the highest floor— the fifth—overlooking the ocean. At night, the water glistened like black diamonds. Lights from other city buildings stretched off to their right, offering a pretty vista in the darkness.

"I can't wait to see this place during the day. It's almost impossible to think you're *dating* the man who will one day be King of all this." Wynn widened her eyes at Chey as the reality of it hit home for her.

"Dated. I dated the man..." Chey corrected. She had the sense of the surreal just like Wynn did, and she'd *lived* it for two weeks.

Wynn waved her off. Like Chey, she'd chosen to travel for comfort: jeans, oversized sweater and lightweight coat in case they hit cold weather. "It's just a temporary break. All epic couples have some kind of separation, then there's a romantic get-back-together thing that makes all the old hearts swoon when you tell the story at Christmas or around a campfire."

"And you're always telling me I'm the one who's dramatic," Chey said with a wry glance at Wynn.

The girl lifted her shoulders with a helpless grin then changed the subject without warning. "By the way, how are we going to get close to this heir to the throne, anyway? We never talked about that."

That very question had been on Chey's mind since before getting on the plane. She looked out the window again, then paced through the room and slouched down on the sofa. "I'm not exactly sure yet. It won't work to take a taxi up to the gates. They'll stop us before we get there and just turn us away. He'll never even know I was here."

Wynn perched on the arm of a plush chair and crossed her arms over her chest. Bird-like, silky hair bobbing around the slender column of her throat, she appeared to give it great thought.

"Does he do public appearances? I'm sure the Royals would advertise that to draw a crowd, right?" Wynn asked.

"I'm sure they all do. Mattias and I went out that one day and he took pictures with a lot of people, but it wasn't announced beforehand. Then again, it wasn't a planned outing like you're talking." Chey considered it. "That would be a good place to at least try and get his attention *if* we knew when he was going out, and *if* we could get close enough to begin with."

"We're here for seven days. We have to make something happen in that time," Wynn reminded her. "That's a lot of 'ifs' and not a lot of real options. What else? Could we draw him out somehow? What would they do if a citizen specifically asked for their presence at some birth or baby naming ceremony or something?"

"I have no idea if he would show up to something like that, and how would we get the news to him anyway?" Chey eyed Wynn.

"Make an announcement in the newspaper. I will dress up and buy a fake babydoll, wrap it in a blanket so you can't tell from a casual glance, and then we wait like snakes in the grass for him to show up. That's when you pounce."

Chey couldn't help but laugh. "You come up with the most outrageous things."

"You forget that you've had your share of outrageous ideas in our time, Chey. You're just on the other side of the fence this time." Wynn cracked a smile at Chey then grew thoughtful again.

Chey couldn't deny it. She'd been the master planner in some pretty hair raising schemes in their time. A glimmer of memory struck her just then.

"You know, Sander told me once that he takes little forays into the towns without his security detail sometimes.

Just goes out among the people. I'm not sure if he meant this town, in particular, or a smaller one nearby," Chey said.

Wynn's gaze narrowed with interest. "Really. It's still risky to count on that for the next seven days. Maybe he'll be too busy or upset with what happened to leave the castle. It's a shot though, one we shouldn't turn down."

"That's what I was thinking. Then I wouldn't have to deal with the guards and someone trying to get me away from him before we can talk."

"We should get a map from the lobby and find out if there are smaller towns that are more convenient that he might visit. This one *is* pretty big. I'd be surprised if he went out too much around here and risked getting Prince-napped or whatever. Word would spread fast."

Chey's shoulders shook with a laugh. Prince-napped. Wynn just didn't know Sander very well. They would have to be wily nappers to simply make off with the Prince. Overall, however, the sentiment made sense.

"Let's go down and grab a map. While we're looking, we can still think of other ideas." Chey got up off the couch.

Wynn slid off the arm of the chair.

"We'll figure it out. One way or another, we *will* run into Sander Ahtissari while we're here."

Chey hoped Wynn was right.

. . .

The hotel boasted a quaint restaurant on the lowest level adjacent to the souvenir shop. After purchasing several maps, local newspapers and two tabloids, or 'rags' as Urmas had once called them, the girls settled into a quiet booth surrounded with a high back that gave them a modicum of privacy on three sides. Made to resemble an alpine ski lodge, the restaurant had little skiers on wires traveling overhead from one 'snowbank' to another. A miniature village of shoppes and houses in alpine style lined the walls high overhead, with the utensils all done in heavy metal resembling pewter. Authentic music spilled out of unseen speakers, low enough to be pleasing in the background without drowning out comfortable conversation.

They ordered chicken and herbs, baked

new potatoes and the house soup that came in a big pot with a ladle for their use. Crusty slices of bread arrived on wooden platters with the knife sticking out of the rest of the uncut loaf.

In her element, Wynn drank beer from a tall stein and laid the maps out over the parts of the table that didn't have food draped across it.

"Okay, so this is Kalev—it's a decent sized town, too," Wynn said. "But there are two little villages between Kalev and the castle, which is over here." She made gestures on the map after wiping her fingers on a napkin.

"Yes. I never visited those while I was here the last time. But I probably saw them from the air when we flew over." Chey recalled a few smaller settlements close to the shore mid-flight. "It makes sense that he might stick to smaller, less busy towns."

"It does. There is also another one up past the castle in the other direction. It's a bit farther though. Probably forty miles or something, if I had to guess." Wynn tried to measure distance with guesses instead of using the grid on the map.

Chey scooped a spoonful of soup into her mouth and leaned forward to get a look at the village further up the coast. She thought it looked like a good bet, too. "There are too many. We can't get to them all in one trip. I mean we can, but how many hours are we going to sit around, hoping he'll walk by the pastry shop we're sitting in? That's not quite as bad as looking for a needle in a haystack, but kind of."

"I say until we have a better idea, or until we hear that the family is going to be at some function where the public has access, then we hit one town a day, starting really early in the morning." Wynn grabbed up one of the tabloids and brought it closer. "Let's see here. This is a lot of stuff about foreign celebrities mixed with the Royals but nothing really jumps out. Most of it's hearsay or wild accusation. Listen to this: *Does Prince Gunnar's wife have a twin? Look-alike spotted in Kalev.* Except the picture they have here is from the back, and blurry. How in the world can they see anything?"

Chey scoffed. "Typical. Nothing about the Royals having a parade or something like that?"

"Maybe in the newspapers. Not these things." Wynn tossed the tabloid onto the seat beside her and reached for one of the newspapers instead. "Let's see. There's a Festival coming up but it's three weeks away and it doesn't say, so far anyway, that the Royals are going. Did Sander ever say anything about it?"

"I don't remember. He might have. Or maybe it was Mattias." Chey frowned, scanning her memory. She'd had a lot of little conversations with them both. A Festival sounded familiar. Then again, it might have come up in passing and wasn't on the Royal's radar to attend.

"Excuse me, can I help you?" Wynn asked three ladies who'd stopped to stare not far from their booth.

Drawn out of her reverie, Chey glanced outward. The women, of middle age and dressed warmly in coats and scarves, whispered among each other. One deigned to wave, almost as if she was nervous. Unsure who they were waving at, Chey looked side to side. The booth blocked the view of any other guests.

One of the women bowed her head and finally, they moved on toward the door.

"What was that about?" Wynn said, slim brows drawn into a frown.

"I have no idea. Do I have something on my face?" Chey turned toward Wynn.

"No. Nothing that isn't usually there."

Wynn brushed at the angles of Chey's cheeks and whisked fingertips across her chin, like there might be crumbs.

"Weird." Chey put it down to a case of mistaken identity.

Ten minutes later, as the girls were deciding on dessert, it happened again. This time a couple, man and wife, both passed their booth with smiles and nods of their heads. As if they knew Wynn and Chey personally.

"Okay, are people here always this friendly?" Wynn asked.

"They *have* seemed pretty friendly during the times I've been out with Mattias and Sander. But not quite this friendly. We could be anyone, but they act like they know us." Puzzled, Chey declined dessert in the end and started gathering up their maps and papers.

"They could just be welcoming strangers. We stick out like sore thumbs, most likely." Wynn insisted on paying for dinner. After signing the check, she grabbed her purse and slid out of the booth.

Chey did likewise. Just as she got to her feet, a pair of younger women rushed up. One burbled out the native language, which Chey didn't understand, and stood right next to her while the other snapped a picture.

"You look like a deer caught in the headlights," Wynn pointed out casually to Chey.

"Thank you!" The girls knew enough English to express their gratitude and hurried away.

Chey stared after them, maps and papers tucked under her arm. "They must think I'm a celebrity or something. Who do I look like?"

"Lucille Ball. You know when her eyes get all crazy and wild?"

Chey laughed and smacked Wynn with a folded paper. "I so do *not* look like that. Ever."

In the lobby, the girls were treated to a few more stares. Someone else snapped pictures.

"I should have asked them who they think you are," Wynn said as they got into the elevator.

"I'm not sure I want to know." Secure in the carriage, Chey leaned against the rail.

"It could be amusing."

"I'm sure it would be amusing for *you.*" Chey stifled a smile at Wynn.

"Of course." Wynn brushed a

nonexistent piece of lint off the shoulder of her sweater. "Are we going out tonight? Hit up any of the local gathering spots to see if he shows?"

"I think we should probably get some sleep. The jet lag will hit you hard in another four or five hours, and you can't believe how early daylight comes. The days get shorter and shorter as winter sets in." Chey could do with a good night's rest herself. All this was taking more of a toll on her than she wanted to admit. She suspected Wynn knew, and that's why the girl kept the conversation light-hearted and distracted Chey at every turn.

Back in their room, they tossed down the maps and papers and prepared to turn in early.

Morning would be here before they knew it.

. . .

Renting a car turned out to be more convenient for the girls, and cheaper in the long run, than hiring a taxi. The proprietor gave them a good deal for the week and signed both girls up for temporary driving permits after thoroughly checking their licenses from the states. The policy dictated that drivers owning licenses longer than five years could apply to drive in Latvala as long as they took a crash course in rules and regulations. There wasn't too much to learn, all told, and considering both girls were seasoned drivers, everything made sense and was easy to memorize. The real test would come on the road and reading the maps so they didn't get lost.

Wynn insisted on taking the wheel first. They departed the rental shop at a snail's pace while Wynn got used to the tiny car and the lay of the street. The weather was overcast and cold, but no snow lingered on the pavement.

For that, Chey was thankful. All they needed was to deal with ice or other bad driving conditions.

"Oh, wait. Before we head up to the other town, let's stop up here and grab today's papers and a few of those tabloids, yeah?" Wynn pulled to the curb in front of an open market with the vendor hawking fresh food and other items that might appeal to tourists.

"I'll get it. Don't turn the car off in case it doesn't start again." Chey didn't have a lot of faith in the little blue sardine can. She got out, leaving the passenger door open. Crossing the sidewalk, she plucked up two of the most prominent newspapers and two tabloids. Chey was less convinced they would find what they needed in the 'rags' but it never hurt to check. She couldn't afford to waste any opportunity to meet up with Sander.

Paying the vendor in his own currency, she turned back to the car and got in. The newspapers went into the back, which wasn't quite a seat but more of a shelf where a few other personal items were stored. Coats, scarves, boots in case the weather turned.

"All right. Off we go." Wynn pulled away from the curb, both hands on the wheel, a car honking somewhere behind them.

It was going to be a long ride up the coast twenty-four miles to the small town they'd decided to visit.

Chapter Seven

"You know, I have to say, Latvala really is a cool country." Wynn peered at Chey above the rim of a steaming mug of coffee.

"I know, right? I didn't have a chance to see much while I was here, but what I did see was pretty neat." Chey, sitting in a chair with her back to the wall, met Wynn's eyes across a small table in a quaint cafe they'd found in the small town just north of Kalev. There was only one main street that ran parallel to the shore, with shops and one old hotel on both sides. People parked out front in slanted slots and hurried from one place to the next bundled up in heavy clothing. It was the sort of scene one expected to find on a postcard for tiny, perfect towns with a total population of a thousand, no more. The buildings were reminiscent of alpine villages with peaked roofs and shutters on windows.

"Seriously. I could move to this town right here and be happy the rest of my life," Wynn announced, twisting a look out the front windows.

"That's saying something for a girl who swore she wouldn't ever leave Seattle for any reason," Chey said, shuffling the newspapers in front of her from an empty seat to her left. They'd stacked their purses and coats on it when they'd arrived.

"I know. But I kind of love how the trees back up against the shops on that side of the street," she pointed with a finger. "Then on that side, is the ocean. Never mind the architecture here."

"The winters can get pretty harsh, from what I understand. Once the heavy snows set in, they last until April or something." Chey took another sip of her coffee and glanced out the windows but it wasn't the shops she was looking at. It was the faces of the few citizens out and about. None of them so far belonged to Sander.

"I love snow," Wynn declared with a girlish grin.

Chey laughed and glanced back across the table. "Yes, I know. Admire the town later, when we're 'off the clock', so to speak. Help me keep an eye out the window."

"I don't even know who I'm looking for,"

Wynn admitted. "I need a picture of this guy."

Chey dug her cell phone out of her pocket. Thankfully, she had transferred a few photos of Sander that she'd taken during their canoe trip. Turning the phone around, she showed Wynn who they were looking for.

Wynn's mouth fell open. "What? That's him? No wonder you're googly eyed over this guy."

"I'm not googly eyed. What does that even mean?" Amused, Chey reeled her phone back, stared at the photo with no small amount of heartache and a little flare of anger, before putting it away. "Watch out the window."

Wynn scooted her chair over for a better vantage, then set down her mug of coffee to pick up a tabloid. "Okay. Hottie search. I can scan the tabloid and look out the window at the same time."

Chey did the same. She moved one newspaper over and unfolded the one beneath, prepared to scan it from front to back for news. A black and white photo at the bottom snagged her attention. A photo she'd yet to see. She gasped.

"What?" Wynn clued in to Chey's distress immediately.

Instead of explain, Chey turned the paper around to let Wynn see for herself. There at the bottom was a palm sized picture of Chey and Wynn walking through the lobby of their hotel. It had to be after their dinner last evening.

"*Back For More! Prince Dare's Consort Returns.*" Wynn glanced up after reading the headline accompanying the photo. "Dare? I thought his name was Sander."

"*Wynn!* Who cares. They recognized me! And I'm not his *consort.*" Chey snorted and ripped the woolen cap off her head. A few haphazard hairs stuck up here and there.

"But you kind of are. Or were. Did they have other pictures of you in the paper when you were here before?"

"I don't know—wait." Chey remembered the snippets left on her bed by the maid who'd tried to kill her. It dawned on her late, very late, that the tabloids and newspapers must have written several stories on her. The innocent shopping trip with Mattias had been quite a public spectacle. More recently was her trip to Monte Carlo with Sander. Holding hands, staring into each other's eyes. "Yes, I guess they did. It's not like I ran to town every day to check the papers, you know?

There's no telling what they printed, or how many pictures there were."

"Fix your hair. It looks like a bird tried to make a nest." Wynn leaned over to swipe strands this way and that. Earlier, after they'd dressed in thick slacks, sweaters and knit scarves, Wynn had french braided Chey's hair.

"I don't care about my hair right now--"

"Trust me. If you could see it, you would." Wynn fixed it as well as she could, then protested when Chey snatched the paper back. "Hey, I wasn't through reading!"

"You're supposed to be watching the window. I wonder if Sander saw this today." Chey could only imagine what he must think. Did he know she was here? Would he try and make contact? "Maybe we should have stayed at the hotel. I never thought of using the media to try and lure *him* to *us.*"

"I didn't either. Then again, I didn't realize you were a celebrity here." Wynn picked up her coffee, propped both elbows on the table, and sipped while watching Chey.

"I'm not a celebrity."

"Apparently those people last night think you are. The ones who paused for pictures and waved all shy and star-struck?"

Chey snorted. "They weren't star struck."

"I'm just saying. I think they were. And for the record, how many Princes read the daily paper? Maybe he hasn't seen it and doesn't know you're here. Even if he does, he wouldn't be expecting you to hang out in a small town like this, where he might or might not show up for coffee and a doughnut."

"He has people for that, I'm sure." Or maybe Sander didn't. Did he? If he'd moved back into the cabin in the woods, he might not receive daily papers. Surely the people at the castle kept track. Whether they mentioned it was another story altogether, and Chey, after another moment or two of consideration, decided they wouldn't tell Sander she was here. Not after wanting her to be gone so bad in the first place.

"What does the article say?"

Chey opened the paper, which only consisted of perhaps seven pages total, and skimmed through to the relevant story. She cringed while she read.

"In a nutshell," she summarized, "Prince Dare's *consort* sneaked back into the country—or never left—in a last bid attempt to win his hand." Chey felt her face flush with embarrassment. "There is a picture of us entering the hotel in Monte Carlo, too. They don't miss anything."

"Let me see." Wynn snatched the paper out of Chey's hands. "No wonder the people here recognize you. He'll be king, right? Of course they're interested in what woman he dates. They probably ran pictures of you two before this, too. While you were back in the states."

"Thanks for pointing that out." Chey picked up her coffee and looked out the window. Seeing the picture made Chey maudlin. They'd looked so happy—had *been* so happy—then. Now the world had tilted out of control once more and Chey couldn't find familiar footing. It seemed this was happening every few weeks and it kept her off kilter.

"I think we're doing the right thing. We just have to be patient. He'll show up, don't worry." Wynn patted Chey's arm, then sat back in her seat, paper in hand, to soak up the news.

Chey couldn't help but worry. This was such a shot in the dark, a long shot if there ever was one. There had to be a better way to make contact with Sander.

She just didn't know what it was.

. . .

Two days passed. Two days where Wynn continued to fall in love with Latvala, and Chey searched for Sander. They hit up the other small town along the coast between Kalev and the castle, spending more than half the day discovering its wharf, shops and beauty. Each day that passed left Chey more worried than the one before it, to the point that she started having trouble falling asleep at night. Acutely aware of the passage of time, and how little of it they had left, she began to think they weren't taking the right approach to finding Sander. Wandering small towns in the hope he might show up for coffee was just too risky by itself.

They needed another plan.

Back in the same cafe where they'd discovered the newspaper article, the girls sipped coffee and contemplated the day. It was early, earlier than any morning they'd risen so far, and the weather report poring out of a static-screened television in the corner promised snow by nightfall. Not knowing how long they would be out, the girls had donned thick pants in wool, boots with heavy tread, and coats to go over knit sweaters that kept the cold from their skin. Chey wore another beanie cap over her french braid and gloves on her hands.

"I think tomorrow, we have to try another tactic," Chey finally said.

"Like what? We haven't come up with another plan besides my hair-brained one with the fake baby." Wynn watched faces out the window.

"Maybe it's time to just drive up to the gates and flat out ask to see him. Let them all know I'm here if they don't already." The mere thought made Chey's stomach flutter with nerves.

"Where do you think that'll get you? I mean, I'm all for it, you know. If nothing else is working, and we're running low on time, then I think we have to pull out all the stops and going straight to the lion's den is definitely pulling out a stop."

"I'm sure they'll turn me away. Unless Sander gets wind. If I'm really lucky, someone will call him and he'll be intrigued enough to make them let me in, at least to plead my case. I think that's farfetched, but still." Chey couldn't decide what she thought the guards would do. Every few minutes, she changed her mind dependent on what knowledge Sander had of her visit to Latvala. He was either still angry and didn't want to see her, or his temper had cooled and he would at least hear her out.

"Okay, tomorrow then. We'll just drive straight to them and see what happens. All they can say is no, in the end, which leaves us back where we started."

"Right." Chey reached up to adjust the edge of her cap.

"That guy is *hot*," Wynn said, muttering against the rim of her coffee mug.

"What guy?" Chey glanced through the cafe. There was a table of fishermen in the far corner, none of them looking this way and none of them really fitting the description of 'hot'. They appeared tired, as if just off a three day shift.

"No, no, *that* guy." Wynn reached over to gently turn Chey's head by the chin toward the window. Toward the vision of a man with broad shoulders in a palomino coat and weathered jeans. Tall, over six-feet, he stood talking jovially with a man and woman who wore welcoming smiles and bobbed their heads in agreement to whatever the other man said.

Even though Chey could only see a sliver of his profile, she would have known Sander anywhere. The shape of him, the way the top half of his sandy blonde hair had been pulled back into the familiar tail. His easy going rapport with the couple suggested he was just another man, coming or going from work.

No Prince here, no Heir to the throne. He was the same as you and you and you.

Although Chey had heard him talk about walking among the people, seeing it was another thing entirely. Even Mattias did not command the jocular charisma that Sander seemed to bleed from every pore. That couple knew exactly who he was, and he knew *they* knew, but he displayed no fear in their presence, no wariness that someone might pull a gun and end him. *These* were not his enemies.

"Isn't he hot? Man, he can light my fire anytim--"

"That's him," Chey said, cutting Wynn off.

"Him who? You mean *that's* Sander?" Shock laced Wynn's question. She snapped a look at Chey, mug hitting the table with a thud and a light splash of coffee.

"Yes. I told you. He's just..." Chey had no good words. When Sander clapped the man on the back and stepped past the couple, it galvanized Chey into motion.

It was now or never. If she missed this opportunity, she might not get another.

"C'mon, hurry. We have to catch him before he leaves." Bustling into the cream colored coat she'd stripped off when they sat down, Chey jerked the lapels together and stood up.

Wynn was right on her heels.

"I can't believe we found him," Wynn said, following Chey to the door.

"Honestly? I can't either. My stomach is in knots," Chey admitted. She pushed outside. Sander was striding along the walk in front of the shops, raising a hand here or there to greet this person or another.

"He doesn't act like any Prince I've ever seen. I wouldn't have recognized him as the man in the newspaper shot of you two at that fancy shindig." Wynn, with her shorter legs, had to walk faster to keep up with Chey.

"I know. I never guessed who he was either, when I first met him." Chey stared at the center of Sander's back. What was she going to say? Should she tap him on the back? Call his name?

He solved the problem of how to approach when he suddenly stopped walking and slanted his chin toward his shoulder, then finished the glance and looked behind him. His jaw was lined with a thin, golden layer of stubble, eyes as vivid blue as they'd ever been.

Chey's heart flipped over. She stopped walking, too, arrested by the direct slice of his stare. Wynn pulled up short at her side.

For a long second, Chey and Sander merely stared at each other. There was still enough distance between them to make a casual greeting awkward. Wynn nudged Chey's elbow with her own.

It motivated Chey to close the gap with small, hesitant steps. Her breath plumed white past her lips, indicative of the falling temperature.

"Sander," she finally said, when the words untangled themselves from her throat. "I've come all this way to talk to you. I hope you'll give me a few minutes to explain."

His eyes never left her face. Chey thought he would turn back and continue on, leaving her standing in her own dust.

She couldn't tell if he was happy to see her, or relieved—or annoyed. He hid his emotions well.

Much to her amazement, he faced her with his whole body. There was still something wary in the set of his shoulders and the way he regarded her as she walked up within a few feet of his position.

"I wasn't aware there was anything left to explain," he said, accent deep and clipped, voice cool and indifferent.

Wynn hustled up just then and stuck her gloved hand out. "Hi, I'm Chey's best friend, Wynn. I came with her all the way from Seattle. You must be Sander."

Chey could have killed Wynn. But Sander didn't disappoint. He turned his incisive gaze on her, clasped her outstretched hand in one of his own, and shook firmly.

"Wynn, my pleasure to meet you. Chey didn't tell me she was returning to Latvala." Sander released Wynn's hand and pushed his own back into his coat pocket.

"I know. It was a last minute kind of thing. Nice to meet you, too." Wynn ramped up a smile, then gestured over her shoulder with a thumb. "Actually, I forgot our newspapers back at the cafe." Wynn followed through with a turn and broke into a little jog the opposite direction.

Relieved, Chey looked up at Sander to find him watching her again. "I think we have a lot left to say. Or I do, anyway. If you'll listen. That night at the--"

An explosion rocked the day, coming from somewhere behind the line of shops near the water. Before Chey knew what happened, she found herself on the ground, Sander sprawled atop her.

This was a familiar scenario.

Instantly his expression was sharp and assessing, eyes darting up and down the street. Chey heard screams in the distance and saw people running from the shops, from trucks and other vehicles, toward the wharf.

"Get inside and stay inside," Sander said in a gruff voice. He got to his feet in a swift motion, bringing her with him.

"But, Sander, wait--" Chey's protests fell on deaf ears. Sander was already running in the same direction as everyone else, cutting through a narrow alley between buildings for the docks.

Chey disregarded his instruction and took off after him. Smoke curled through the air and the screams intensified. There had been some sort of horrible accident. She smelled gas, too, and burning rubber.

"Chey! What was that?" Wynn was not far behind her, running for all she was worth.

"I don't know!" Chey didn't need to look back to know that Wynn would keep up. Cutting down the alley, she was in time to see Sander bolt across a paved road and onto a wide dock. Beyond him, flames. Black smoke. People fleeing in all directions.

Emerging from the alley, Chey came upon a scene of horror.

A barge had impacted another boat, pushing it half onto the wharf and into a small seafood shanty that had collapsed and exploded. Men and women trapped on the barge, the damaged boat and beneath fiery debris from the shanty screamed for help. Sander shucked his coat on the run and threw it down over a man on fire, using his hands to roll him along a part of the wharf that wasn't burning.

Wynn bumped into Chey with a startled gasp of shock, one hand flying to cover her mouth.

In the next second, Chey bolted

forward, aiming for the flailing, small arm of a child buried under a charred slab of wood.

Every other minor worry and fear evaporated in the face of such disaster.

All she could think about was reaching the child before it was too late.

Chapter Eight

"Grab my hand! Hold on!" Chey kicked at the slab of wood smothering the child. She could hear tiny gasps for breath between screams. That the child was still alive after such trauma was a miracle. She doubled her efforts to get the wood off. Black pieces splintered away from her boot after another kick. Finally, the heavy piece fell away, clattering over the edge of the dock into the water.

Blonde haired, with big blue eyes, the child—who was no more than five—stared up at Chey in terror. Burns made holes in the thick layers of clothes, blood oozed from a gash in her forehead and soot streaked her otherwise porcelain skin.

Chey gathered the girl into her arms and wheeled away as a sharp crack sounded under her feet. This section of dock was ready to go. Stumbling, Chey got her balance and ran toward a knot of Latvala citizens setting up a trauma area for victims. People were still streaming in from businesses and nearby homes, bringing blankets, dry clothing, food. It was a concerted effort, with other men and women charging down onto the docks to help save lives.

Several women took the child from Chey's arms, rattling off what sounded like words of gratitude in their mother tongue. Turning back, Chey took stock: one barge, a trawler and half the dock were on fire, more people were trapped between the boats under heavy pieces of wharf that had snapped like sticks under the weight of the collision. Sander and Wynn were nowhere to be seen. Several people were burned, more were unconscious, and still more floated in the water, flailing and crying. At some point, snow had started to fall, painting the scene in a surreal swirl of flakes and haze.

She darted between smoking pieces of rubber, around a slab of demolished wood, and down into a crack in the dock. Hopping from one piece to the next, she gripped the sections, thankful for the gloves still on her hands, and slipped closer to the water. Without dipping even one toe in, Chey knew it must be frigid. Those in the water wouldn't last long at all.

"Hey! Swim over here. Grab this!" She tugged a length of loose pipe free and extended the end toward a struggling swimmer. It wasn't much to hold onto, but other than shredded wood, there wasn't anything else to use. All Chey could see was a shock of wet, red hair, red eyebrows and a wealth of freckles. The splashing woman fought her way closer to the dock, hindered by heavy winter clothes. A nondescript coat weighed down her arms while the ragged end of a scarf trailed on the surface. She went under twice, causing Chey to consider actually going in after her. The tenacious survivor resurfaced both times, fighting her way toward the pipe.

"Good, good, just grab the end and I'll pull you in." Chey shouted to be heard over the roar of fire somewhere to her left and the din of panicked voices calling out into the day.

The woman reached for the pipe and missed. Teeth chattering, a gust of breath rushed from between lips beginning to turn blue from the cold. She surged and reached. Missed again.

"You've almost got it. Come on!" Chey allowed herself to skid another foot closer to the water. At the sharp angle of the collapsed dock, she was on the verge of falling in herself. Clinging as best she could to an edge, she leaned further, the end of the pipe wavering just out of reach of the swimmer. Finally, the woman grabbed hold.

Chey hauled her in, bracing her feet and using the grip on the dock as leverage. The soggy coat felt like wet carpet, heavy and awkward to maneuver. Chey went hand over hand, grabbing a sleeve, the lapel, whatever she could to bring the woman to safety. Grunting, breath freezing in her lungs, Chey twisted her body to make room. The redhead flopped down, gasping and wheezing.

"You climb up right here. Take the pipe if you need help," Chey said. She decided to come behind the woman and push instead of pull. If she lost her grip, the lady might wind up right back in the water again. Chey put all her weight into providing leverage while the woman sought a more level section of dock.

It was precarious going, with several setbacks, before the woman made it up to a point where waiting men could haul her the rest of the way.

Slipping on the damp, slick wood, Chey

sought a better hold. Her face felt numb, like her hands, which didn't want to grip things with the strength of even five minutes ago.

A fisherman leaned over the crack above, beanie askew on his head, beard so thick it obscured his mouth. He shouted at Chey and made 'come here' gestures.

She scrambled up the wood, or felt like she scrambled. In reality, she realized she was barely moving. How had the wet woman done it? She must have been twice as cold and even more immobile than Chey.

The dock cracked.

Chey slipped further. Her feet, then her legs, went into the water. The angle of the damaged wharf was too steep, too slippery. She couldn't get traction and had nothing else to hold onto. The water was even colder than she imagined it would be. Needles of ice pierced her calves and thighs and seeped down into her boots.

The fisherman shouldered out of his coat, tossed it aside. He peeled out of his suspenders and dangled them down to her, keeping a tight grip through one loop. Flat on his belly, he inched forward until his balance started to tip. He shouted, making more gestures, his eyes sharp and concerned.

No matter how far he stretched, the distance seemed like miles to Chey. Surely it was a matter of feet, a reasonable gap to handle. Staring up, snow landing on her cheeks and forehead, the fisherman looked smaller and smaller by the minute. Was she sinking and didn't realize it? Fear galvanized her into motion. She surged upward, straining and reaching, praying the dock didn't crack and sink in with her attached.

If she could just grab the suspender. If she could just move her legs, get a boot on the wood. Her entire lower half refused to function as it needed to.

Mind over matter, Chey. Push harder. The other woman did it and she was submerged longer.

Just past the fisherman's shoulder, another blonde head came into view.

Sander.

He stared down, then flattened to his stomach and scooted dangerously forward over the edge.

The fisherman handed off the suspenders, braced his feet at angles, and grabbed onto his Prince's coat and pants at the back.

Chey watched the men work in unison without any communication at all. One would think the Heir to Latvala did this every day of his life. What was more, the *people* acted like it was normal.

"Grab the suspenders, Chey," Sander called down. He wasn't shouting, wasn't yelling. A shock of hair fell over his forehead.

"I don't know if I can reach it," she called back. The drag of the water on her legs made it hard to move at all.

The dock cracked again; she slipped another foot into the water. Scrambling, sure that the chunk of wood would just slide under the surface with her on it, Chey fought to reach the suspenders. She met Sander's eyes. His were intense, focused, worried.

"I'll get it," she said, and with a surge in her flagging energy, she lurched up to make another grab. The water lapped at her ribs now, soaking her coat.

Sander slipped down a foot when the fisherman lowered him. He was the only thing keeping Sander from taking a header onto the wood, and then into the water.

"I've got you no matter what," Sander

said with steely determination, as if he wasn't hanging all but upside down over a busted section of wharf.

Chey's fingers hooked through the suspenders. Immediately, Sander started reeling her up. He barked words over his shoulder to the fisherman, who hauled the Prince back by his coat and pants. With a reach and clasp, Sander grabbed hold of Chey's wrist and forearm. His grip was firm, undeniable.

He wouldn't let her go.

With the help of two more fishermen, their anchor pulled Sander and Chey to the wharf. Chey rolled onto her back, legs numb, chest rising and falling with the effort of holding on and kicking against the water.

Sander peered down over her, shucking his damaged coat to lay over her torso.

"We'll get you into a tent and into some warm clothes. Are you hurt anywhere else?" he asked with brisk efficiency. Sander might have been one of the doctors for how thoroughly he assessed and treated her.

Through chattering teeth, Chey said, "I don't think so. If you'll just get me some new boots, I can--"

"No, no. Lay back," he said, using his

palms to press her down when she tried to sit up. "You're in no shape to help. You've done more than enough."

The fishermen brought a stretcher over.

"This is ridiculous," Chey said, brushing at Sander's hands. She missed, misjudging the angle. "I'm fine."

"You're bleeding," Sander informed her. "And you look a step away from hypothermia." He lifted her onto the stretcher, giving more orders to the fishermen.

"Bleeding?" That was a surprise to Chey. She didn't know she was bleeding. From what wound? Disconcerted and disoriented, she felt the world tilt when the stretcher lifted off the ground.

"Don't worry, you're in good hands," Sander said. He paced by the stretcher as the men ferried Chey toward a newly erected tent. The people of Latvala had worked quickly to establish an emergency work center close to the docks.

"But, Wynn--"

"She's helping the nurses out. She's fine." Sander squeezed her shoulder a last time, then parted away from the group. He headed back toward the wreckage at a jog.

Chey turned her head to watch him go before losing sight of him in the teeming mass of bodies. She wanted to go with him. Help others injured by the accident. The fishermen had other ideas.

Toted inside a tent, they transferred her to a military style cot and exited with the stretcher in tow. Nurses dressed in civilian clothing swarmed around her, bringing warm blankets, hot tea and bandages.

Chey gave up the struggle to rise and finish what she'd started.

The nurses would have it no other way.

. . .

Nine hours after the wharf ordeal began, Chey and Wynn climbed into the little blue car and headed back to Kalev. Both girls were exhausted, sore and mildly injured. At least their sopping clothes had been exchanged for dry ones brought by volunteers at the site.

Neither said anything as Wynn parked in the garage. They lumbered their way through the lobby and up to their room.

One by one, they took steaming

showers and changed into soft pajamas that felt like heaven on their skin. They ate a late dinner of fruit, toast and oatmeal, with hot spiced cider on the side.

All of Kalev was abuzz with news of the accident. They sat on the couch and watched television reports, warm mugs in their hands and blankets pulled to their chin. A ticker tape in English running at the bottom of the screen kept the girls informed of the details.

The cause of the accident, they discovered all this time later, was a heart attack suffered by the driver of the barge. He'd slumped over on approach to the wharf, bumping the lever forward that sent the barge speeding faster than it normally would have. One impact led to another, resulting in the explosion.

Eight people perished in the aftermath, with dozens more hurt. Amateur videographers captured much of the rescue effort on film, from the fiery blaze to fishermen working together, to the tents set up by volunteers. Several times, Sander was shown on the screen, a vaunted hero who had saved a handful of lives.

Twice, Chey's image flashed into view. One shot showed her pulling the child free from under the charred slab of wood. It was an image the networks would use over and over, like so many others. Of course several mentions were made about her status with Prince Dare—or rather the lack of status. No one was sure.

Chey wasn't sure how she felt about the extreme gratitude the people of that small community had shown her. After all, she'd only done what anyone else would do in a time of crisis. She'd thrown concern for herself out the window and done what needed doing to save those who couldn't help themselves. But the citizens expressed an outpouring of thanks to both her and Wynn for their aid.

It was touching, and endearing, since Chey felt the same gratitude toward the people for helping *her* when she'd needed it most. After recovering for a few hours in the tent, Chey, in new, dry clothes and a bandage or two on her wounds, had gone right back to giving her time to assist the nurses as more patients came in. There were many who needed stitches or salve for burns and any number of smaller injuries suffered from daring rescues.

She hadn't seen Sander again. Even after a thorough search outside, as the snow had fallen heavier and the day waned, he wasn't to be found among the survivors, workers or those in the tents. It could have been that Chey simply missed him coming or going, but she suspected he'd slipped away after the last of the victims had been pulled free.

Her chance to thank him, to talk to him, vanished when he did.

At least he knew she was here.

"Can you believe all that happened?" Wynn finally asked, breaking the comfortable silence. She stared at the television as if not really seeing the images broadcast there.

Chey glanced at her friend. She was proud of Wynn for the hours of tireless aid she'd given. "Not really. What a shame about the ones that died, too."

"Oh, I know. The people were so torn up. I wonder if we should go back tomorrow."

"What for? It'll take days to clean up the mess at the wharf," Chey said.

"I don't know. It just feels like we should go back and do something." Wynn sipped her hot cider.

"We can go back if you want. I'm not sure we'll help. Might be more in their way at this point." Heavy equipment would have to be brought in to deal with the remains of the wrecked boats.

"I don't know if we'll be able to get through. Look at the forecast," Wynn said next, as the weather flashed in through the reports of the accident. Eight to ten inches overnight, said the weatherman, with temperatures dropping into the single digits.

Chey shuddered. "It must be an early storm. I didn't think that kind of snow came this early in the season."

"Yeah. It'll hamper driving, for sure." Wynn grumped between swallows of cider.

"It'll hamper a lot of things," Chey said, mostly under her breath.

Wynn picked up the remote and turned the television off. She looked at Chey. "Do you think he'll find you?"

It was the first they'd spoken of Sander since the crash. Helpless, Chey lifted a shoulder. "I don't know."

"I can tell you one thing. It's easy to see why you fell for him. He seems like a really great guy, Heir and Prince aside."

"Yes, he's great. Considerate, thoughtful, boisterous—listen to me. I sound smitten." Chey smiled at her own praise and looked down into her mug.

"You sound like you're in love with him

to me," Wynn pointed out. Like Chey, she rarely minced words.

"I guess I am." Chey didn't bother to deny it. Exactly when she'd known, she couldn't be sure. She just knew that she was, and that she wanted a fair shot at making things work between them. Even if she was filled with dread at having to deal with his family, and what being involved with Sander meant for the long term.

He was worth it.

"I bet you first thing in the morning, he shows up here with a huge bouquet of roses and sets everything straight." Wynn matched Chey's smile, then tilted her head back against the couch.

"That's probably asking a little too much, too soon. But we can hope." Chey felt as tired as Wynn suddenly looked.

"I'll hope for you on my way to bed. I feel like I could sleep for a week." Wynn closed her eyes.

Chey laughed and set her mug aside. "Same here. Let's go get some rest. I have a feeling we're going to need it."

. . .

"Look at this, Chey. The news on TV says that *members of the Royal family plan to show solidarity with the families of the victims of Vogeva by attending an honorarium today at noon.* The only reason I can read that is because they have the ticker tape in English below the news anchor again," Wynn said, standing in front of the television in her Betty Boop pajamas.

Three hours after the alarm went off, Chey and Wynn were still in their nightwear, plotting what they were going to do for the day. In her trusty velveteen pajamas with the candy canes emblazoned over the pants, Chey walked her fresh mug of coffee closer to the TV. Order in breakfast had been taken care of, as well as checking the roads to see if they were clear of snow.

The plows had been busy; every street they could see from their hotel window was scraped down to the asphalt.

Chey's heart hammered in her chest when flashes of Sander's face came and went on the screen. The news station had chosen to show the ones of his soot streaked jaw and clothes from the accident yesterday, reminding viewers once again that their Prince cared deeply for his people.

"Did it say Sander specifically would be there?" Chey asked.

"No, just members of the Royal family. But you'd think, since he was a part of it, that he would show up." Wynn glanced at the digital clock on the nightstand. "Since we got up so early, we still have three and a half hours to decide if we want to drive to Vogeva."

Chey opened her mouth to reply but a trio of hard knocks on their hotel door stopped her cold. Remembering Wynn's prediction that Sander would show up with flowers and apologies, she snapped a look across the room, eyes wide.

Could it really be him?

"Oh my God, I told you!" Wynn set down her mug and darted past Chey, apparently forgetting they were still in their nightclothes. She didn't hesitate to unlatch the chain and swing the door wide. "Hi--"

Natalia gave Wynn a thorough looking over before brushing past with a snort of derision. Coiffed, dressed to immaculate perfection, the youngest Royal's nostrils flared when she got a look at the cozy hotel room and the dark haired woman staring like a deer in the headlights. Natalia raked Chey with a cold, mocking glance. Two members of her security detail entered behind her, while three more remained in the hallway.

"I didn't believe the reports that you had actually dared to return on your own merit," Natalia said, peeling her gloves from her hands in a way that suggested she wouldn't be touching anything. Not in *this* room.

Chey, recovering her wits, took another sip of her coffee and twisted to set the mug on the little table at the end of the couch. She couldn't have felt more exposed, or ridiculous, if she'd been stark naked.

"Then I suggest you get new intel," Chey said with a healthy dose of sarcasm. She was in no mood to deal with Natalia.

Natalia met her eyes, then perused the candy cane Pjs with a telling look of disgust. "Listen, I'll make this brief. You were war--"

"Excuse me," Wynn said, interrupting. She stalked across the room toward Chey and Natalia as if she wasn't wearing Betty Boop's face on her chest. "Who the hell are you again?"

Chey bit her tongue. Why make it

easier for Natalia? Except Natalia didn't give Wynn the time of day. She picked up right where she'd left off before the intrusion.

"You were warned, were you not, to stay away? Is it not enough, then, that my brother *sent* you home after he discovered you're just as conniving as I've always said you were? Hm?" Natalia arched a sleek brow in question.

Wynn gasped when she realized who was standing in front of her.

Chey, gripped with a sudden devilish tongue, leaned in ever so subtly. She sniffed in Natalia's direction. "Pardon? I'm used to you blathering drunkenly, so I'm not quite sure I understood what you said."

Natalia's expression shifted, growing impossibly colder. Her eyes caressed Chey's face in the same way a butcher might a chicken right before he wrung its neck.

"You're to leave Latvala immediately. Heroics aside, the Royal family finds you a threat and has ordered your departure. *Today.* Here are the tickets for a three-thirty flight this afternoon. Make sure you're on it," Natalia said, delivering the news with obvious relish. One of her guards stepped forward and extended a classy envelope with the Royal seal on the front.

Chey glanced at the envelope and felt her heart sink into her stomach. Natalia—perhaps the whole Royal family—wasn't playing around. They meant business. Had Sander been a part of this decision, too? Just because he'd saved her didn't mean he forgave her. The few second hesitation gave Natalia another opening.

"If you decline the tickets, we'll be forced to arrest you. Now. It's your choice," Natalia said.

Left with little else to do, Chey plucked the envelope out of the guard's hand.

"You've made your point, Natalia. Now get out," Chey said. She couldn't find it in her to even pretend diplomacy.

Natalia breathed a little laugh, clearly relishing Chey's reaction. "You're hereby banned from ever entering Latvala again, by the way. If you attempt to pass through customs, you'll be arrested as a terrorist and indefinitely jailed."

Wynn gasped again.

Natalia smirked, pivoted on a heel, and stalked from the room. Her guards followed, closing the door in her wake.

Chey stood there as if a freight train

had just run her over. Breathless with shock, she couldn't make her legs move, couldn't look at the tickets or even glance at Wynn. The reality of the situation kept hammering at Chey's insides. *Banned. Forever.* There would be no reconciliation, no tentative talks between her and Sander to fix things. And once she left, she could never return.

The iron thumb of the ruling Monarchy had her trapped between a rock and a hard place.

Wynn stepped in front of her, mouth agape. She clasped Chey's biceps with both hands and just...stared. *Did that just happen?* said her expression.

Chey met Wynn's eyes. She nodded, not needing Wynn to ask the question aloud.

She glanced down at the envelope in her hands and opened it. Of course, the outer leather was high quality, the Royal seal stamped in silver. Natalia had spared no expense to drive her point home. *They were Royalty, Chey was not. She wasn't welcome here.* The tickets inside, printed in two languages, backed up Natalia's threats. There were two, one for Chey, one for Wynn. Someone had been snooping in the hotel's database. Three-thirty was the scheduled departure time, which meant they needed to be at the airport at least an hour early.

Chey wondered if security there would call someone if she didn't check in before her flight. Would they go so far to arrest her at the hotel?

"What's that look?" Wynn asked, still holding onto Chey's arms.

Chey closed the envelope and smoothed her thumb over the seal on the front. She glanced up. Met Wynn's eyes. She said, "Feel like going for a drive?"

Chapter Nine

"Now *this* is what I'm talking about. Right here. Not allowing that little wench to kick you when you're down. We'll show her a thing or two about American tenacity. Yeah?" Wynn rubbed her hands while the little blue car warmed up. She exhaled, breath pluming white against the windshield. Then she glanced sideways at Chey.

"American tenacity is likely going to get me arrested. We'll probably hit ice between here and Vogeva. Even though the road's been plowed," Chey said, studying the map in her lap. Natalia could kiss the snowy bottom of her boots. She wasn't giving up now.

"Don't worry about the ice. I can handle it. Seriously, though, if her men see you when we get to Vogeva, you get out of the car and run, okay? I'll lead them away, hopefully give you a head start." Wynn turned the heat up another notch. Parked in the hotel's garage, the windshield was already clear, the tires dry.

"I don't want you to end up in jail, Wynn. I wouldn't put it past her," Chey said. It wasn't worth Wynn being imprisoned because of Chey's willful plan to put herself in Sander's path regardless of Natalia's threats.

"Don't worry about me. Daddy's a lawyer, or have you forgotten? He'll spring me—and you—free if we get into trouble."

"That's *if* they let you near a phone." Chey didn't trust that Natalia would follow any International rules.

"We'll be fine. You'll catch up to Sander, explain it all, and you two will get back together." Wynn ground the gear into reverse and backed out of the parking spot.

Just as Chey thought, there were slick patches on the road despite the salt and recent plowing. Wynn slid the car to the first stoplight, Chey's arms braced against the door and dash in case they went right through against the red. Thankfully, the little car came to a stop. Chey and Wynn glanced at each other at the same time.

It was going to be a long drive to Vogeva.

Three turns later, Wynn hunched up

against the rather large wheel, she suddenly veered the car into a right turn. The wheels skidded, the back end swinging out into the oncoming lane.

"Wynn!" Chey clenched her teeth, prepared for impact. They missed another car by inches.

"I think we're being tailed," Wynn said, giving the car gas. She shifted from first to second, glancing left-right-left for a place to pull in.

"What?" Chey twisted around to look out the oval shaped back window. She saw three cars, only one of them a sedan that might or might not have belonged to a security detail. "How can you be sure?"

"Because that black car is still behind us. It started back at the hotel."

"Since when did you go all Mission Impossible?"

"The second some Royal wench showed up at our hotel door, threatening to turn you into a terrorist," Wynn said, tone dry. She eased the little car around a corner, then into someone's single car garage with the door still up.

"Wynn, what are you--"

"Just wait." Wynn watched the rear view mirror.

"Sure. They won't get us for terrorism,

they'll get us for trespassing on private property." Chey watched out the window. A few moments later, the sedan rolled by, doing at least thirty miles an hour.

"Think they saw us?" Wynn asked.

"I don't know. They're out of sight and I can't tell if they stopped."

"We'll give it another five minutes, then we'll back out and go on."

Five minutes felt like an hour to Chey. Any moment, she expected to see the sedan back up and stop outside the garage. Either that, or several silhouettes darken the garage doorway.

Nothing happened. The sedan didn't return, and no men approached.

Wynn backed the car out of the garage, sliding into the street before she could get the car to stop. Putting it in first, she went the other direction, taking several back roads to reach the main artery that would ferry them to Vogeva.

Finally, they were on their way. The bigger streets were clearer than the smaller, less driven ones, and once Wynn reached the two lane highway, she had an easier time controlling the car. Sitting forward, tense and on alert, Wynn drove them toward their destination.

While Wynn concentrated, Chey

thought ahead to their plan. To what she would say to Sander if she could get close enough to speak. Reaching into her pocket, she pulled out a handwritten note she'd penned before leaving the hotel room.

It read: *Sander. Things aren't what they seem. We desperately need to talk. Your sister has threatened to have me arrested if I don't leave Latvala and has banned me from ever returning. Please listen to me. I know you sent me to Seattle, and maybe I deserved a cold shoulder for allowing that man to maneuver me outside when I felt so woozy from the wine. But I don't deserve not to be heard out. He drugged me. I'm sure of it. Something is going on. If I can't contact you today, please think on what I've said and find me in Seattle. Give us the chance you fought so hard for. I love you. Chey.*

She hoped it wasn't too dramatic. But it *was* honest, and she thought he needed to know what his sister was up to. Chey only hoped Sander hadn't been an agreeable participant in the plot to send her home again.

Vogeva was much the same as when they left it. The wharf was still being sorted through by local officials as well as ones from Kalev. Volunteers had made the trip to help clear the mess, though the snow wasn't helping with clean up efforts.

Wynn drove slower down a side street. The main thoroughfare had been closed down in preparation for the Royal's arrival. Parking in a small lot behind a merchant store, Wynn cut the engine and exhaled a long breath.

"You did good," Chey said, patting her best friend on the shoulder. "So you still think the best place to wait for the entourage is that little bar a few spots up from the cafe we usually sit in?"

"I think so. Just in case someone mentioned to that girl's people that we've been visiting the cafe. I'd hate for them to find us there and haul us out before you have a chance to talk to Sander." Wynn smiled, then pulled the keys out of the ignition. "I'd pull that beanie down a little more, too, and try to stay undercover. People might recognize your face."

"I've got it." Chey put the note back in her coat pocket and flipped the collar up high on her neck. She'd chosen a cream colored peacoat with navy accents on the lapels and cuffs to wear with jeans. Tugging on the matching beanie, unsure just how much more it might disguise her than yesterday, she opened the door and disembarked.

Wynn climbed out her side and closed her door with a rusty thump.

Wary and alert, Chey hunched down into her coat and traversed the pathways until they crossed the street to the other side. It was snowing again, though the flurries spiraled down slow instead of fast. Taking the route behind the line of shops, they approached the bar from the back. Most of the businesses had either side entrances or back ones where more parking was available to customers.

The interior of the gloomy pub provided seating along one entire wall, with three booths up near front windows overlooking the street. A bar ran the length of the right side, with a mirrored back that made the area seem bigger than it actually was. Beams arched up to a point in the high ceiling, adding a rustic flair to the otherwise spartan décor. After procuring mugs of coffee, the girls sank down into a booth near the front window to wait. So far, only four other tables were occupied, indicating people were waiting until closer to the time the Royals were scheduled to arrive, or had chosen other places to hole up.

"You feeling okay?" Wynn asked.

"I guess. Nervous, you know? I'm not sure what to expect." Chey made sure not to stare out the window so that she was easily seen from the street. No sense advertising that she was ignoring Natalia's direct order to leave the country.

"We have about an hour and a half before they're due to make an appearance," Wynn said after checking her watch.

"At least it's comfortable in here. It won't be a hardship to wait," Chey said. A potbelly stove in the back corner spewed enough heat to keep the pub decently warm.

"We've even got stuff to read. And they're in English." Wynn picked up a few newspapers and a tabloid some other customer had left on the booth seat. She slapped them down on the table and plucked the top one off for herself. Laying it open in front of her, she propped her temple in her hand and started scanning through.

Chey glanced at the pile, then stared at the wall beyond Wynn's head. Her mind was too busy with thoughts of Sander to be preoccupied with news she'd probably already seen on the television. The accident was still the most talked about story around.

An hour crept by. Chey, then Wynn, took bathroom breaks and ordered another round of coffee. More people trickled into the bar, as well as other establishments along the row of shops. A few lined the walkways in anticipation, bundled in heavy coats, boots and hats to ward off the snow.

On the third newspaper, Wynn paused at a story on the front page. She checked the date twice.

"What is it?" Chey asked, noticing the shift in Wynn's demeanor.

"See for yourself." Wynn turned the paper around. There right at the top, was a black and white photograph of Princess Valentina and Sander Ahtissari. They were separate pictures situated side by side. The headline, however, left no doubt as to the content of the article. *The Prince Chooses A Bride.*

Chey rubbed her forehead and skimmed the story. In summary, it said what she expected it to say. That Sander had chosen his intended for marriage. The wedding, as Valentina had predicted at the hotel in Monte Carlo, was in the spring. This was cause for celebration, obviously, for the citizens of Latvala.

"They really aren't making this very easy on you," Wynn finally said. "I have to admit—if it was me, I'd probably throw in the towel. How are you going to fight that off?"

"Sander and I already talked about this. We knew there would be obstacles. He made it clear though when he saw her at the hotel that he hadn't agreed to anything. Their *people* had, but Sander had not. Apparently, he changed his mind, or the council went ahead and printed it anyway." Chey wouldn't put anything past them if this was the outcome they really desired. She turned the paper over and tossed it down on the seat so she couldn't see the picture.

For once, Wynn was silent.

Chey met her eyes across the table.

Wynn sipped at her coffee, then glanced out the window. "Should we go outside soon and wait on the sidewalk with everyone else?"

"Probably. Sitting in here won't do me any good." Chey sipped her coffee as well, preparing herself mentally for the coming meeting.

"We want to get a good—oh crap. Is

that them, already?" Wynn set her cup down with a thump.

Chey looked out the window, mug at her lip. Five black Hummers cruised down the street, tires kicking up bits of snow that had fallen since the plows cleared the road. Each one slanted into an open parking space that had been left open for Royalty.

"That's them." She set down her cup and slid out of the booth. Other patrons in the bar headed for the door and pushed out into the cold. Chey got on their heels; Wynn closed in behind her.

Three Hummers spit out security that fanned around the fourth. The men were dressed in all black, with heavy coats, boots, hats and weapons attached to their belts. Chey, standing just behind the first row of people, kept her eyes on the fourth car.

The doors opened. Mattias, Paavo and Gunnar got out. Resplendent in military uniforms, they looked sharp and solemn, considering the nature of their visit. Sander came last, his uniform a step up from the rest, with a royal blue sash across the front and silver double buttons holding the coat closed. Clean shaven, hair scraped back into a low tail, he wore gloves on his hands and a sober expression as he greeted the growing crowd with a crisp nod of his head. The Royal brothers marched along the street itself, flanked by their security. Another car had arrived at some indeterminate time with staff who carried wreaths in memory of the lost.

Chey knew this wasn't the time to call out Sander's name. She couldn't make a scene in front of all these people, especially when the men were so obviously set on a course.

The Mayor of Vogeva met the Royals at the end of the row of shops and saluted the brothers before shaking each of their hands. By this time, hundreds had turned out at the far end of the main street to watch the Royals pay their respects. The wreaths were lined up along an empty stretch of ground with the damaged wharf in the background and a podium someone erected for announcements to be made.

Chey stood half behind Wynn among the crowd, watching as the Mayor took the podium first. The Royals flanked him, two on each side, with their security making a loose circle around the whole. Chey didn't know what the mayor was saying, couldn't take her eyes off Sander.

But she understood the gist, knew by the way a few women around her wiped their eyes that the Mayor was remembering the victims. He'd probably known some of them personally.

Sander stood tall, hands clasped behind his back, distinct in his slightly different uniform. He dominated the male population in sheer presence alone, even more so than Mattias who stood to his left. Chey's breath caught in her throat when Sander looked directly at her. She couldn't tell if he actually saw her, or if he recognized her, or whether she was just another pair of eyes in the crowd.

He took the podium next, his mother tongue slipping eloquently past his lips. The warmth and rasp of his voice over the speaker sent a chill down Chey's spine. Suddenly, the crowd surged with a cheer, several people's hands jutting up into the air. It surprised a twitch out of Chey.

Wynn glanced back; Chey shook her head. She had no idea what he'd said.

The wreaths were gestured to, and then the Wharf, before Sander closed out his personal remarks and stepped away from the podium toward the crowd. People stepped forward to shake his hand, some crying, others as sober faced as the

Royals.

Mattias, Gunnar and Paavo all dispersed to do the same. The security seemed a formality; the Royals didn't look wary at all to walk among the people and share condolences and other quiet sentiment.

"This is it," Wynn whispered over her shoulder, breath gusting white past her lips.

"He's making his way around toward us," Chey replied. "I'm going to move forward when he's just in front of you."

"Got it," Wynn said.

Sander shook hands and stepped on, trading quiet words with people. The closer he got to Wynn and Chey, the more Chey fretted. She gripped the folded note in her gloved hand and held her breath as Sander came within touching distance.

Moving up shoulder to shoulder with Wynn at the last second, she extended the hand with the note trapped against her palm by her thumb. And then he was there, masculine and broad and heart-stopping.

He clasped her hand—and paused. Snow flurried from the sky, fat flakes that decorated the shoulders of his uniform. Chey locked gazes with him, her note crinkling between their palms. He'd saved her yesterday, why shouldn't she be here?

"Please read the note," she whispered, giving his hand a squeeze. She wished they were skin to skin. The subtle scent of his cologne only enhanced his virility. "We need to talk, Sander."

He stared, hand still caught in hers. Chey noticed one of the security paying more attention with Sander frozen in place like that. Taking initiative, Chey removed her hand from his and eased back a few inches.

"Meet me at the cafe in a half an hour," he said. After meeting Wynn's eyes and giving her a curt nod, he continued along the line of people, shaking hands after tucking the note away.

Chey eased back and, with Wynn at her side, navigated her way through the throng toward the sidewalk running in front of the shops.

"It worked. Now you've got your shot to explain," Wynn said, striding double time to keep up with Chey.

"Yes. I probably don't have very long to make my case, but this is more than I'd hoped for." Chey headed inside the empty pub when she came to the door and found the first vacant table near the window.

Wynn sank down into a chair on the other side.

Now, all Chey had to do was wait.

. . .

"Ten minutes before he should be here. I wonder how he's going to manage that with so many people watching his every move," Wynn said, gazing out the window.

The crowd had not dispersed much since they entered the pub.

"I don't know. As long as I can have a few minutes of his time, I think I can make him understand that something went wrong that night in Monte Carlo." Chey, a bundle of nerves, rubbed her gloved hands together. This was her shot, her chance to get through to Sander and beg for more time to discuss things. In private, rather than a pub where anyone might see them.

The back door of the pub opened and closed.

"It's amazing no one recognized you," Wynn added, tucking her hands down between her thighs.

"Yes. But they're not focused on me,

they're focused on the tragedy." Chey's gaze caught on Mattias when the crowd parted just so. She hadn't dared shake hands and say hello, but she realized she missed his friendship. Missed their conversations and how easy he was to talk to. If anyone could understand her plight besides Sander, it was him.

A pair of hands grabbed Chey by the shoulders. Another covered her lips with a cloth that smelled sickly sweet. Chey only had time to draw in a startled breath before the world went hazy past her lashes. She saw vague images of Wynn being hauled out of the booth before her whole world went black.

Chapter Ten

The steady drip of water was the first thing Chey heard when awareness returned. Groaning, slitting her eyes open, all she saw was darkness. Had she passed out at the hotel? Was it the middle of the night? She couldn't recall going to bed. Couldn't even recall, at first, what she'd done last. The hard surface beneath her back and hips made her bones ache, and she reached down with a gloved hand to feel what appeared to be a slab of solid stone.

What the hell?

Sitting up, disoriented and confused, she tried to get her bearings. Struggled to remember why she was here in a place that smelled musty and dank.

"Wynn?" Chey's voice echoed off the walls. Blinking away the blurriness from her vision, she saw a rectangle of light straight ahead, broken up by black lines running up and down the length. Were those vertical blinds? The hotel didn't have them.

Standing up, she discovered she wasn't as steady on her feet as she would have liked to be. Shuffling forward, she bumped into the black lines and realized they were bars. Iron bars. Grunting in surprise, she gripped them in her hands and gave a shake.

It didn't budge. And it was a door, or a gate, she could see that now. A flicker of candlelight out in the corridor beyond was the only source of illumination. The walls there were also stone, reminiscent of underground tunnels.

Turning around, she moved aside so the light would spill past the bars.

She was in some sort of cell. A cell with no other window, no door, only a slab of stone that apparently served as a bed. In the corner sat a rusty pot that Chey didn't want to consider the implications of.

"Hey! Hello? You can't keep me down here!" she shouted, turning back to press her face against the cold iron.

Images rushed back, filling in the blanks of her memory: the Royals in town, Sander making a speech, Chey passing off her note. Their plans to meet. A hand over her mouth and Wynn—oh God, where was Wynn—dragged from the booth.

"Wynn, are you in here? Wynn! Hello?" Chey raised her voice and shook the cell door.

This was impossible. It couldn't be happening, not in today's times. Unless she missed her guess, she was in the dungeon beneath the main Ahtissari castle.

No one answered her calls.

Had Sander set her up? Arranged for someone to grab her? He wouldn't have. He could have ignored her, and her note, and been on his way.

"Hello? *Hello?*" Infuriated, Chey shook the bars again, then let go. Pressing the heels of her gloved hands against her forehead, she tried to wrap her mind around what it all meant. Surely, whoever perpetrated this crime couldn't hold her long.

Maybe Natalia had been at the meeting and paid her guards to grab them. She seriously wanted to throw down with Natalia, Princess or no.

Chey alternated between pacing and sitting on the edge of the stone slab, one knee bouncing in spastic fits as nerves got the better of her.

An hour went by. And another.

Finally, Chey heard a shuffle out in the

corridor. Surging to her feet, she stalked to the bars and shook the door. "Hey! You cannot keep me down here. I'm not a prisoner!"

A long shadow grew from one end of the hall, coming closer. Tall, broad, imposing.

Chey thought she might be sick. Please, oh please no. It couldn't be Sander. Betrayal threatened to make the sudden nausea real.

"My wife has had the devil of a time with you," the King said, striding slowly into view. He had his hands clasped behind a long cape that scraped the ground at the heels of his boots. White fur draped the shoulders, and a gold chain with an ornate clasp fit snug across his chest. Salt and pepper hair had been combed carefully away from the refined but rugged angles of his face, his goatee neatly trimmed.

Chey stared at Aksel, trying to understand what he was saying about his wife. Helina. The woman who had been such a thorn in Chey's side the whole time.

"I don't know what you mean," Chey said. Except that she did. She knew Helina didn't want her dating Sander or being in any part of his life.

"I think you do," Aksel said, coming to a halt on the other side of the bars. He studied her with sharp eyes. "I am King. This is my Kingdom. Sander, my first born, will someday inherit all this, become the ruler I have raised him to be. It comes with great responsibility, something you know nothing about. My wife has tried to warn you away, but you're stubborn, are you not?"

Chey didn't bother to answer what was really a rhetorical question.

"Even my daughter has not been able to keep you away, which, I must admit, is rather surprising."

"You can't keep me here. I'm not a prisoner. This isn't the dark ages and trust me—someone *will* know I'm missing," Chey said, struggling to keep her voice from shaking.

"Really," he said, and it wasn't a question. "Your parents are dead. You have no siblings. Who then, besides the girl who unfortunately accompanied you here, will care?" He arched a thick brow.

Chey was sure the King didn't mean to hit below the belt, but being reminded of the recent death of her parents felt like it. She looked down, away from Aksel's face.

The ugly truth of it was...only her friends would realize she was missing. Chey had an estranged aunt who lived on the other side of the world who hadn't bothered to even attend her own brother's funeral. She wouldn't know or care if Chey disappeared from Seattle.

Both sets of grandparents were gone, and she had no siblings to fall back on.

How galling to know he was right. Aksel appeared to know it, too, and pressed his advantage.

"That's what I thought," he said. "You've painted yourself into a corner, Miss Sinclair, and you're wrong when you say that you're not my prisoner. That's exactly what you are. Any threat to the crown is dealt with swiftly and harshly and you, Madam, have proven to be just that."

Chey looked up. Met Aksel's keen gaze. "Because I'm dating your so--"

"Were. *Were* dating."

"You have no right--"

"I have every right. It says so in the laws of this country. I may hold you indefinitely, without representation, so long as you fall under the category of direct threat to the Monarchy. It's my word against yours, Miss Sinclair. Who do you think the police will believe?" He paced a few feet away, then back again, the end of his cloak trailing the ground. "You should have gotten on the plane."

Chey didn't know what to say. The thought that they could keep her here indefinitely made her stomach ache.

"What, no snappy comebacks? No witty repartee? I'm disappointed, Miss Sinclair. I thought you would have at least lashed out over your treatment." His gaze scanned the circumference of the cell, then found her face again.

"What do you plan to do with me, then? We're in disagreement about my intentions, but you're right. No one will believe me over you. Or your wife." Chey conceded the point.

"Warnings and threats have failed. Returning you to your own country failed. Murder, failed. What would you suggest I do next?"

"Murder?" Chey followed Aksel with her eyes. What was he saying?

He laughed. Low, quiet. Resonant. "Viia was a decent scapegoat, was she not? A pity, though. My wife had grand designs for her and Mattias. It pained Helina greatly to name Viia as the culprit behind Elise's attack. It had become apparent, however, that Mattias was merely stringing the woman along, so the situation only stepped up the progress of having Viia removed as a possible candidate for a wife."

Chey felt dizzy at the duplicity of the Royals. Of the Queen. It shouldn't have surprised her, yet it did. Helina, not Viia, had been behind the attack at the castle. The woman was a snake. And what of Viia? The woman was in jail, would probably spend another ten years or maybe even the rest of her life behind bars, all because she'd been convenient to blame murder upon. A good target to shuffle attention away from the Royal family. Forever changed, damaged, through no fault of her own.

It shook Chey to her core to know that these people were Sander's parents.

"Is control that important, then? Did you arrange Gunnar's wife, too? Aurora for Paavo?" Chey asked.

"That you even need to ask that question is the answer itself," Aksel said, lips thinning. He stopped just outside the bars and studied her face. "The only reason I have taken time out of my busy schedule to visit you in person is because few people know the truth of Viia, and I believe you will take what I have to say next to heart coming from the King instead of security."

Chey waited to hear her fate. She knew that's what came next. Her hands tightened on the iron until her knuckles turned white.

"Your little friend, Wynn, and her lawyer father pose a significant annoyance. Yes, we could arrange to have him taken out and make it look like an accident, a father-daughter catastrophe that would remove the problem once and for all. It is a tedious business, however, eradicating inconveniences, Miss Sinclair. Therefore, I will take the next two days to decide whether you will suffer an unfortunate accident here in Latvala on your way to the airport, or if, one more time, I will send you packing in the hopes that this time, you understand better that I *will* take your life if you so much as consider entering Latvala's borders again. No warning, no capture-and-coerce. You will simply cease to exist, and that will be that." Aksel wore a no nonsense expression, eyes cool and indifferent to the idea of murder.

It was his threat against Wynn and her family, along with the indifference he

184

delivered his plans, that turned Chey's blood cold. She realized then just how out of her depth she really was, and that there were bold plots churning beneath the Royal family of which even some security were not aware. Chey amounted to a wad of gum on the sole of his expensive shoe. One he was having trouble scraping free.

"If you send me home, I promise I'll never set foot here again," she said, licking her lips. Chey felt it important that she fight for her life. "I didn't understand how serious this was, but I do now. Wynn and I won't ever talk about any of this and Sander will never hear from me once I'm gone."

"Things are not so cut and dried as all that, Miss Sinclair," Aksel said. He took a step closer to the bars. "My son fancies he has some shot at 'real love' with you. It has made him take action he would not normally take. Seeing that he is being groomed to one day take my place, it disturbs me that he would challenge our authority over his need to procure an outstanding wife. Your death, arranged just so, would also provide me the necessary tool to press *my* point home to Sander. Which is—it insults me to have my authority questioned, and that he is not in control here. I am. Finding the wreckage of your 'accident' would not be mistaken by Sander for anything other than what it is: taking you out of the equation while teaching him a lesson I thought he had already learned."

Chey took a discreet step back from the bars. Chilled, afraid that it was too late to save her own life, she wanted to put as much distance between herself and the King as she could without making him angry. He'd been right about one thing, too. Hearing this from his own mouth made it a hundred times more potent.

A thousand.

She didn't doubt for a moment that he meant every word.

"While I ruminate on it, someone will be down within the hour to move you to more acceptable accommodations. Regardless what you may think, I'm not *that* much of a heathen." He rumbled a laugh, winked, then stalked away down the corridor.

Chey stared at the place the King had just been, horrified beyond comprehension. It would do no good to cry, or scream, or protest. There was no one to hear. No one who cared. Whatever guards he sent down were surely in his pocket, immune to her pleas or her truths.

The only thing left to do was wait to see if she lived—or died.

. . .

The two security guards who arrived an hour later to escort her to a new holding room were ones Chey had never seen. They wore standard business suits in black and white and did not make eye contact as they guided her through the maze of tunnels to a more updated section of the dungeon. Here, cement floors replaced the dank stone and the walls were covered with paint.

Although spartan, the room they left her in had its own private bathroom and a narrow trio of windows at the very top of the wall near the ceiling. The cream colored paint offset a twin bed with royal blue covers and sheets.

Chey spent forty-eight hours there, alternating between tears and fury. Just when she thought she had control over one emotion, the other rose up to take its place. She saw no sign of Wynn—or any other 'guest' for that matter. Only the guards who came to deliver her meals.

When they arrived in the early afternoon of her second full day, Chey knew the decision had been made. They escorted her down the corridors, up a flight of stone stairs, and out into a side parking area away from the main courtyard. Snow had been plowed off the asphalt, leaving the drive clear. Chey noted that although it wasn't snowing now, the sky was heavy with clouds that promised more in the near future. She wondered if she would die beneath the brooding heavens.

This, then, was what a death row inmate must feel on his final leg to the executioner's chair.

Escorted into the back of a Hummer, Chey buckled in and fidgeted with the edge of the seat. She sent prayer after prayer that this wasn't her end, unable to wrap her mind around the torture of the unknown. Would she make it to the airport alive?

Intrigued as she had once been with Ahtissari castle, Chey discovered she didn't want to so much as glance at it upon her departure. She didn't care to have a last view of its impressive turrets and decorative arches. Natalia was probably staring down from on high, a smirk on her petulant mouth, counting the seconds until Chey was forever banished from her life.

Tense the entire drive, expecting a crash, or explosion or some other horror, Chey watched the shoreline whip by out the window. How different this trip turned out than how she imagined. Just now, all she wanted was the relative safety of her Seattle apartment and a year or two to recover from her inadvertent misery.

They passed through one small town and approached Vogeva from the north. Surprised when the Hummer pulled up in front of the quaint hotel on the main strip, she sat forward and reached for her belt.

The guard in the seat in front reached back to stay her motion. Moments later, a harried looking Wynn rushed out the front door with two guards carrying their luggage at her flank. She made her way around to the passenger side door and climbed in.

"Chey! Oh my god, you're all right. I wasn't sure what to think when they separated us. What happened? Did you get--" Wynn's immediate questions got cut off when Chey shook her head. *Not now. Ask later.*

Wynn's mouth shaped an 'oh' of understanding. She reached across the Hummer once she was in to embrace Chey anyway.

Holding tight to her best friend, Chey saw this as a good sign that perhaps Aksel had decided to let them both go home instead of the alternative. She wouldn't ever be so glad to see Seattle again.

The Hummer made good time from Vogeva to Kalev. Chey and Wynn said little on the way. When the vehicle approached the airport, Chey closed her eyes with relief. Her shoulders were tight with tension, her head aching from stress.

On the sidewalk, the guards passed the girls their luggage, which seemed to be intact and accounted for. One handed each a fresh ticket with their name printed on the front.

Chey glanced beyond the guards after taking her envelope with a murmur of thanks, and silently bid Latvala—and Sander—goodbye. It just wasn't meant to be.

An hour later the girls were in the air

on their way back to Seattle.

Chapter Eleven

Chey stared at her reflection in the mirror and halfheartedly applied a thin layer of peach lipstick to her mouth. Three and a half weeks had gone by since arriving back in the states, and Chey was listless as ever. Tonight, Wynn intended on dragging her to a Halloween party in an upscale neighborhood, where the promise of mystery and surprise awaited. The masked ball was invite only, catering to a select group of people, one of which happened to be an acquaintance of Wynn.

To combat her gloomy mood, Chey had chosen a frail ballerina costume, whimsical and white, with tiny crystals sewn around the low neckline and the hem of the tulle skirt. Ballerina shoes with ribbons wrapping her ankles and calves added character, as well as the sheer white stockings Chey encased her legs in. Little pearl pins dotted the riot of dark curls she'd styled her hair into. A bun was too much work, and she knew her hair would likely spring free of the bobby pins and hair spray anyway.

The mask was the crowning jewel. Made of white porcelain, the maudlin, almost sorrowful expression cast a sharp contrast to the whimsy of the outfit. Only Chey's lips, jaw and chin could be seen. The rest of her face was hidden away. Cut outs allowed a person to view the dramatic make up Chey applied that accentuated her long lashes and blue eyes. White feathers created a fringe around the forehead.

Exhaling once she was through with the finishing touches, Chey snapped off the bathroom light on her way to the kitchen to collect the white cloak that she swirled around her shoulders. It was chilly out and the extra layer a necessity with such a revealing outfit.

Gathering her keys, Chey exited the apartment, locking the door behind her. The night sky was rife with rainclouds and Chey sent up a silent plea that they wait to downpour until she was safe in Wynn's car.

In the parking lot, it wasn't Wynn's Cadillac waiting, but a limousine with Wynn standing beside it, glancing at the sky as if she too were pleading for the deluge to wait. Wynn, decked out as a Steampunk Girl, wore clothes reminiscent of the Victorian era with slight deviations, like suspenders and bits of metal adornments that accented the machine built construction of her mask. It appeared as if gears and gadgets from a large watch had been what the mask was made out of, topped by a tall hat with a small machinery crafted buckle. Wynn wore goggles over her eyes and gloves on her hands.

"What's with the limousine?" Chey asked when she arrived.

"I didn't want us to have to worry about drinking and driving, so I rented it for the evening." Wynn cut Chey a smile below the edge of the mask and climbed in when the driver opened the back door.

"You're so excessive sometimes," Chey said, and followed suit. Being inside the limousine reminded Chey of Latvala, of the Royals, and of Sander. It put a fresh pang in her heart that she tried to stifle as the driver got them under way.

"You have to admit, it's a relief not to worry about it." Wynn pried the goggles up far enough to expose her eyes. "Are you still brooding?"

"What? No." Chey glanced aside, met

Wynn's eyes, then looked forward again. The limousine sped up to get on the freeway.

"Yes you are. After all these weeks. At some point, you're going to have to move on, you know?" Wynn patted Chey's knee with sisterly affection. She had been horrified to learn what happened to Chey in the dungeons on the flight back to Seattle. Since then, Wynn had done her best to take Chey's mind off Sander and the fiasco in Latvala.

"I've moved on,"Chey said, protesting. But she hadn't. Her days were filled with crying jags or indifference. She wasn't up to looking for a job yet, although she knew she needed to. The other half of the photography money wouldn't be coming in after all this.

"You're languishing and thinking 'what if'. I expected it for a week, maybe a week and a half. I'm kind of surprised you're still here almost four weeks later, though," Wynn said. "You dodged a bullet where the King and Queen are concerned. I'm not sure the greatest guy in the world is worth all that."

Chey glanced out the window. "I'm sure you're probably right. If he'd just been a regular guy..."

"There you go again with the what ifs. C'mon. Let's look forward to the party."

Chey tried. Her mind kept veering back to the same place it had for the last three or so weeks.

Fifteen minutes later, distraction came whether she wanted it to or not. The limousine pulled in past a modest gate toward a good sized mansion nestled on its own five acre lot. Lamps lined the curving driveway toward the broad front steps leading to the doors. Trees dotted the dark landscape to the side of the mansion, in front beyond the wide drive, and off in the back.

Bringing the limousine to a stop, the driver let the engine idle while guests unloaded from a vehicle in front of them.

"There are supposed to be like a hundred and fifty people here tonight," Wynn said, positioning her goggles back over her eyes.

"That's a big crowd." Chey wished she was looking forward to the party.

"Very. Okay, it's our turn." Wynn disembarked after the limo pulled up and the driver got out to open their door.

Chey followed, flicking the edge of her cloak to release wrinkles. She tucked the key to her apartment into a small pocket on the inside of the skirt at the waist. Otherwise, she had no purse, no phone, nothing to worry about leaving behind or losing.

Four white, tall columns marched along the porch on either side of the steps. To the side of the double doors sat a coffin with half the lid propped up. Inside lay a vampire, hands folded neatly over his double breasted coat. Pale skin offset ink black hair and bloodless looking lips. As the girls approached, the vampire sat up and smiled just enough to expose the glimmer of sharp eye-teeth.

Wynn laughed and hurried Chey along, giving her name to another vampire just inside the foyer. One had to be on the list to get in.

The mansion spread out in three directions, with a dining hall to the right, an enormous living area to the left, and a double staircase straight ahead leading to the second floor. Spider webs, caldrons and dry ice were just a few of the decorations that transformed the mansion into a scary haunt. Purple lights replaced regular bulbs in a high chandelier and a ghost greeted them at the archway to the living area. Any and all regular furniture had been removed; in its place, tables with chairs lined the walls and a glossy dance floor made up the middle. Two more chandeliers sat over the dance floor, replete with purple lights. Swags of purple silk draped the walls and candles in tall floor holders flickered in four corners. Sheer panels of silk and gauze hung from the ceiling, creating floating wisps of material that added mystery to the overall décor.

Already, the party was in full swing.

Every type of costume was represented, from zombies, to Dorothy and Toto, to the Creature From the Black Lagoon.

A zombie took possession of Chey's cloak just before they entered the room, and also discreetly took her name so she could retrieve it at the end of the night.

Wynn glanced back with a broad smile on her mouth, and led the way deeper into the throng.

Chey returned the smile, even if hers felt hollow and forced. She stuck on Wynn's heels, catching glimpses of herself in gilded mirrors situated every so often among the swags. Once, she saw how haunted her own eyes looked. Even make up couldn't hide the veil of sorrow she had existed in for the last three weeks.

When a ghoul in flowing robes swept

Wynn out onto the dance floor, Chey diverted to a bubbling cauldron for a glass of neon green punch. The first sip told her it was heavily spiked. It didn't stop her from consuming the entire thing and going back for seconds. Walking away from the cauldron lest she be tempted to drown all her sorrows in liquor, Chey wove in and out of the costumed guests, admiring an elaborate get up now and then. Some had gone to extremes, including none other than the Headless Horseman, replete with a pumpkin tucked under his arm. A fake flicker of fire showed through the cut out eyes and jagged mouth.

She was halfway through her second glass when someone touched her on the shoulder. Chey twisted a look back—and up. A man in an elaborate gold mask, red cape draping from his shoulders to the floor, gestured toward the dancers with a gloved hand. The mask was full faced, giving her no glimpse of his nose, mouth or jaw.

Chey hesitated, glancing toward the swirling bodies, about to deny him. She wasn't in the mood, just wasn't ready to pretend like all this was okay. Like *she* was okay. Where she should be was home, out of the limelight, licking her proverbial wounds. They were many.

He touched her elbow with gentle encouragement. Chey set down her glass and allowed him to escort her onto the floor. She didn't care that her hesitance was obvious, nor that her eyes past the mask probably expressed her desire to be elsewhere. Swung into his arms, Chey picked up the steps to the waltz easy enough. Of course it just reminded her of the dance she had with Sander in Monte Carlo, which did nothing for her desire to be out here now.

With spare tolerance, Chey followed his excellent lead, ignoring the prick of pleasant masculine cologne and the weight of his hand at the small of her back. When she glanced up into his eyes, she found she couldn't easily see them for the shadows cast by the mask. He twirled her, instinctively threading through other dancers without having to wrench looks over his shoulder.

She was loathe to admit how good he was. Which mattered here nor there in the grand scheme of things. Many men were decent dancers.

"You could at least pretend to enjoy this," the man said. His velvety accent was only slightly muffled by the mask.

Chey snapped her gaze up to the shadowy holes for eyes and gasped. "Sander?"

"Shh. Say my name too loudly, and you'll tip someone off."

Breathless, shocked, Chey couldn't unscramble her mind. How could he be here? How had he known? Her steps faltered for the first time. Sander guided her into recovery with smooth hands and swift feet. Elegant, the cape swirling around his ankles, he followed the rotation of the couples until he could easily guide her off the floor without interrupting the rest.

Assaulted by all manner of emotions, Chey allowed him to lead her by the hand through the room and around a corner into a shady niche. He turned her toward the wall and crowded close, blocking her in with his body. Only then did he push the mask up to expose his face.

Reaching for hers, he inched it up until her face was as bare as his.

Chey experienced a spike of lust and passion so sharp that she didn't think twice before sliding her hand around the back of his neck to pull him in for a kiss. A kiss he was already leaning down to claim. From the get go it was electric and hot, the taste of his mouth familiar and heady. Her tongue tangled with his, dipping into the hollows, and a groan escaped her throat when he returned the same.

She knew she shouldn't be doing this. Shouldn't let him obliterate everything in her world except Sander. But it was as natural to be in his arms as it was to breathe, and she'd missed him more than she could ever explain.

Breaking the kiss, he braced one hand on the wall behind her head and stared down into her eyes. "I shouldn't be here, not after you stood me up at the cafe, but--"

Pulse racing, Chey lifted trembling fingers to her lips. Then they fled to his, cutting his words off. "I *was* there. Waiting for you. Wynn and I were in a booth," she whispered, suddenly frantic to tell him what happened.

He frowned. "You weren't when I got there."

"I know. Sander—you might not believe this, but your father had men take me from the cafe, unconscious, and put me in the dungeon. In one of those older cells with the stone slabs." Chey saw his eyes narrow in the gloom, heard the harsher rasp of his breathing.

"Go on," was all he said then.

"He came down there. The King. He told me that Viia was never behind Elise's attack." Chey swallowed. Oh God. Sander wasn't going to believe her. "Your mother was. She framed Viia because Viia was convenient."

Sander grated words out in his native tongue.

Chey decided they must be curse words, as terse and clipped as they were.

"See, your sister came to the hotel Wynn and I were staying at before all this. She handed me tickets for Wynn and I to leave Latvala. Told us that if we didn't get on that flight, she'd have us labeled as terrorists and arrested. She said I was banned from your country, never allowed back." Chey paused a moment to catch her breath.

Sander looked furious.

"What else?" he asked, voice tight with anger.

"I decided to hell with her, and went to Vogeva with Wynn anyway. To give you that note. Right after, when we were waiting for you in the cafe, is when your father nabbed us. He threatened my life, told me that he'd arrange a horrible accident for *you* to find, because he thought you needed to relearn a lesson--"

"*He said that?*" Sander said, breaking into her explanation. His fury grew until his cheeks were ruddy, even in the gloom.

"Yes. I wouldn't lie about something like that. He kept me there for two days—not in that cell exactly, he moved me to a better room down there—while he decided whether I would live or die. Sander, if I didn't know better? I'd bet they were behind what happened in Monte Carlo, too. With that guy. He drugged my drink, I know it. I felt strange, not myself, and I shouldn't have ever let him lure me outside for any reason when I was so out of it like that." The confessions poured forth, and it felt wonderful to clear her conscious, above all else. Carrying around the weight of those things had been difficult for her to bear.

Sander closed his eyes. He seemed to be fighting for control of his temper. Not at her, but at the way they'd both been played. "I don't understand why you left, then."

"Left where?"

"Latvala. Why did you demand to be taken home?"

Chey frowned. "What? When? In Monte Carlo?"

"Yes. I expected you to come home with me, but the guards told me you demanded to go back to the states. Why?"

Chey palmed her cheek. "I never demanded to go home. They told me *you* ordered me escorted back to Seattle. That you gave your apologies that it could never work out. That we were over. They brought me all the way back here, right to my apartment even."

Sander ripped out another few words that must have been more curses in his language. Then, "You're right. Monte Carlo was a set up. I bet the whole 'security breach' was fabricated for the event, so they could put their little plan into place."

"Sander, they're dead serious about us. About you not being with me. I meant what I said in the note—I love you. I do. More than I can even say. But I was scared out of my mind that your father was going to have me murdered on the way to the airport, and I can't live like that." It hurt Chey more than she cared to admit to say these things. To deny her heart, their heat and passion.

Death, however, was a permanent

consequence that she wasn't ready to face.

He stared down at her, expression pensive. "This also explains why they have moved forward too aggressively with the wedding between Valentina and me. Several articles proclaiming I've 'chosen my wife' or my bride or whatever it says were not sanctioned by me. In fact, they never even ran it past me before printing."

"I can't say I'm surprised to hear it." And she wasn't.

"Give me a little time to look into things," he said. "I'm going to weigh some considerations carefully over the week that I'm here in the United States, try to come up with an alternate plan. During that time, I'd like to see you. Maybe take you out, though expect to keep a low profile. I think it's best if you don't tell anyone, Wynn included, that I'm here."

It astonished Chey that Sander still wanted to find a way to make it work, even after he heard what he'd just heard. Even though, like her, he knew in the long run that the King would have his say. This close to him, she was tempted to make a pact as they had before. To agree to buck the system, to find a path around. Aksel's warnings sounded in her head, driving spikes of real fear into her stubborn streak.

"Isn't it just going to hurt us more, Sander? God knows I want to be with you more than anything—but at what cost? My life? Is it really worth risking that if your father finds out? I won't tell anyone you're here." Chey gnawed on her lip. They were costumed and enclosed in a shady niche, and she was still fretful the King's spies were out there somewhere, ready to report back that she was once more engaging Sander.

"Don't be so quick to think I don't have ways to protect you," he said, voice low. "He might have his loyal employees, but I also have mine. They are loyal to me and me only, and I trust them all with my life. They will do as I say, not my father, because they know that one day soon, the throne will be mine. You need to give me a little more time. See me this week. I'll make sure we do it in a clandestine manner that won't put your life in jeopardy. Besides. You're not on Latvala land. You didn't seek me out, I sought *you* out, which pretty well negates all his current threats."

Chey leaned into the trail his fingers made along her cheek. When he cupped her jaw, she rested a hand on the middle of his chest. She wanted to put her faith and trust in him. *Did* have faith and trust in him. The question still remained; was it worth risking her life? Could it work out in the end, even if he found a way to strong arm the King and Queen into accepting her as his? Chey envisioned a life of hell in the castle. Constant sniping and undercutting and outright hostility. She wouldn't ever feel safe under their roof.

Still, when he touched her, looked at her like he was doing now, she wanted to throw caution to the wind and just *live.* Be with him. Enjoy him. Their draw to each other was undeniable.

Rising up on the toes of her ballerina shoes, she kissed him. It was the kind of kiss a woman gives when she expects more than just a meeting of mouths. Demanding, aggressive, urgent.

He rose to the occasion, threading his hands through her hair, pins flying every which way. He didn't just kiss her back, he *took* her mouth with fiery need, coaxing gasps and groans out of her before a full minute was up. There in that shadowy alcove, where anyone might walk by and discover them, he had her with a ferocity that knocked the breath from her lungs. All male, driving hips, clothing coming undone under the rough tug of his hands. He imprinted himself all over her, biting her throat, leaving bruises on her skin.

Pinned to the wall by the time it was over, sweat dotting her brow, Chey buried her face in his neck and fought to get her wind back. Her lips felt raw and swollen, her body shuddering randomly from aftershocks.

Into her ear, he whispered, "I don't care what anyone else says. You're *mine.*"

. . .

Sander left the important parts of her costume undamaged, and for that Chey was thankful. Ten minutes after he left the hidden spot, she followed. Mask in place, she fixed what she could of her hair, but knew anyone paying close attention would realize the once neat style now looked sex-tousled.

Music vibrated through the speakers, dancers packed the dance floor, and more guests crammed the sides near the food and drink tables. She navigated the throng, smoothing a hand along her hip over the tulle layers of the ballerina skirt.

The strong hand that landed low on her spine was immediately familiar as Sander's. Chey slanted a coy look up and aside; he was put back together much neater than she, hair slicked into place, cape lapping at his boot heels.

Without asking, he guided her into another waltz. He held her closer, touched her body more intimately, gazed down at her from behind his mask. She only saw the burn of lust in his eyes when the light hit just right. Daring to brush her pelvis against him during a turn, she smiled when he groaned.

At the end of the dance, he whispered near her ear. "Dance with others if they ask. Mingle. I'll find you for another dance in a while."

"All right." Chey parted from him and went to find a drink for her parched throat. Wynn caught up to her then, a sparkle in her eyes when she lifted the goggles for a moment.

"Girl, who is that guy you're dancing with? He seems like a great partner," Wynn said. She'd been engrossed with several partners of her own.

"I don't know, but he's skilled and enjoyable to waltz with," Chey said. She was careful not to appear too happy or altered mood-wise from when they'd arrived.

Wynn reached up to touch a wayward, tousled lock of Chey's hair. It was just that, a touch, almost as if Wynn was asking a silent question.

Chey quirked a wry smile and lifted a hand to smooth back the mussed strands. "That's what I got for trying to slide the mask up without lifting it away from my head first."

Wynn laughed. "It's easy to forget. Are you having a little bit of a good time, at least?"

"As much as I can, Wynn. I'm not sorry I came." Chey poured herself another glass of the green spiked punch.

"Good. Now then. That Devil over there has been giving me the eye again," Wynn said, turning Chey by the shoulders to view a man in a Devil costume. Horns spiked up out of his red mask and a spaded tail curled behind his legs. Otherwise, the Devil wore a suit that strikingly resembled Armani.

"You go dance. Or whatever he wants. I'll see you on the floor," Chey said, turning back with an exaggerated brow wag for Wynn.

Wynn eased her goggles down over her eyes. "You bet you will."

Chey watched Wynn sashay herself toward the Devil, who playfully twitched his tail in anticipation. It really was great to see Wynn enjoying herself. However, Chey's attention hopped to the other guests, searching for a particular costumed man.

Before she could find him, someone asked her to dance. Chey drained her drink and allowed no less than three different costumed men to whirl her onto the floor. One after the other, all in varying stages of inebriation. The whole time she kept watch for Sander, hoping he would interrupt and step in.

He did. Two dance partners later, when Chey was about to get perturbed at the delay, she suddenly found the mummy in her arms replaced with the gold masked, caped man once more.

Chey cautioned herself not to smile or otherwise give herself away. Sander pulled her indecently close and guided her through the steps with effortless ease. His cape lapped at her ankles, his scent tickling her nose. He was all consuming, all engrossing.

"Keep looking at me like that," he said at one point. "And we'll find ourselves back in the alcove."

Chey's breath hitched in her throat. She wouldn't have minded round two with him between her legs. What a wanton thought.

"You must like the idea. I don't hear you complaining," he pressed with a deviant tone.

"Of course I'm not complaining. I can barely get my mind off the things you did to me in there," she confessed, earning a laugh from Sander. The rasp and warmth shivered over her skin.

"Good. I can't either. By the way, expect me tomorrow night, late."

"Where?"

"Your place."

"You know where I live?" She stared up at the holes in his mask, wishing she could see his eyes easier.

"I make it my business to know many things," he replied. "Yes, I know where you live."

Chey wondered what he thought. It was modest compared to what he was used to. She told herself it didn't matter. He knew she didn't come from Royalty herself, or an affluent background. Sander got what he saw with her, which was perhaps why he kept coming back.

"I look forward to it. Are we staying in?" she asked, twirling away from his body before he pulled her back.

"For tomorrow night, yes. Unless there is somewhere you'd like to go."

"Not especially. This was a little more than I wanted to do for Halloween, but I'm glad I came. How did you know I would be here, anyway?" Chey asked. There was no doubt now that Sander had known she was attending.

"I never tell all my secrets," he said with a low laugh. "It was too good an opportunity to pass up, what with the masks and costumes."

The music seamlessly changed over to a slower beat, a couple's dance that invited more swaying than waltzing. Sander switched holds on her body and led her into a languid rock of hips.

"Why now? Why three and a half weeks later?" she asked after adjusting to the new pace. The spiked neon punch relaxed her, made her paranoia a little less stark. It wasn't the same kind of buzz she'd had in Monte Carlo, which enforced her theory that she'd been drugged.

"Because it took me that long to make legitimate plans to come to America without raising red flags. At first, I didn't know what to think when I didn't find you in the cafe. I thought you might have changed your mind. But I kept your note, and after several rows with father, I began to plot my departure."

"Legitimate plans?" she inquired, careful to keep her voice to a whisper.

"I had a meeting with some prominent people in Sacramento yesterday. I have another at lunch tomorrow. Those keeping an eye on my whereabouts believe I'm still there. The plane has not left the private terminal we use, which will enforce the idea I haven't gone anywhere." He stroked his fingers low along her spine.

"Then how did you get here? Certainly not driving."

"No. We chartered a different private plane to go back and forth under another name. I told you. I have those loyal to me that will keep my cover. There are a few back in Sacramento ready to waylay anyone if need be until I return."

Chey realized just how many precautions Sander was taking. It made her believe the situation was as precarious as she imagined it to be.

"So you'll fly back tonight, have your meeting, then come to Seattle tomorrow evening again?" she asked.

"Yes. I can stay two days, if you'll put me up. Then I'll need to fly to California for my last three engagements. Unfortunately, I won't make it back to Seattle again after that before departing for Latvala. The meetings are too close together, with an evening event that will likely last far into the night, making it impossible for me to go between states without being late. That will wrap my week in America."

"I can put you up for two days. That's not a problem." It appealed to Chey to have Sander to herself, regardless of the danger she might be putting herself in. If she was going to agree to any of this, then she was going to go all the way, no holds barred.

"Excellent. I promise I'll make it worth your time."

"You better."

Chapter Twelve

Chey paced her apartment, straightening this, straightening that. Nothing needed it, she'd already done the same thing ten times before. The bathrooms were spotless, as was the kitchen. Standing behind the loveseat, she examined her modest domain and wondered what Sander would think. Nothing here sported gilded frames, or ornate carvings, or cost more than a year's salary. Much of it came from flea markets, at that.

Parting from him last night at the Halloween party had been bittersweet. He left before it was over with promises to return. Wynn, feeling no pain from the spiked drinks, had chattered on and on during the ride home, never suspecting a thing. She'd tried to pin Chey down for another evening out tonight, which Chey declined with complaints of an oncoming headache.

Wynn had been too blitzed to question

or hassle.

The storm that threatened the previous day was still present, lashing the trees around the complex and pouring rain in buckets. Thunder boomed through the sky and lightning caused bright flashes of light beyond the windows. For once, the violent weather made Chey feel safer holed up in her home. She decided that anyone spying on her would have a much harder time getting a good look at any visitors, might be deterred altogether of lurking on the street with binoculars.

"That's really reaching, Chey," she muttered to herself. But was it? After death threats and attempted murder?

She decided not.

A series of hard knocks jerked Chey out of her reverie. Crossing to the door, she took a deep breath, then turned back the bolt and opened it. Sander stood there looking nothing like himself. A baseball cap sat low on his brow with the hood of a sweatshirt tugged up over that. Jeans worn white at the knee and crease of his hips had seen better days, as had the lace up boots soaked from the rain. He held the straps to a duffel bag that was slung over his shoulder.

"Hi," he said with a wry grin.

"...I almost didn't recognize you. Come in." Chey stepped back, pulling the door wide. He dwarfed her stepping across the threshold. Closing the door once more, she threw the bolt and turned in time to see him drop the duffel on the small square of tile at the entryway and shove the hood down before removing the baseball hat.

"I figured it wouldn't hurt to have a little extra coverage, seeing as my father has had people attempting to verify my whereabouts lately," he said. Sander tossed the cap down onto the duffel bag.

"Oh no. He's not suspicious, is he?" Chey wondered if she should jam the back of a chair up under the knob of the door.

"I don't think so. My men covered my tracks well." He strolled deeper into the apartment, taking a good look around.

Chey smoothed her hands over the sage green shirt she wore with a pair of cotton yoga pants in gray. They weren't going out; she didn't see any need to doll up when he was likely to remove what she had on eventually anyway. She was under no illusions about the activities their night would entail.

At the moment, all she could do was

fret that he would find something lacking about her personal space. He paused in front of several pictures on her mantel that she'd taken of her parents. One was a formal portrait of all three of them before their death. Although her apartment was small, it was still on the larger side of most in town. Being on the top floor, her ceiling arched high and the square foot was nothing to sneeze at.

Despite all that, Sander overflowed the room. Even in street clothes, he exuded a powerful presence that made her apartment feel tiny and cramped. Compared to the castle—well. There was no comparison. Even to the suite of rooms she'd stayed at in the family seat, this apartment was miniscule.

Still. Sander made it seem like a two-by-four tree house.

"That's good. About your men, I mean. Are they waiting in the parking lot?" Chey asked after a loud crack of thunder.

He glanced across the apartment and unzipped the hoodie. For the first time, he looked her over head to foot. "They're alternating shifts. Some are staying at a nearby hotel and they switch out every so many hours."

"Good. I mean it's not good that they

have to sit out there in the cold, but it's good you're covered." She smoothed her hands down her hips in the wake of his gaze. "Do you want something to drink? Eat?"

"They have heaters," he said offhand, though he wasn't dismissive or cruel. Just honest. "No thanks, I ate on the flight. This suits you," he said with a gesture around the living room.

"You think so? I like it." Chey had seen apartments while searching for this one that offered much less in the way of amenities and charm. Just then, it seemed like a sardine can. She watched Sander's expression, trying to get a bead on what he was thinking. Just because compliments passed his lips didn't mean he meant them.

And wasn't that cynical? Chey quashed her internal skeptic and concentrated on Sander.

"It's very close to what I imagined." He shucked the hoodie, exposing a shoulder holster with a gun tucked neatly into a sheath. This he removed and set on a cushion of her couch. That left him in a plain tee shirt of heather gray and jeans. As the night before, his jaw was clean shaven, the top of his hair pulled back into a familiar little tail.

Chey watched him approach, feeling smaller by the second.

"You look like a deer in the headlights," he said, coming to a stop before her.

"I can't believe you're actually here, I guess," she admitted. Her skin prickled under the thin shirt. Dropping her gaze, she skimmed a look at how his shoulders stretched the material of the tee, and how lean he was comparably in the hips.

In short, he was staggeringly handsome. Virile.

"All yours for two whole days. What *will* you do with me." His accent dipped into a lower range, the syllables edged with a rasp.

Chey laughed and pretended to think, rolling her gaze upward toward the ceiling. "Well, let's see. There's a light in the kitchen that needs replacing, and the fireplace could use cleaning--" Chey's tease got cut off when he stooped and lifted her over his shoulder like a sack of potatoes.

"Listen, you, I didn't come all this way to *clean* things or replace lights. Not fifteen minutes in your door and already I'm forced to go caveman on you." He exaggerated a sigh and walked straight into her bedroom like he had a right to.

"I never dreamed you wouldn't be thorough in all your tasks," she chided, laughing.

"My tongue is thorough. I'll give you a demonstration you'll never forget," he promised, and bumped her door closed with the heel of his boot.

. . .

November 2

Let's just forget that it's been six months or so since I've written here. Okay? Diaries are forever, or some claptrap like that. It's dark, too dark to see what time it is because the lights went out some time between sexcapade one and sexcapade two. I'm pretty sure it's not long before dawn, though with this storm still blowing, I don't think anyone will notice when it arrives.

Why have I decided to write? His name is Sander. I've been remiss penning anything about him because I've been too busy living. Right now, he's lying in my bed with the covers tangled around his hips. I can just see the swell of his ass. For a Prince, he's built quite nicely. But back to the more important thing: he's a Prince. Heir to the throne. No, I haven't lost my mind and no, I'm not drunk. I wish I could say that it's all been very fairytale like, but I can't.

I'm writing here because my nerves are shot and I need some place to vent. I can't tell Wynn that he's here, or that Sander and I have made up. I can't tell her that Sander wants to find a way to be together even though the King and Queen would prefer that I'm dead.

Thirty years from now, I'll look back at this entry and snort at what will seem like wild exaggeration. Death. Except I'm not exaggerating, and it's not funny. I just spent the most blissful five or six hours of my life in a man's arms, and all I can think about in the aftermath is whether there are people spying on my apartment and planning some sort of 'accident'. The King promised me he would do that if I didn't leave his son alone.

Sander came looking for me this time, although I seriously doubt the King and Queen care about those kind of semantics. I'm wrecking their plans, have put a kink in their designs to have Sander marry some well appointed Princess who will no doubt spit out heirs from her vagina like bullets.

I'm being unnecessarily crass, and I don't care. This is what stress does to me. I'm not even sure this entry makes sense, or that I've covered all the things that need covering. If I was a smoker, I'd be through three cartons in two hours, easy. I'm not even sure what the point of this entry is—oh wait. Venting. That's right. This is relieving my stress.

This is my carton of cigarettes, my bottle of whiskey, my Xanax. I can barely read my own chicken scratch, and it's not the fault of the darkness.

I'm sure I should have ended things with Sander when I realized how serious certain people are about keeping me out of his life.

But you know me, diary. I've never done anything the easy way, and the second someone tells me I shouldn't, I'll do it anyway. I have to learn all my hard lessons through bitter experience.

Not everything with Sander is bitter, though, and while I'm not sure I'll live to see my twenty-fifth birthday, I don't regret all the sighs and moans and growls we make between us. I don't regret his skin under my nails or his fingerprints on my hips.

If you don't hear from me again, it's because I'm buried somewhere six feet under.

Yours,
Chey

Closing the journal, Chey set it aside on the nightstand. The pen went on top. She considered ripping out her latest sarcastic entry, then decided against it. There was truth to what she'd written, and expelling some of her angst was much needed catharsis.

Curled into a chair at the side of the bed, she leaned back and sought Sander's silhouette among the covers. He was out cold, both arms up under his pillow, one knee pulled up toward his chest. It put strain on the sheet that just barely covered his backside. Doing nothing more than sleeping, he was still a presence not to be denied. This was the kind of man painters shaped into Gods on cathedral ceilings, with their bronzed skin and ripped muscles. Here was divine inspiration, the stuff of dreams and girlish wishes.

And what a wreck he might make of her life.

Chey knew what the trouble was. She knew why she wanted to backpedal from her earlier *throw caution to the wind* mentality. Down deep, she was afraid that she would fail him when it counted. When he needed her to be crafty around diplomats and silver tongued with politicians, she feared her inexperience would cost them both. The last thing she wanted was to make a fool out of him—or herself.

These were not invalid concerns. She'd mingled twice with the upper echelon, witnessed how it worked. Only on the surface, sure, but her imagination could fill in the rest. Was she up to the task? Would her wit and worldly knowledge fail her at a critical time?

"Your mouth looks pensive," Sander rumbled. His voice sounded heavy, drugged.

Chey glanced toward his face. She couldn't see anything from the shadow his shoulder cast down. "That's because I *am* pensive."

"Second thoughts?"

"Not exactly."

"That's not the answer I wanted to

hear." He rolled over. The sheet slithered indecently low on his naked stomach. There was just enough natural illumination to see the cut of his abdominal muscles and the bone of his hip.

"I don't know. I keep thinking about later. Like at events in Monte Carlo. I'm not experienced enough dealing with foreign leaders and their ilk," she said.

"Then it's a good thing you don't have to be. We have our own Ambassadors and Diplomats for that."

"I saw how people treated Valentina. You told me yourself that she's a force to be reckoned with in circles like those."

"You weren't born into Royalty, Chey. They understand you won't be versed in the same things."

"And they'll take advantage, right?"

"They'll try. Some of them. Learn how to double-speak—that is, answer without telling them anything they want to hear—and you'll be fine. As long as you're cordial and polite, there isn't a thing they can do if you won't give up state secrets. You're smart enough to hold your own."

"You have a lot of confidence in me that I don't even have."

He rumbled a laugh, smoothing his

palm absently over his chest and stomach. "Look, I know it's intimidating. But if I'm not worried, then you shouldn't be, either. I won't throw you to the wolves, you know. I'll break you in slowly until you feel more secure." He turned his head on the pillows to look toward the window, then at the nightstand.

"Power is still out," she said when he searched for the time. "You make it sound so easy. The mingling part."

"It's never easy. Not even for me, and I grew up with it. But you'll adapt."

"What if I don't?"

"You'll need to, to a certain degree. Not necessarily with foreign dignitaries, but with the people of Latvala. They'll expect to see you, hear from you."

"Oh, well that's not a big deal." Chey was thinking in simple terms. She was thinking, in fact, of the catastrophe at the wharf. Mingling then had been natural and right.

"Good. Now tell me if you'd like to go somewhere today. If so, it's better to leave while it's dark."

"You won't be interested in doing what I'd like to do." Chey gladly set aside her concerns about other things in favor of concentrating on the now.

He said, "Try me."

Chapter Thirteen

Milford's was a pancake house located between the library and the police station. The building took up three lots, had a tin roof and food to die for. The interior, filled with booths and tables in navy microsuede and a beige tiled floor, sprawled around a gigantic stone fireplace positioned directly in the middle of the room. Flames cracked and hissed behind the grate. A large kitchen took up the back half, leaving more than enough room for three to four hundred guests on its busiest days.

Chey sat across from Sander in a corner booth, far away from three other customers lined up at the long counter. The remains of their breakfast— strawberry waffles for her, and everything on the menu for him—sat between them. He sipped coffee in the aftermath, while she had her hands wrapped around a small glass of orange juice.

"You have an impressive appetite," she

informed him, as if he didn't know.

"I was hungry. We probably burned another thousand calories in the shower this morning."

Laughing, she blushed. They'd nearly missed the window of opportunity to leave the apartment. "That's not my fault."

"It's directly your fault. There I was, trying to take a shower, when I was accosted--"

Chey balled up her napkin and tossed it at him, laughing again. The wad bounced harmlessly of his shoulder. "You, sir, have got a faulty memory. Because it was *you* who accosted *me* after I politely informed you I would take my shower first."

Outside, the rain, which had battered the landscape during their entire meal, came to a stop.

"I didn't hear you complaining," he said with rakish good humor. Taking another sip of his coffee, he set the mug down and slouched in the booth. He'd chosen to wear toned down clothing again: a flannel open down the front with a white shirt beneath, jeans, boots and the baseball hat that he kept low over his eyes.

"So you admit that I'm right." Chey wore jeans as well, with a long sleeved shirt in canary yellow with a heather gray hoodie over that. The dark layers of her hair had been scraped back into a ponytail.

"I admit nothing." He dipped into an accent like a vampire might use, then glanced around the restaurant. "So tell me why you chose this place out of all the rest. I'm guessing you have personal memories attached."

Chey's lips ticked with the start of a smile. Then she glanced at the interior of *Milford's* before finding Sander's eyes again. "You're astute. My parents and I used to come here every Saturday morning. Without fail. We loved it especially in the winter because of the fireplace."

He nodded, meeting and holding her gaze. "It's comfortable. Which makes me wonder what's next on our agenda."

"You'll just have to wait and see. At least the rain stopped." Chey finished off her orange juice and set the glass aside.

"So, something outdoors, then?" He reached over to pick up the check that the waitress dropped off on her last visit. Taking money out of his pocket, he dropped more than enough to cover the tab and a healthy tip as well.

"Thanks," Chey said, when he paid. "And I told you. You'll just have to wait and see. You're impatient."

He snorted. "You're welcome. Let's go then. As patient as you think I am, I'm still curious as hell."

They departed the booth and left the restaurant after a round of goodbyes with the waitresses. The lone guard who had loitered inside drinking coffee at the counter followed them out a few minutes later.

The SUV made good time across the city, ferrying the group of five toward a destination that Chey guided them to. It felt good to be doing something on a whim, to show Sander the little habits that made up her life. He fit into the schedule without trouble, never complaining that the activities were too mundane or boring.

Fifteen minutes later, they pulled into a parking lot with rows and rows of slots for vendors surrounding a warehouse in the middle. The slots outside were vacant thanks to the rain, which kept the surprise going a little longer. After parking in the guest section, Chey disembarked with Sander and two guards. They seemed like any quartet of friends on an outing, drawing little to no attention as they crossed toward the large smoked glass doors closed against the weather.

Sander quirked a brow at her when he opened one and gestured her to go in before him. Entering, Chey turned to walk backwards so she could see his reaction.

Spread out over thousands of square feet was the flea market she so dearly loved to visit. The vendors had pulled their wares inside due to the weather, but the haggling between them and the customers continued. This flea market happened to cater to those with a love for antiques and collectibles rather than newer, cheap merchandize that one could find at any dollar store. Trunks with leather straps and iron hinges sat next to Victorian lamps and tapestry chairs that looked as if they had come straight from a French parlor. Dividing screens, end tables, paintings, ottomans, rocking chairs—the variety was staggering.

Sander took it all in with a vague grin on his mouth.

"And this," she said, turning to walk beside him again, still watching his face. "Is where we spent Saturday afternoons after breakfast. Usually the goods are spread out through half the parking lot as well."

"I can't say I'm surprised," he said, sliding his hands into the pockets of his jeans. "This is exactly the kind of place I'd expect to find you."

"Why do you say that?" Chey ran her fingers across the top of a fifteenth century dresser with baroque accents. "My apartment isn't stuffed with things like this." She had one or two precious pieces, but not a hoard.

"If you had a house with places to put them, it would be," he said, taking a guess.

Chey laughed and nudged him with her elbow. "You know me too well."

"You'd be surprised." Sander bent his head down to put that comment at the shell of her ear.

She shivered and glanced aside. "What, how well you know me already? I'm still figuring you out."

"Yes." He straightened. "You're not supposed to know me that well already."

"Why can you know me, but I can't know you?"

"I didn't say you can't know me. I said you're not supposed to know me *that* well already. You might become bored of the man without the mystery and intrigue

236

attached, which means I would have to show you my dark side." His voice lowered at the last, like there were deep, dark secrets that might scare her off if she found out about them. It was so contrived that Chey laughed and bumped her shoulder into his.

"You're so full of it. I was kind of hoping to find a little half table to go against the wall in the dining room. In that empty corner," she said, giving him insight to why she was here. Beside the desire to immerse him into her routine for the short time he would be in Seattle.

Sander surprised her then. As they walked, he began to point out specific pieces that were more important than others from a historical angle. He also knew his way around antiques, correctly naming styles and designs and from which parts of the world they hailed. They spent two hours wandering up and down the rows, heads bent together while they discussed the appeal of an armoire over there, and a chest of drawers over here.

When Chey came upon a little half table with carvings in the surface and clawed feet, she fell instantly in love with it. After a thorough examination to make sure it was intact, Sander paid the vendor and arranged to have it delivered to Chey's apartment later that day.

Her delight knew no bounds. Just watching him deal so expertly with the vendor heated her blood, as well as the easy way he handled the payment and delivery details.

"I know you want that bureau back there, too," Sander stage whispered, after the current transaction was done.

Chey laughed and glanced across the market toward a dresser she'd lovingly caressed with her fingers on the way by. "Yes, but that thing is twelve-hundred dollars."

"And your point is?" he said, offering her his elbow as they moved on.

Chey slipped her fingers into the crook of his arm and rested her cheek against his biceps. She could almost believe that he wasn't a Prince, and that they would go back to her apartment and live a life like everyone else. Without worry of plots and intrigue, without having to look over their shoulder. He was just Sander, and she was just Chey, a couple out on the town for the day. Later they would make love on the floor in front of the fireplace after a dinner of steak and wine, with nothing more pressing on their agenda than to spend hours in one another's arms.

Her daydream shattered when one of the guards stepped up, phone to his ear, and murmured to Sander.

"Sir, it's the King. There's been an accident."

. . .

Just that fast, Chey's world tilted on its ear. She snapped a look from the guard to Sander, wondering if she was standing next to the new King of Latvala. Although Chey knew he was destined for the role, that he had been groomed his whole life to ascend the throne, she'd thought it would be years yet before it actually happened.

Sander's gaze sharpened. His mouth thinned. Something else shifted in his demeanor, shoulders bracing to take the weight of a responsibility that few men would ever have to bear.

"And?" he asked in a curt, no nonsense voice. Asking, outright, if he had just become King.

Under her clothes, Chey's skin broke

out in goosebumps. She glanced from Sander to the guard, breath in her throat.

"They're recalling everyone immediately. We must return to Latvala." The guard shook his head, indicating that Sander wasn't King. *Yet.*

Sander tightened his elbow to trap Chey's hand against him, and started moving for the doors. The guards walked at his flank, a little closer than they had going in.

Chey wanted to ask what it all meant. That Sander's visit to America just got cut short was obvious, but that didn't explain what happened next. It didn't explain what kind of accident the King had been in, nor what was expected of Sander if his father was still alive but in a vegetative state. Now wasn't the time or the place to have that discussion.

On the drive back to her apartment, Sander spoke on his phone to several people, voice terse, his native language rolling smooth from his tongue.

Chey hated that she couldn't understand a word. She couldn't tell if he was talking to Mattias or some other head of state. Once, the guard in the front seat twisted a confused look back at Sander, who ignored him in favor of another call.

The guard eyed Sander as if he'd just lost his mind.

Chey's curiosity churned into overdrive. She conjured all kinds of scenarios, from the dramatic to the not-so-dramatic, and everything in between. A short time later, the SUV pulled into Chey's apartment complex and parked near the foot of the stairs. Engine idling, it was clear the driver meant to wait right there until the Prince was done. Still on the phone, Sander helped Chey down from the vehicle and followed her up to her apartment.

Once inside, with two guards standing on the landing outside, Chey gave her curiosity free rein. "Sander, what's going on? Who were you talking to?"

He ended the call and pushed the phone into his pocket while he started gathering his things from her apartment. What fit into the duffel bag he crammed in without folding.

"I don't have a lot of time. As you heard, I have to leave for Latvala immediately. So far, I can't get any straight answers about how bad it is, so I'll have to call you after I arrive and find out firsthand. I'm sorry my visit got cut short." He yanked the zipper closed after removing the hat and stuffing it atop everything else.

"Will you be taking over if he's incapacitated? What does that mean for you and your duties? I don't mean to be insensitive about the King, but I'm more interested in what's happening with you," she said, shooting for honesty. The King had considered having her murdered. Chey didn't have a lot of sympathy for him.

"It's not like he has inspired trust and love with you, hm?" Sander said, correctly guessing what was on Chey's mind. He paused with her near the door and cupped her jaw in his hand. "Right now, I don't know what it all means. I wish I had more to give you. It's possible I'll get there and he'll recover and things will be fine. It's also possible I'll have to fill in as his proxy for a while, which will definitely incrcase my duties and what the council expects from me. These are just guesses though."

Chey stared up into his eyes, resting her hands on his hips. "Please don't wait too long to call me and let me know, okay? I have no other way of contacting you."

"I know, and I'm sorry about that, too. I

can't give you my new number because they're probably watching who's calling me. It pisses me off, but there isn't much I can do about it other than call you from an undisclosed line. That's what I'll do, but it still doesn't leave you a way to get in touch with me. If I can set it up on the trip home, I'll try and get a separate email account so that we can write back and forth until I figure out what's going on. All right? I need a little time to work all this out."

"Something is better than nothing. I'll take the email account whenever you can get it. I--" Chey paused when one of the guards knocked three times on the door, indicating it was time to go. Sander pulled her against him and kissed her like there wouldn't be a tomorrow, all searching tongue and sizzling heat. She arched into him, wrapping her arms around his neck, desperate to make these final seconds last.

It was over too soon. He broke away with clear reluctance and stared down into her eyes. "I'll get in touch as soon as I can. Take care of yourself, Chey."

"I will. You too. Be careful." Releasing her hold around his neck, she slid her palms down the breadth of his chest. How she hated to let go.

He unlocked her door and stepped out onto the landing. After a lingering look, he followed the guards down the stairs to the waiting car, got in, and was gone.

Chey stepped out after them, leaning against the rail while the men filed into the vehicle and drove away. It was one of the harder things she'd ever had to do, knowing that she now had no way of getting in touch with Sander again.

Retreating inside her apartment, she threw the bolts and leaned her spine against the door. Pressing the heels of her hands against her eyelids, she exhaled a long breath and prepared herself for a long wait.

Chapter Fourteen

Chey stared at her bedroom ceiling, one arm flung across her forehead. It was the wee hours of the ninth day after Sander left, and still no word. No text, no phone call, not even an email update. Nothing. She didn't know whether to be worried or annoyed, and settled for a little of both.

Any information she'd been able to pull up on the computer about Aksel's health was vague and largely unhelpful. Certainly there was no mention of an accident, nor that Sander had replaced his father as King. In fact, there was a distinct lack of stories barring human interest pieces that had nothing to do with Royalty. She decided it was probably a planned blackout, so the news didn't circulate among the elite of the world until the Latvala Royals were ready.

Glancing at her window, she stared at the milky stream of moonlight falling in through the panes. It reminded her of how she'd sat at the side of the bed that night and studied Sander's shape among the sheets. How the same moonlight bathed the contours and illuminated muscle. She wondered what he was doing, and whether he was thinking of her, too.

A hard series of knocks at her door startled Chey into an upright position. Clutching the covers against her body, eyes wide, she listened for sounds of the knob jostling. Panicked that someone might be trying to break in, she reached for her cell phone on the nightstand. Minutes crept by. She heard no more knocks, no knob being twisted with someone's intent to come in.

Had it been someone at the wrong door? Once, and only once, a stranger had tried to walk in after confusing her apartment with someone else's.

Sliding out of bed, she put her feet on the floor, phone in hand, and inched toward the doorway. Peering around into the living room, she saw nothing out of place. Glancing at the door itself, she saw the corner of what looked to be a manila envelope poking through the crack. The weathering on the frame of the door wasn't so great that a sliver of paper couldn't be pushed through.

246

Wary, she tiptoed to the door and eased the envelope out of the crack. Looking through the peephole, she saw no one on her landing. No body, no silhouette. Drawing back, she took the envelope into her bedroom and snapped on a small Tiffany lamp. Sitting on the edge of the bed, she turned the envelope over. On the front, someone had written her name in slanting script. It was a bold stroke, with black ink.

Opening the latch, she held her breath and fished around inside. What she pulled out was a thin stack of money and a folded piece of paper. Setting the money aside, she opened the note and read.

Under intense pressure. Cannot contact you any other way than this. Be prepared for bad news in the coming week. This is to see you through while I contend with the K.

Chey read it three times. It had to be Sander, although he hadn't so much as signed his initial to the paper. *K* stood for King, unless she missed her guess. Uncomfortable with the idea that bad news was coming, she set the note aside and picked up the bundle of money. Five thousand dollars in one hundred dollar bills was the sum of his gift.

Unsure how she felt about accepting it, she nevertheless understood his intent. It came across as charming and caring instead of overbearing and domineering. He knew she was out of a job, and perhaps whatever bad news was on the horizon would affect her ability to find one.

What the hell was going on? Frustrated at being kept in the dark, Chey tucked the money back into the envelope and brought the paper he'd written on to her nose.

It smelled like him. The scent was subtle, but definable.

Had he left one of his trusted men behind in the United States to do his bidding while he was half a world away? That was the only scenario that seemed plausible. He wouldn't risk sending cash, plus the note, to just any delivery service.

Rubbing her head, Chey slid the note in with the money and placed the envelope inside her nightstand. Turning out the light, she flopped back against the bed and pulled the covers to her chin.

At least she didn't have to worry about keeping the power on or buying food.

Small comfort.

. . .

Five days after the arrival of the envelope, Chey returned from a trip to the grocery store and let herself into the apartment. Everything she'd needed fit into one bag that she carried into the kitchen. Putting away fruit, lettuce for salad and fresh chicken, she was just about to make herself a cup of tea when her doorbell rang.

Leaving the kitchen, she walked back to the door and peered through the peephole. It was just before noon, which told her it was either a salesman, the mailman or another mysterious delivery.

It was neither.

Chey opened the door with a smile for Wynn and stood aside to let her enter. "It's been a week since I've seen you, what's up?"

"I know, that's what I told myself this morning when I went to work." Wynn paused to hug Chey on her way inside. She worked for her father in his law offices, and pretty much set whatever hours she wanted to. If she needed half the day off, she took it.

"It's good to see you. I just got home like ten minutes ago." Chey glanced along the landing and out to the parking lot, but didn't see anything familiar or suspicious. Closing the door, she engaged the bolt and followed Wynn into the living room.

"I know. I was out in the parking lot, waiting. Except I got a call from mom and you know how that goes. Tough to get her off the phone." Wynn dropped her purse on the floor, smoothed a palm down the hip of her black slacks, then peeled out of the crocheted sweater of ash gray and draped it over the back of the couch.

"I didn't see your car." Chey kicked her shoes off, walked to the kitchen to shut the light off, then headed back into the living room. She felt bad that she'd not told Wynn about Sander at the Halloween party or the ensuing note. Sander wanted her to keep a low profile, however, so she adhered to his wish.

"That's because mine's in the shop. I have Dad's today." Wynn sat on the edge of the sofa and removed her sunglasses. Setting those aside, she glanced at Chey again in a way that indicated she was searching for something.

"What?" Chey glanced down at herself while at the same time running a palm over her hair. The ponytail swayed past her nape, free of twigs or other unexpected debris. The jeans she wore with a sweater in autumn colors, nothing special or notable, lacked stains, rips or bugs that might be causing Wynn to watch her so curiously.

"I take it you haven't been on the internet yet today," Wynn said.

Right away, Chey knew this was the 'something bad' Sander had cautioned her about. Wynn would have blurted whatever news it was otherwise without hesitation. She reminded herself that Wynn didn't know about Sander's visit and pretended that she knew nothing about what was to come. Which wasn't all a lie; Chey didn't have specific details, only a generic warning.

"No, I haven't," Chey said. "Why?"

Wynn rubbed her hands together. "I stumbled across it by accident myself. I figured you might need a shoulder to cry on or something."

"Wynn, what is it?" Chey braced herself. Scared senseless that Wynn would tell her Sander had been the one in an 'accident', she hugged her arms around her middle.

"The article was dated several days ago,

but it announced that the Heir to Latvala's wedding was going to be streamed live on the internet. Like...tomorrow. I think it's happening tomorrow." Wynn winced.

Chey sat forward, shocked. *"What?"*

"I know babe, I really do. It's a good thing you've cut all contact with him, right? I mean, obviously he was lying to you when he said he wasn't going to marry that Princess."

Feeling like her head was going to start spinning around Exorcist style, Chey buried her forehead into her palms. This couldn't be happening. Sander, marrying Valentina. Why hadn't he told her? He must have known when he'd spent the night in her bed.

"It must have been a mistake, Wynn. An old article from--"

"No, it was recent. Published a few days ago. I'm sure of it," Wynn said. "That whole thing is a mess. It's probably better that you're not involved anymore."

Chey surged up off the couch. "But I am involved! He was here, Wynn. That man I was dancing with half the night at the Halloween party? That was Sander. He spent time here with me, spent the night after flying to Sacramento and back.

We went to *Milford's,* went to the flea market. We had *plans."*

Wynn's mouth fell open. "*That* was Sander? Why didn't you tell me? This whole time, I thought you were getting over him and moving on." She paused, then added, "He spent the night here?"

"Yes. Yes. He planned to spend two whole days with me, except he got a call while we were at the flea market that his father had an accident. We weren't sure that he hadn't just become King. I still don't know if he is, or he isn't! King I mean. I never found any information about Aksel when I searched online." Chey paced through the living room, distraught and disturbed. Sander wouldn't have lied to her. It didn't make sense. He needn't fly across the world to be with a lover for one night. Sander had his pick of women and he didn't have to set foot out of the castle to get them with the way they flocked to his side.

"Oh man, I can't believe I'm hearing this." Wynn slouched back against the cushions.

"He sent a delivery person to my door in the middle of the night about five or six days ago. There was five grand in cash he wanted me to have, along with a note. He predicted that this week would be rough—I guess this is what he was talking about." It was rough all right. Chey didn't know what to think, what to believe.

"I hate to play devil's advocate here," Wynn said. "But are you sure that's not a payoff? To keep quiet, to keep your legs open whenever he wants to get laid while he's in town?"

Chey stopped pacing and stared at Wynn. "Absolutely not. He doesn't *need* to do those things. He can get any number of different women at any time, all without having to leave the comfort of his home. I'm sure the same applies when he travels. Women make it known when they're 'open for business', you know?"

Wynn flashed her palms. "I'm just saying. It's something to consider. If you really think he's serious about you, then maybe this whole wedding thing is just..."

Chey waited for Wynn to continue. She didn't.

"I don't know what it is. All I can think is that the King succeeded in brow beating him to the altar. Maybe he didn't know how to tell me. Didn't want to hurt me." None of it made sense to Chey.

"Maybe. Are you going to watch it tomorrow on the internet?" Wynn asked, pushing to her feet.

"I'm...I don't know." Chey considered it a moment. "I suppose I will, if it really happens. I'll need to see it for myself." Morose at the thought, she decided it was a necessary evil. That way, she could once and for all put Sander behind her. Whatever else she was or wasn't, Chey would not sleep with a married man. Vows were vows and a trip down the aisle meant Sander was off limits forever. Chey couldn't decide whether she was feeling heartbroken or homicidal.

Had Sander known the whole time, and neglected to tell her?

Chey pressed a palm against her forehead. She felt hot. Sick. Dizzy. Denial raged around inside like a dervish.

Wynn stepped over and pulled Chey into a hug. The women embraced for long minutes.

"I know it's hard, Chey. I know you're suffering. Maybe this is for the best, although I'm sure that's not what you want to hear. This thing needs resolution and it needs resolution *now*." Wynn leaned back with a compassionate smile. "I'll stop by tomorrow, okay? We'll watch together."

"Yeah. I'll figure out what time and

everything and text you later, all right?" Chey couldn't work up a smile for Wynn in return. She couldn't meet her best friend's eyes, didn't want to see the sympathy she knew must be lurking there.

"Good. I'll be waiting. I'm going to get back to work so I can get off a little early and stop by to have dinner with you." Wynn kissed Chey's brow in a sisterly manner, then gathered her things and headed to the door.

"It's just chicken and vegetables," Chey said. She wouldn't be eating a thing. Her stomach wouldn't allow it. But she would make it for Wynn regardless.

"It'll taste like sawdust, but you have to eat. I'll bring dinner instead, how's that? Some deli sandwiches so you don't have to cook." Wynn paused at the door.

"All right. Drive safe." Chey hovered near the couch. She watched Wynn head out, then crossed the room to throw the bolt over. Tilting her forehead against the door, Chey closed her eyes and swallowed back more tears.

Could it be real? Was it true?

Was Sander Ahtissari, one of ten most eligible bachelors in the world—*her* lover —walking down the aisle tomorrow?

Chapter Fifteen

Thanks to the time difference, Chey got out of bed at three a.m. the next morning, not that she'd been asleep, and wandered into the kitchen to make coffee. Hair a mess around her head from tossing and turning, she yawned and dumped water into the reservoir before adding two scoops of coffee grounds into the filter.

Research yesterday afternoon led to the discovery that the Ahtissari wedding would begin at three p.m. Latvala time, which meant Chey and Wynn needed to be parked in front of the laptop by five.

Dressed in her favorite candy cane pajamas, she got the coffee brewing and went out to the living room. She'd left her laptop on the coffee table the night before; it glowed to life when she woke it out of sleep mode and pulled up the link to the site hosting the nuptials.

The whole thing felt like a bad nightmare. She'd cried for hours after Wynn went back to work, had cried half the night while she laid in bed and stared at the ceiling. All the information she'd pulled up had proven to be recent and authentic. There were even photos of Sander and Valentina—not together, but separate—on the loading page. His face stared out at the world, jaw tight, blue eyes keen. Valentina, in her regal pose, looked almost smug. The sight antagonized Chey to the point that she'd positioned a sticky note over the woman's face so she didn't have to see it. It was still there, a big pink square, blocking out part of the screen.

In anticipation of the event, the site was already showing pre-video shots of snowy Kalev, people in bars ready to watch the wedding and celebrate. There were several links available for different videos, though Chey wasn't prepared to press any. One in particular was all about Sander. A glowing montage, she was sure, from boyhood to manhood with sentimental music that would probably make her want to scream or stab things.

Getting up, leaving the laptop on, she scraped back her hair into a messy knot and brought two mugs down out of the cupboard. She sniffed, then rubbed her stinging eyelid with a knuckle. Crying had rendered her lids puffy and itchy.

Pulling the pot out before it was half full, she poured herself a half cup and set the pot back. Wynn would want some the second she got there.

Walking the coffee back out to the living room, she curled down on the couch and drew the laptop onto her knees. She clicked onto a link against her better judgment, and choked on the first sip of her coffee when one of the photos she'd taken of the entire family popped up.

Those bastards, using her pictures after all this!

It was the one taken the day she'd discovered Sander was actually a Royal, with the men in their uniforms. Two more clicks proved the family was using several of her shots, not just of the King and Queen, but of the castle and the grounds.

Snorting, she took another sip of coffee and tried not to let the images upset her more than she already was. She wondered, too, if they'd used the photos on purpose, because they knew she'd be watching. Bastards.

She refused to check and see if they gave her credit anywhere on the site. It would be a boon for any photographer to have their name associated with a project this big. At this point, she really didn't care about credit. She had no desire to photograph any other elite group of people, ever. Small weddings, birthdays, graduation ceremonies, that was her ticket.

Several short videos showed Valentina's family arriving in grand flair at the airport, with snippets of Valentina smiling for the camera. Personable shots that she knew were supposed to help warm the Latvala people to her.

Chey felt sick all over again.

This was really happening.

The video cut away to a zooming shot of a stunning cathedral. Gray stone, with a peaked roof and heavy carved doors that the camera swerved down into. It was a great special effect, Chey had to admit, never mind that she was getting a bird's eye view of the route Valentina would walk to marry Sander. Up the aisle it went, where pews on both sides were decorated with all white bouquets of calla lilies and sheer white ribbon. At the altar stood a podium flanked by enormous sprays of more calla lilies tucked into waist high, fluted vases. In that exact spot, not long from now, Sander would promise himself to another, effectively severing any chance of a future for himself and Chey. The picture had a dreamy quality, fitting for a Prince and Princess's romance.

Chey looked away from the screen down into her mug. The whole ordeal was making her bipolar. Half of her wanted to sob her sorrow into the pillows; the other half had an epic rant sitting right on the end of her tongue, ready for a blistering delivery. The scorching diatribe would only fall on the deaf ears of her apartment instead of pertinent Royal members of the family, making it useless and pointless.

She felt the inevitable sting of tears and refused to let any more fall. If she didn't need to see with her own eyes that Sander was really taking a wife, she would turn the whole thing off now and save herself hours of torture.

Forty-five minutes later, Wynn let herself in the front door.

Chey was on her third cup of coffee, the laptop perched once more on the coffee table instead of her thighs. The screen was dark.

"Hey. Have you been watching?" Wynn asked. Dressed in yoga pants of black and two layers of long sleeve shirts in gray and white, she dropped her purse near the door and went straight to the kitchen to help herself to coffee.

"I was," Chey said. She heard the listlessness in her own voice and didn't care enough to correct it.

"I know it's hard. I caught glimpses while I was getting dressed. Have you heard anything from him? A call, text, another delivery?" Wynn walked her mug out to the couch and curled down next to Chey.

"Nothing, no." Which made it worse, in Chey's mind. "He could have at least sent a note via his messenger that it was over. That he was sorry he'd lied, or whatever, and that he was getting married."

Wynn rubbed Chey's shoulders, then reached over to wake the laptop. "I know. Let's see where things are. We've got...what, an hour left? They should be doing more of the pre-stuff. Letting people into the church even, maybe."

The screen glowed to life, refreshed to the front page of the wedding site. As Wynn guessed, more things were happening now. While Chey had clicked links to get to pre-recorded videos, a live streaming one was now rolling on the main page. The camera angle, pointed so it took in a view of the curving driveway leading to the door, picked up several official looking people hovering in front of the church. Security members, Chey decided, from their clothing.

A foot of snow lined the drive, which had been shoveled clear for cars that dropped off dignitaries and other prominent guests as the event wore on. More and more people were arriving now, everyone smiling, dressed to the nines. Closer to three o'clock Latvala time, limousines pulled to the curb and out stepped the Royals. Natalia first, with some man or another on her arm, dressed appropriately with a knowing, smug look on her face. The King and Queen came last. They paused to wave to the crowd gathered out on the other side of the street from the church before entering and following the procession of people down the aisle toward their prominent seat in the front pew.

Once seated, the groomsmen filed out a side door toward the front of the church. Mattias, Paavo and Gunnar took their positions, dressed in immaculate military uniforms, gloved hands caught behind their back.

Music made of pretty, lilting strings

filled the background.

Blowing her nose, Chey watched it all like she was having an out of body experience. Nothing felt real, or it felt *too* real, she couldn't be sure which.

When Sander stepped out of the same side door moments later, Chey sobbed into a tissue. Resplendent in his uniform, he had his hair pulled back into a tail, face clean shaven, shoulders square and broad. He wasn't smiling when he took his place at the head of the groomsmen and faced down the aisle toward the now closed doors.

Chey wanted to turn it off. There was no stopping it now. Whatever she'd hoped to see, it wouldn't happen. No last minute intervention or change of plans. The church was full, cameras on, the Priest in place.

All they needed now, was the bride.

. . .

To a flare of dramatic but soft music, the church doors opened. The camera, looking down the aisle in one shot, then cutting over toward Sander's face in another, faded in and out from one scene to another.

Valentina stood there, finally, with her father on her arm, ready to walk down the aisle. Poised and perfect, she paced him toward the front of the church, the close ups of her face behind the veil giving glimpses of her obvious pleasure at the event. She almost gloated, it seemed to Chey, before the image faded for one of a softer Valentina at a different angle, lashes batting coyly as they arrived in front of Sander.

Wynn groaned and wrapped her arm tight around Chey. "I'm so sorry," she whispered.

Chey had nothing to say. Couldn't speak. This was nothing but torture. Her mind, busy for hours coming up with every excuse in the book for Sander, turned to anger at the end. No note, no call, no other forewarning than a cryptic note in the middle of the night that could in no way prepare her for this.

What the hell was she supposed to think?

Sander Ahtissari was getting *married.*

It meant the absolute end to everything she thought of having with Sander. No more nights in his arms, no more strolls through the flea market. There would be no immersion into each other's lives.

As Sander accepted Valentina's hand onto his arm, his expression remained stoic, unreadable. He was unbelievably handsome, which was no doubt why Valentina looked so smitten and so smug.

She'd caught him, just as she'd wanted.

In front of hundreds of guests—and an untold number of thousands watching from their homes in Latvala, Sander Ahtissari took a wife. He said his vows, placed a ring on her finger. When the Priest announced he could kiss the bride, he lifted Valentina's veil and covered her mouth with his.

The church exploded into applause.

Chey had never been so miserable in her life. Tucked into Wynn's arms, she closed the laptop lid and cried. For the better part of an hour, as twilight broke over Seattle and dusk claimed Latvala, Chey Sinclair sobbed her heartbreak onto her best friend's shoulder.

The love of her life was now married to another.

Chapter Sixteen

Thanksgiving Day dawned cold and white. Overnight, four inches of snow had fallen, blanketing the landscape and the trees.

Chey bundled into jeans, a heavy sweater, and a coat of white over that. She wrapped a cashmere scarf of blue around her throat and pulled a beanie over her hair. She didn't bother with make up.

Four days had passed since the wedding. Four horrible days that she'd spent in misery in her bed, wallowing in self pity. Wynn had been there after work for much of it, forcing her to eat, and just being by her side when she couldn't.

Today was high time to stop feeling sorry for herself and get on with the business of living. She'd declined Wynn's offer to come to her parent's house for dinner, begging the need for time alone.

Chey had plans to spend this Thanksgiving elsewhere.

She drove through the streets toward a wooded section set back away from homes and highways, a secluded patch of twenty acres overlooking part of the city. The only time she stopped was for flowers at a convenience store still open for the holiday.

Pulling in past the wrought iron gates, Chey followed the drive to one of four designated parking spots. Pulling in, she cut the engine, gathered her flowers, and exited the car.

She took a deep breath, then started walking. It had been several weeks since her last visit.

Threading her way along a narrow stone path, she kept her gaze down, breath pluming white past her lips with every exhale.

Finally, she came to a stop off the path in front of a large headstone.

"Hi Mom, hi Dad." Her voice wobbled. She set her purse down on a little curving bench and walked the flowers up to a small holder built into the stone just for that reason. Returning to the bench, she sat down and huddled into her coat.

"Of all the places I thought we'd meet for Thanksgiving, this wasn't one of them," she murmured with a laugh, although nothing at all was funny. It was just a way to fight off a sob. She sniffed, took a moment to get control, then continued.

"I've done something incredibly stupid. I fell in love with a Prince. Now, I know what you're thinking. A 'real' Prince? Well, yes. A real one. One who just happened to marry another girl about four or five days ago. I thought he and I had a shot, and I let myself fall. If you had both been here, maybe you would have cautioned me against it. Told me what an impossible dream it was. Then again, maybe, if you'd met him, you would have advised me to do whatever it took to keep him." Chey swallowed down more tears.

This was much harder than she thought it would be.

"Anyway. It didn't quite work out like I hoped. But I'm still alive—I know, that's a whole different story and it involves a King—and that's what matters. Right? I'm still here, having Thanksgiving with my parents in a graveyard. I forgot to bring food, but that's here nor there. I'm not hungry. Maybe later I'll fix Ramen."

Fishing a tissue out of her coat pocket, she blew her nose, wadded it up, and walked it to a trash can set out for guests to use. Probably for things just like this. Back at the bench, she sat down and gazed out at the cemetery.

"I'm not really sure what I should do next. Part of me thinks I should pull roots and move. Try to start over somewhere else. But I don't want to move that far away from you. It's silly, I know. I shouldn't have a problem. I can talk to you anywhere, not just here. Still. I'm not even sure where I would go, and I don't have enough savings to make it happen." Chey didn't consider for a second using the money Sander left her.

She stared at the headstone, at the engraved names, the dates of birth and death. Her heart ached. Just then, she wanted nothing more than the warmth of her father's bear hugs and the sweetness of her mother's gentle coos.

"I think snot is starting to freeze to my upper lip though, so I guess I should go." Chey stood up off the bench, shivering inside her coat. The iron sky promised more snow before the day was over. She picked up her purse, walked to the headstone, and pressed a kiss against the ice cold marble. "I love you. I miss you. You'll see me again around Christmas, I'm sure."

Then she turned back toward the path, following it past a few trees, eyes cast down. She didn't want to think about her first Christmas alone. Thanksgiving without them was bad enough. Sniffing again, wishing her stomach would settle, Chey pulled her keys out and glanced up to her car.

A gleaming black SUV parked behind it snagged her attention. The man leaning against the side, leonine and long, caused her to stumble on the stone path. Chey caught her balance at the last second, still staring.

Sander, wrapped in a heavy wool coat of navy, with jeans and boots, watched her with the same stoic expression he'd worn on television when he'd married Princess Valentina.

Married, that's right Chey. He's someone else's husband now.

Pressing her lips tight, fighting off a bout of irrational anger, Chey turned back to her car and jammed the wrong key into the lock. Struggling with it, she pretended not to notice that Sander had pushed off from the SUV in her direction.

"Chey," he said, voice warm and resonant.

She got her door unlocked after finding

the correct key. "I have nothing to say to you."

"That's fine. But you need to hear me out." He caught her hands with one of his before she could open the door, effectively blocking her from getting inside.

Chey snapped a hot look sideways and up. She refused to acknowledge the heat spiraling through her veins at his nearness, or how his scent, musky and masculine, did strange things to her pulse.

"Actually, *Dare,* I don't have to do anything. Now release me."

"No."

"...no? Are you kidding me?" Chey jerked her hands away from his and stuffed her keys into her pocket. All she needed was to drop them and lose them in her distraction.

"I'm not. I have a hotel here. Come back to my suite with me so we can sort this out. There is a lot I need to tell you." He crowded her space, looming and staring down.

Chey pushed against his chest, just once, to put a bit of distance between them. He was being obnoxious using his size to his advantage like that.

"Shouldn't you be warming your new

wife's bed, instead?" she spat, failing to curb a spike of white-hot jealousy at the very thought of him bedding that smug little Princess.

He narrowed his eyes. "This isn't the place to have that discussion."

"But your suite is. How convenient. I don't think so. Now get out of my way." She shouldered into his chest and fought to get her car door open. Sander was crazy if he thought she would tromp off back to his hotel with him.

He used his body to blockade her door. "Chey, I don't have a lot of time. You need to trust me and come along. Right now."

Chey yanked her hand back away from his body and glared up into his eyes. "And *you* need to realize that I'm done with this. With you. If there was ever a chance at anything, you ruined it when you walked down the aisle with another woman."

"I sent you a note, warning you something was going on," he said, voice just this side of a snarl.

"Oh yes, the note!" She flailed a hand. "The infamous note, where you couldn't have just said, by the way, Chey, I'm getting *married* in a few days!" Her exasperation knew no bounds.

"No, I couldn't," he said, moving his face closer to her own by inches. "There are very good reasons I was so vague."

"What, that Valentina might have read them over your shoulder from bed?" She snorted.

Sander growled and suddenly bent forward, tucking his shoulder into her middle. He was gentle but firm when he slung her up and stalked back toward the SUV.

"Sander! Stop right this second! You can't just kidnap me from a cemetery!" Aghast, she pounded a fist against his hip.

"Just be quiet. You're coming, and you're going to hear me out, and that's the end of it." He stood aside while a guard opened the back door. Sander dumped her onto the seat, then chased her inside and sat next to her. After the guard closed the door, he got into the front passenger seat and the driver pulled away from the curb.

"This is ridiculous. You won't change my mind about anything, Sander. You're married. While you might not think that's a binding act, *I* do, and I won't be swayed into any more 'dates' or whatnot." She whispered sideways, loathe to have this conversation in front of the guards. In front of anyone.

Sander said nothing. He crossed his arms over his chest and sprawled in the seat.

Seething, Chey looked out the windows and did her best to ignore him for the duration.

. . .

They spent the entire ride in silence. Which suited Chey fine. The hotel the SUV pulled into was a five star, of course, and Sander growled a warning at her before they disembarked at the VIP entrance.

Don't make a scene, don't make any trouble, or else.

Or else what, she'd wanted to shout. What would he do, throw her over his shoulder again? Carry her caveman style through the marble floored lobby to his private hallway and elevator?

In an effort to keep the situation under some kind of control, she said nothing as they entered the hotel and headed straight for the elevator bank. Sander's guards flanked them the whole way. Acutely aware of his presence on the way to an upper floor, Chey remained silent, arms crossed over her chest, purse dangling from her wrist.

Spit out into a long hallway with red carpet, the walls adorned with classy paintings and niches with faux marble statuettes, Sander led her all the way to the doors at the end. A guard produced a key before they got there and opened one for them. Sander gestured that Chey precede him.

Entering, she found what she expected to find inside: lush furnishings, tapestry chairs, gilt framed mirrors. Windows overlooked a balcony which in turn overlooked Seattle and the water. Chey plunked her purse into a chair and recrossed her arms.

To her surprise, Allar and Hendrik, the first two security members she'd ever met when they came to her apartment door, strolled out of a bedroom with phones to their ears. Both hung up at the same time.

"Hello, Miss Sinclair," Allar said with a smile. He looked dapper as ever, with his short dark hair styled just so and his suit without wrinkles. Hendrick looked savage with the scar cutting through his cheek.

"Hello," Chey said, unsure their presence here was a good thing. Weren't they in legion with the King? She glanced at Sander.

The men traded a bit of conversation in their own language before all the members quit the room, closing the door behind them.

"Won't they turn me into the King?" Chey asked Sander, blunt and unrepentant about it.

"No," Sander said, pausing at a side bar to pour himself a drink. The fireplace had a fire going, the wood hissing and cracking. "Want something?"

Chey could have used a drink all right. "I don't feel especially relieved at your answer. And no, thank you."

"Their loyalty is to me. It has been for years. But they still go out on missions for the family, which is how they ended up at your door to begin with." Sander lifted the tumbler and pulled a long drink from its confines. He leaned a hip against the little bar and regarded her with an almost truculent expression. As if he was the one put out here, not her.

"We better hope so. Because if you just think they're loyal to you, and they're really not, then you've just put my life in direct jeopardy." Chey turned away to stalk through the suite. The finery did little to lift her mood. In fact, seeing proof of their status differences annoyed her.

"You think I would be so cavalier about your safety, hm?" Sander finished off his drink and poured another.

"I think you're doing all kinds of things that might not be in your or my best interest," she snapped. Her mood had reached a dark place after all this.

"That's a pretty brazen statement, considering what I've just put myself through for my own benefit as well as *ours.*"

"Ours? Ours? Have you lost your mind?" Chey turned on him, shouting through the room. "How in the hell is you marrying another woman a benefit to us whatsoever?"

"I can't explain everything to you right now. You need to trust me. You need to realize that there is a lot more at stake here than your hurt feelings." He tipped the newly poured glass up and had a drink while he stalked away from the bar.

"So I'm just supposed to go on blind faith? I'm supposed to...what. Sleep with you after I saw you marry her with my own eyes? I don't think so, Sander. I don't care what you have to say—*you're married.* That negates everything else." She made a slashing motion with her hand through the air.

Sander moved his sleeve up and checked the time. He'd not bothered to remove his coat.

"What are you doing?" she asked, indignant.

"Wondering how in the hell I'm going to convince you to pack everything you'll need for six months and get on a plane with me for Latvala in the next ten minutes."

Chapter Seventeen

The man really had lost his mind. Chey's mouth fell open in shock. "You want me to what?"

"You heard me. The longer we stand here debating, the more likely I am to be found out."

"You want me to pack--"

"Yes. The sooner the better. Get everything you'll need that you can't live without. Pictures, scrapbooks, whatever. You can call Wynn when we get there and ask her to put the rest in storage, or send you packages through the mail." Sander set the empty glass on the side bar. He still hadn't removed his coat.

"There is no way I'm going to Latvala with you. Your father will have me knocked off before we can even get to the castle. I--"

"I'm not taking you to the castle. Well, not that castle. I'm taking you to *my* castle, which sits on one of the islands just off the coast of Latvala. It's my holding, procured under pressure and duress with my marriage to Valentina."

"No."

"Chey..."

"No. I will not go to Latvala to be your mistress while you and that whore go about the business of securing heirs for the good of the kingdom and--"

"Chey," Sander said, a warning edge to his voice.

"Don't Chey me! You're asking me to commit adultery! I won't do it, I shouldn't *have* to." Her fury knew no bounds. The nerve of him!

Sander glanced at his watch and exhaled a frustrated breath. He spat a curse, or what sounded like a curse, in his own language. "We're going to be late! I can put off leaving for *maybe* another twenty minutes, but that's it."

"No."

He broke away from the couch he was standing next to and strode toward her, expression determined.

One thing Chey had never been was afraid of Sander, and she wasn't afraid of him now. He wouldn't hurt her, at least not physically. Emotionally, well. He'd already done that. She stood her ground, chin lifting with just as much determination as he.

Once he was right in front of her, he placed both hands on the outsides of her shoulders and stared down into her eyes, pressing his point home with quiet urgency. "Do you trust me?"

"Sander, I--"

"Do you?"

She exhaled in frustration. "I did before you said I Do."

"No, I mean do you trust me. Can you overlook what you think you know, judging by what you've seen, and have enough faith to just do what I ask, so I can explain it all later? Time is a real issue right now. I need you to trust me." His words were sincere, his gaze pleading.

It threw Chey off to see him so intent. She smacked her hands on the outsides of her thighs. "So you're asking me, really, to move to Latvala. With the clothes on my back, so to speak."

"Yes. At this point, you might have to ask Wynn to send you clothes or your personal things. We can't miss the take off window."

"Sander, you're making this very difficult. I'm banned from your count--"

"Chey, we don't have time. Don't you think I know all that already? What do you think I've been doing since I left? Now come on." He slid his hands down to hers and took a step back. There was vague desperation in his eyes, along with a sliver of hope.

She knew this was a bad idea. A really bad idea. Why was she even considering it all of a sudden? It would lead nowhere good. He was married. *Married.* Or was he trying to tell her that he'd set the whole thing up? And if so, did it still change the base fact that he was now spoken for? He'd said vows. He was even now wearing a ring. Valentina's ring. She took a step forward when their arms couldn't stretch any longer without breaking the clasp of their hands.

"Trust me. I'll explain everything on the plane," he repeated, taking another step back. His hands, warm and strong, tugged hers.

With reluctance and warning bells going off in her head, she closed the distance by a foot. Then another.

"Good. Come on. Get your purse and let's go." Sander laced his fingers with hers, turned, and gestured toward her bag on the way to the door.

Chey balked at first, digging her feet in. A thousand questions and worries plagued her mind. She snatched at her purse as they passed it, and followed him to the door.

This wasn't a good idea. Something awful was going to happen, like her head nailed to a spike outside the Ahtissari family seat when Aksel found out she was back.

The desperation she'd seen in Sander's eyes, however, worked magic on her. She found it, and him, hard to resist. Especially with him spouting all these things about trust. She did, didn't she? Trust him.

Yes.

Against her better judgment, she allowed him to hustle her out the door of the suite and down the hallway of the hotel.

Once she got on the plane, there would be no turning back.

. . .

Chey engaged in a staring contest with Sander as the plane leveled off and hit cruising altitude. He lounged in the luxurious seat across from her like a lion.

"Any time would be good, Sander," she finally said, attempting to prompt him into some kind of explanation. She still felt mildly hostile and every mile that the plane put between her and Seattle only increased the sensation. To prompt him, she started with a point of curiosity. "What happened to the King?"

He made a sound between a scoff and a grunt, then raked a hand back through his hair. "He used what amounted to a sprained ankle to set his incredible plans into motion. None of us saw it coming."

"So you're not King," she said, stating the obvious.

"No. But what I've been doing the last week and a half or so will cement my right to take the throne once I overthrow him."

"And that involved getting married to a woman you clearly seemed against marrying not so long ago?" She arched a brow and wished she had a stiff drink to help her through this conversation.

"Yes. You see, the King had been quite busy in the interim, behind all of our backs. Remember when Valentina said that our 'people' had made an agreement, one I distinctly said I had not agreed to?" He didn't wait for her to answer. "Not just an agreement, but plans, including dates and press releases that went out while I was gone. They released news of the wedding without my knowledge. Valentina had to have been aware. In fact, she was as complicit in all this as my father and mother."

Chey frowned and decided not to interrupt with questions while he got rolling with details.

"Everyone but Mattias had been sucked into the ruse. The King called an official meeting, including all four brothers and Natalia along with the council and the highest legislators. During the night, unbeknownst to us, the King made a decree that unless I honored the strategic marriage set between Latvala and Weithan Isle, a marriage already announced in both countries, he would bequeath Kallaster Castle to Paavo. *Paavo,* of all people. Aksel went so far as to skip Mattias after me, which is beyond incredible." Sander's expression took a dark turn.

"I'm not sure what that means," she admitted, though she could tell by the look on Sander's face that it wasn't good news. Not for him, not for Mattias.

"Historically speaking, no heir has ever ascended the throne without Kallaster

Castle being one of their holdings. Kallaster has been considered mine for the past four years. I've filled it with my belongings and staff, though I don't live there full time. So for him to strip me of what everyone has accepted as mine, my *birthright,* was shocking to say the least. See, ascension starts long before a King assumes the seat of power. There are a hundred small steps before the big one. Unofficially giving me Kallaster is one— doing it *officially* is another step altogether. What it all amounts to is the King flexing his muscle. Suggesting I might be overlooked for the throne didn't work. I ignored his threat. No one believed he would actually take action, least of all me." Sander gestured with a hand; the stewardess arrived and he ordered vodka for him, a Tequila Sunrise for her.

Chey considered everything Sander said so far. Once the stewardess was gone, she said, "So this was his way of forcing you down the aisle. It's pretty blatant and ugly of him, I agree." She leaned forward a few inches, holding his eyes. "It still doesn't change the fact that you're *married.*"

"What matters more to me—and the King is aware, because all Kings and

Queens care about this—is public perception. He didn't just throw down an ace, he threatened to undermine the trust I've spent my whole life building with the people of our country. If I would have balked, or backed out, the King would have made it seem like I didn't have my countrymen's best interest at heart. Everyone is convinced this 'match' with Weithan Isle is necessary. There was no way I could have gracefully bowed out. Not with Valentina doing her part, playing as if this were already a done deal and that she knew I would follow through for the love of Latvala. I can't tell you how pissed off I was. *Am,*" he amended. He paused when the stewardess returned with their drinks.

Chey murmured her thanks and had a sip right away. Then another. "That's understandable. I saw the way the people responded to you in Vogeva. Without your security around and things."

Sander, on the other hand, swigged half his tumbler down.

Between the hotel drinks and this one, it was the most Chey had ever seen Sander imbibe.

"Yes," he said. "We—Mattias and I— had very little time to come up with a plan. A workable plan. Because I couldn't risk Kallaster falling into Paavo's hands, nor risk my reputation undergoing a thorough tarnishing thanks to the King, I agreed to the marriage while the council was still in session. I had to give them *something.* Anyway, once the meeting was over, I scrambled to set my plan in motion. Part of my condition was that I wanted to arrange the man who would marry us and our agenda after the ceremony. The council, the King and Valentina agreed. So I flew to London in the middle of the night and hired a stage actor I'm very good friends with. I knew I could trust him to keep his mouth shut about the act of treason he was about to perpetrate."

Chey choked on her drink. "You hired an *actor?* That man wasn't really a Priest?"

"No." He smiled, but the humor didn't reach his eyes. "While I was doing that, Mattias had a fake marriage certificate created. The scribe wrote it in a pretty but hard to read hand so that no one would be able to make out the words unless they sat down with it and scanned it personally. What Valentina signed was a confession of duplicity, not a marriage contract. Her people were so busy planning all the frivolous frippery regarding her trousseau—or whatever the hell it's called—no one bothered to read the fine print, as it were."

Stunned to her core, Chey studied Sander's features in disbelief. "So wait, are you saying you're not actually married?"

"Not technically, no. I said vows, I went through the motions, but I was acting right along with the Priest. I meant none of it. But I covered my ass publicly, and I also obtained this." He reached into the pocket of his coat and withdrew a digital recorder. After a moment of pressing a button or two on the screen, Valentina's cultured voice came through amidst faint laughter in the background.

"Well, Prince Dare didn't have a choice. Who knew that such a man could be manipulated with a few well placed decisions and limitations. I guess I know what to do when we're man and wife."

A titter of feminine laughter followed, as if a group of women hid their amusement behind their hands.

"I *am* surprised to hear he's threatening to pass it to Paavo, though. Mattias is now one of the ten most eligible bachelors thanks to you finagling Dare off the market," one woman said.

Valentina replied, "Paavo has the ambition. He's already engaged to a woman approved by the Crown. There won't be any bucking of the system. Dare should have known he couldn't get his way."

Another woman asked, "Don't you feel the least bit guilty about going behind Dare's back with the King?"

"Would *you,* if it brought you the title of Queen?" Valentina replied. "I would have done a lot more than twist his arm to gain that. I'll never rule Weithan Isle—but ruling Latvala will be so much better." Valentina muffled another laugh with the women. It sounded like they were at some sort of gathering.

Sander clicked the recorder off.

Chey glanced between the device and Sander's eyes.

"This is just a small part of the conversation. There's more. A lot more. She gloated about her success at a party *I* arranged and had infiltrated with people whose mission it was to get this very thing. I turned the tables on Valentina and the King both," he said, sliding the recorder away.

"But how will you use it?" Chey asked, more than a little amazed at the intrigue and deception going on with both sides. Not that she blamed Sander after what almost happened.

"Blackmail, of course. Valentina will not like the idea of her name being tarnished in all the high circles, which is exactly how I'll work the whole thing back in my favor. She has a big secret to hide, which I will expose when the time is right." Sander gestured to the stewardess for a refill. She came to claim his glass and stepped away.

"What secret is that?" Chey asked, settling back in her seat. The whole thing was much more complex than she would have ever imagined. Sander hadn't just gone home and forgotten her. He'd gone home and been under siege as he called it, fighting for his political—and personal —life.

Sander accepted the new drink, took a measured sip, then said, "She's pregnant."

Chapter Eighteen

Chey felt like someone had kicked her in the gut. *Pregnant?* Her shock knew no bounds.

"It's not mine," Sander said a moment later, when Chey failed to respond. "But it's someone's, which is why this whole thing got a rush job on it. Valentina undoubtedly put restrictions on time, because she knew she could only hide it for so long. The King and Queen obviously don't know, or they never would have agreed, since that would make a bastard the King or Queen of Latvala one day. Valentina's been playing us all." He paused, then added, "But not for much longer."

"Are you sure it's not yours?" Chey asked, blown away by the news. She couldn't recover from the sheer magnitude of what was happening.

"No. I've never slept with her. Not on our 'wedding night' or any day after. She's knocked up by some playboy who isn't titled, I'm sure, and this is her best shot at avoiding a scandal that will bring Weithan Royalty into unwanted limelight. It must have happened after Monte Carlo, since she'd been content to wait until Spring before then."

Falling silent, Chey absorbed everything Sander told her. Many things now began to make much better sense. Finally, she said, "Were you afraid they were watching you, is that why you couldn't get word out sooner?"

"I didn't just suspect it, I *knew* they were monitoring me. It was tricky to just get the note out that I did. The King put a few of his security team on me, and they stuck like glue. I could hardly breathe for the way they suffocated my personal space. Anyway, we only have a small time frame to sneak you into the country, so that's why it was critical to go now."

"Why such a small window?" she asked, remembering to take a drink from her glass.

"Because I have the current customs official in my pocket as well, but not the ones three shifts after. Nor the one before. I can only make so many trips stateside before someone gets suspicious, which makes slipping you in precarious to say the least." He arched his brows and finished his fourth drink of the day.

"You should have just told me all this at the cemetery," Chey said. "I wouldn't have given you such a hard time."

"Would you have believed the very abbreviated version of this story?" he asked with a droll lilt to his accent.

Chey actually laughed. "Well...now that you mention it, probably not. I would have thought you were just saying anything to get me to go with you."

"Right." He nodded once, then tilted his head back against the chair, watching her through the slats of his lashes.

"Where will I be staying then, if not the family seat?" she asked, imagining some cabin in the woods far from prying Royal eyes. Then she recalled mention of another castle.

"Kallaster Castle. You won't need to fear the staff there will turn you in, or relay information that you're in the country. Still, everyone will need to be mildly vigilant for a while until I blow this whole thing wide open. Visitors rarely come without prior warning, considering it's on an island and passage can get dangerous in bad weather, but extra attention will have to be paid. I think you'll like it there," he added, knees parting wide when he slouched down. Sander looked tired in that moment, as if the long hours and days of the past weeks were finally taking a toll.

"This feels risky," she admitted, of her return to Latvala. "How long will we have to keep a lid on it? I mean—how long until I won't have to feel that my life is in danger?"

"It's less risky to me to have you where I can see you, so to speak, than to have you half way around the world. Honestly, I just don't trust that Valentina or the King and Queen won't try to finish you off. They won't be expecting me to do something so bold. In my mind, Kallaster Castle is the last place they'll think to find you." He paused, reaching an arm up over his head to clasp the seat with his hand. "Like the rest of us, you'll always have to be a little cautious. But I plan to make sure the King and Queen are shut down with any plans to harm you again. Maybe...three weeks? Four? Mattias and I are still figuring when and where to expose this mess. We need to do it at the right time, get as much bang for our buck as we can."

"That makes sense," Chey said,

following the line of his arm with her eyes. She trailed down to his chest, then his stomach, to the way the jeans fit over his muscular thighs. Turning her thoughts back to more serious things, she glanced at his face to find him watching her as if he knew exactly what she'd been thinking.

She quirked her lips at him.

He smiled, lazy and leonine.

"You're not completely off the hook, you know," she said. "I'm still smarting over seeing you get married. Well, watching your fake marriage."

His shoulders shook with a silent laugh. "What will it take to get me back in your good graces?"

Chey hated the way the velvet rasp of his voice brought shivers down her spine. "That's for me to know and you to find out."

"Does it involve the bedroom in the back?"

"Sander!" Chey glanced over her shoulder; the stewardess was nowhere in sight.

"I'm only saying what you're thinking," he drawled.

Chey glanced back. "You look about as capable for a romp as I look to go walking down a Milan runway."

He exhaled, as if she would just never get it. Then he leaned forward, snatched her out of her chair, and hauled her back to the bedroom.

Sander shut the door with a decisive thud of his boot.

. . .

Chey hadn't lied when she said he wasn't completely off the hook. In the aftermath of lust that had left them both shattered and breathless, Chey stared up at the ceiling of the plane, one arm tucked behind her head, and wondered whether Sander would succeed in besting Valentina and the King. He seemed to have all the chess pieces necessary, and, at least from her vantage, was closing in on a check-mate.

One of the lessons she'd learned in life was that you could never count on anything going to plan. There was always some juggernaut waiting to throw a wrench into your well oiled machine. The wrench in this case could be that the King himself had a counter to Sander's blackmail. Maybe he had something powerful in his coffer Sander couldn't envision, hadn't foreseen.

You're such a paranoid skeptic, she chided herself.

Wynn hadn't been happy to hear of Chey's plans. On the way to the private airstrip, they'd found a payphone for Chey to make a quick call, and she'd informed Wynn what she needed her to do in less than thirty seconds.

Wynn's protests rang in Chey's mind. *Have you totally lost all good sense? You really believe that nonsense he's probably selling you? What if he can't protect you like you think he can?*

They'd talked over each other, until finally, Wynn had given up and agreed to do as Chey asked.

Of course Chey had doubts and fears. Sander's plan had worked so far—maybe he would see it successfully through to the end. The *what ifs* plagued Chey while she rolled onto her side to face Sander. He was out cold, on his stomach, one arm flung wide.

What if he *couldn't* protect her, and Aksel and Helina discovered she was in the country? Would they send her to jail— or plan something more sinister? Even if

Sander orchestrated the blackmail to its highest advantage, would it really keep her safe?

She trailed her fingers over the warm skin of Sander's back, tracing muscle, tracing bone. He rumbled, but didn't waken.

On the other hand, reverse to her worries and fears, was the blossoming sensation of pride and affection that he'd taken the time to fit her into his plan. That he was concerned enough over her well being that he'd risked seeking her out in public at the cemetery, and taking her to the hotel. Once they were on the plane, he'd explained as he said he would—and what a tale it had been. It pleased her to know that Sander hadn't taken Valentina to bed on their fake wedding night.

What excuse had he given? *I have a headache* rolled through her thoughts, in Sander's voice, and a laugh accidentally bubbled past her lips. Oh, to be a fly on the wall for that conversation!

Dealing with Royalty was proving to be every bit as complicated as it appeared from the beginning.

For now, she decided to come to peace with the turmoil, the grief. She truly believed Sander meant to set aright the wrongs so that they could be together.

What it meant for the country of Latvala, or the rest of the family subject to the fallout, she couldn't say.

Chapter Nineteen

The transfer from plane to helicopter happened as dusk fell over Latvala. After the customs official pretended not to see her and signed off on the jet, security swarmed around Sander and Chey to shield them from sight, creating a tight cocoon of bodies that dispersed once the pair were ensconced in the second aircraft.

Snow blanketed the region in a pretty swath of white, a stunning sight as they flew over the landscape. Chey stared down out the window at her side, enchanted with the transition from ground to water that the setting sun painted with shades of orange and deep pink. The choppy surface reminded Chey of rippling material until it smoothed out to something like glass as they left the shoreline behind.

Her first sight of the island, which took them only minutes to reach, caught Chey's breath in her throat. It was bigger than she thought it would be, with a clear peak from a small mountain and trees that choked the terrain up to the creamy shoreline where a wide swath of sand took over. She could see an inlet this high up with a dock where several yachts were moored. As the helicopter flew over the middle toward the other side, where Sander said the castle was located, she saw flat patches of land that must be used for farming when the weather was right. Houses peppered the island here or there, though most were not clustered together in the way track houses would be. Each one seemed to have its own little private pat of land.

Her first glimpse of Kallaster Castle came in the shape of high walls and soaring turrets, with spires reaching for the sky. Nestled into an unknown amount of acreage on the northward side of Pallan Island, the castle dominated the entire bay which it presided over. Flanking it was the high peak, providing cover along one whole side. Chey realized a person wouldn't be able to see the coastline of Latvala from this vantage, only the wide open sea.

"This holding was built to be the first bastion against attack from invading countries," Sander said near her ear. He had to speak up to be heard above the chop of the copter blades. "It's a fortress in the truest sense of the word, although of course we don't worry about invasion of that nature these days."

Chey could see from this perspective how difficult, if not impossible, it would be to 'sneak' up on the castle and attack it. Several towers for lookouts provided advance warning of any incoming sea vessels, and the island itself had sections of hostile coastline that made it hazardous to anchor in, as Sander pointed out next.

Awash with wonder, she studied what she could see of the structure that would be her home for the next several months until the helicopter descended toward a landing pad adjacent to the castle itself.

Disembarking as the sun sank lower against the horizon, Chey noticed the security didn't swarm as they had during the last transfer. Probably because they needn't worry about spies in such a secluded area.

Sliding into the back seat of a glossy sedan, Sander at her side, she set her hands in her lap and marveled at the scenery.

"What do you think so far?" Sander asked.

"I don't have words to describe how beautiful I think it is," she admitted.

The sedan pulled away from the helipad and cruised along a single lane road that wound toward a tall arch protected with an enormous gate. The landing pad wasn't far at all from the castle itself, giving easy access to arrive and depart at will.

"It's always been my favorite holding," Sander confessed. When they came to a fork in the road, he gestured the other direction, where the coastline swerved in the shape of a half moon. "That building there wasn't in the original plan. My grandfather added it on for days when he wanted to linger on the beach but didn't want to be enclosed behind the castle walls."

Chey caught the barest glimpse of a structure built on rock just at the line of the sand, almost a mini-castle in the way it was made of the same color stone as the big one and sported dominant, regal architecture. One could stand right on the broad covered portico and stare out at the water, unimpeded.

"That's no small building," she pointed

out, as the structure disappeared from sight when the sedan passed through the open gate.

"Six bedrooms, with a large porch and an even larger balcony. It has its own little garden, a back patio with a great view of the mountain and windows all along the front. I'll take you there soon and let you wander around." He glanced aside, taking her reactions in.

"I'd like that, yes," Chey said. The grounds past the gate seemed manicured and well appointed despite the layer of snow covering it all. If she had to guess, she would have thought the walls here were at least twenty feet high. The castle itself rose far above that, ensconced behind the protective barrier, with obvious balconies, arches, and niches easy to see from the bailey.

When the car pulled up to the entrance, footmen came to open the sedan door. Unlike the family seat, the security here all wore suits, as if none were military, and the staff's attire was simple black and white, easy to maneuver and move in.

Chey got out after Sander, exchanging a quiet word of thanks before taking the hand he offered to follow him up a shallow flight of wide stairs, through a high arch, and toward double doors that another staff member opened.

Right away, Chey sensed the difference in this castle compared to the other. Despite its more medieval architecture, there was still something casual and inviting about it. A foyer opened up from the doors, with a soaring dome ceiling and a great hall stretching to the right. On the left, a spartan table that sat at least thirty represented the dining hall. Arches carved into the walls were filled with stained glass overlooking the bailey. Colored light slanted across gray stone floors, only adding to the medieval feel.

Ahead, a long hallway led deeper into the structure. Aside it, a stone staircase that spiraled up out of sight into higher floors. There was so much mystery here that Chey was enthralled, her imagination set afire. She wanted to explore every nook, every cranny. How she wished she had her photography equipment with her.

"This is incredible," Chey said, voice just a whisper. She didn't see any other staff members at the moment; the security had dispersed outside somewhere, rather than follow them inside.

"I'm glad you like it. I'll give you a proper tour in the morning, hm? For now, let me show you where you'll be sleeping." He cut a dashing wink aside and led her toward the staircase.

"I thought that would be with you." Chey marveled at her brazen tongue.

He laughed. "Exactly."

From brazen to surprised, Chey parroted his laugh. "Really? Actually, I was joking. I figured I'd be shown to a suite like I had in the other castle."

"Well, you *can* stay in another room if you like." Deviant, he smiled.

"You're a devil," she declared with another quiet laugh.

"I keep saying it's what you like best about me."

"What I like best about you isn't proper for a lady to say."

"Damn. It's all about the body, instead of the mind." He lamented his circumstance with a put upon sigh.

Amused, Chey tilted her cheek against the muscled strength of his arm.

Chuckling, he kissed the top of her head.

After ascending two flights of stairs, they finally emerged onto the second level. Immediately to the left was a large, arching window. It dumped waning light across an open area with several hallways leading different directions.

"Wait, I want to glance out here a second," she said, veering toward the window. The vista of castle, shore and water from this height was impressively beautiful. She could see angles of stone that made up the structure, part of the surrounding wall, and all of the half moon bay.

"You should see the view from the master suite," Sander said, standing at her elbow.

"I will in a second. This is amazing, though." Chey stepped back and let Sander guide her toward the hallway to the right. This was more private, with no rooms intersecting on the left. It was a shorter hall than the others, with two doors tucked into a niche halfway down.

"I'm glad you like it." He opened one door and released her hand to let her walk through. "This is where you'll be sleeping."

Chey crossed the threshold and sucked in a breath. The entire opposite wall facing the bay was made of more large arches with windows between columns at least three feet in circumference. A balcony with a carved stone rail followed the length of the suite, which appeared to take up the entire rest of the floor on this side. An enormous bed situated against a wall sported masculine covers in shades of cocoa and red with accents of fur draped across the foot and around some of the smaller pillows. Rugs covered the stone floor in specific spots, and more furniture sat in clusters near bookcases stuffed with old and new tomes. Swords and sheaths along with a large metal family crest took up space on the wall, along with a few tapestries taller than she was.

The effect, again, was distinctly spartan and medieval. Chey half expected a knight to come wandering out from one of several arches leading to other chambers in the suite. A fireplace across from the bed snapped and cracked, the flames flickering around several pieces of burning wood.

Behind her, Sander closed the door. He stepped past her and gestured to one arch on the right. "That's the bathroom and closet in there. I had some clothes and other feminine things brought in, just in case we weren't able to grab enough of your things before we left the states."

"You were pretty sure I'd come with you, weren't you?" she asked, distracted by the décor.

"I wasn't about to take no for an answer," he said.

She followed his gesture through the archway to the right that sat next to the fireplace. It was obvious that at some point, the castle had been updated to accommodate running water and more modern amenities, like a shower, toilet and jacuzzi tub tucked into the floor in the middle of the immense bathroom.

Entering the closet, she felt around for a light switch and flipped it on. Sander hadn't done justice to his declaration that he'd had some things brought in. Fully ten feet of a thirty foot section had an array of feminine clothing. That was just 'her' side. The other was 'his', stuffed to the gills with suits, shirts, slacks, jeans, khakis, hunting gear, several types of boots, polished shoes and more. In the center of the space stood a piece that served as one gigantic dresser. Flat on the surface, it had rows of drawers for folded items and even cubbies for shoes.

"I've never seen a closet this big," she admitted. The back wall had a higher rod, where already a few long dresses hung.

Chey turned around to find Sander leaning against the door frame, one arm propped above his head. He glanced past her as if he'd seen it all too many times before.

Of course he had. He'd grown up with this kind of luxury every day of his life.

"I'm sure you'll find ways to put it to good use," he teased. Then he retreated, letting her follow as she would.

Chey, too nosy for her own good, went to check the hanging clothes. There was a selection of jeans, casual tops, fancier tops and dresses present. Handfuls of each, enough to see her through at least two weeks without wearing the same thing twice, all in her size. There were three coats in varying stages of elegance or usefulness to choose from. She found underthings in one of the dresser drawers, socks, scarves and pajamas.

He'd thought of everything.

"Sander, why did you even want me to bring anything? There's already enough here for half a month," she asked, leaving the closet after turning off the light. She went back into the main part of the bedroom. He was out on the balcony, hands in his pockets, staring out over the sea.

Curbing her curiosity to see what the rest of the suite contained, she stepped out onto the balcony with him. Up here, a stiff, frigid breeze gusted against her skin. She huddled into her coat and glanced at his profile. He stood with his head slightly tilted back, eyes lidded, hair lashing around his neck. Chey decided he'd never looked more like a Nordic conqueror than he did right then. She could easily superimpose him against the backdrop of the castle into another time, another era. One he would just as easily reign in.

In that moment, Chey was so very thankful that he'd come back for her. Regardless of her broken heart and fury over his 'marriage' to Valentina, and being left in the dark for weeks, it was all worth it to be here, right now, watching a future King gaze out over his domain.

Her future King.

"You look like a man who has a lot on his mind," she said.

"I am a man with a lot on his mind," he replied. After a few seconds, he glanced at her without breaking his stance.

"You know what's on my mind right now?"

"What?" His mouth quirked like he suspected he knew what she might say.

"Thanksgiving dinner. I was going to have Ramen or something, but maybe we can improvise and have something a little nicer. I'm sure you don't celebrate that holiday, but it can't hurt to eat and be thankful at the same time, can it?" She smiled what she hoped was a charming smile.

He laughed. "If it's a Thanksgiving dinner you want, then that's what you'll get."

"For starters, that'll do."

"Greedy." Hooking her around the neck with his arm, Sander tugged her inside and closed the doors against the cold.

. . .

Disoriented by the time change, jet lag and the unfamiliar bedroom, she sat up out of a dead sleep and reached for Sander among the sheets. An urgent question dawned on her, perhaps in dreams, one she needed an immediate answer to.

"Sander? Wake up. Why didn't I think to ask you this last night?" Mumbling to herself, she discovered his side of the bed empty. Knuckling the sting from her eyelids, she got out of bed and nabbed a robe from a nearby chair to cover her nakedness with. Tying the belt around her waist, she padded over the cold stone floor in search.

"Sander?"

"In here," he called from somewhere beyond an archway and down a short hall.

Chey followed his voice, bundling deeper into the warmth. Rounding yet another arch—the entire chamber was separated by large rooms divided by these archways—she found him sitting in what appeared to be an office. A great mahogany desk sat in front of a wall bearing a floor to ceiling tapestry, with bookshelves and another desk for printers and the like taking up yet a different wall.

He sat in a tall leather chair, dressed in an immaculate suit of dark gray and white pinstripe. The coat, shed at some point when he began working, hung from a coat rack near one of the book cases. Golden hair pulled back into a low tail, he glanced up from the sheaf of papers in front of him.

"What are you doing up so early?" she asked, wondering how she'd missed his departure from bed. She curled into a plush chair on the other side of his desk, facing him, and drew her feet up onto the cushion. The morning after their impromptu Thanksgiving dinner found Chey feeling a little nauseous. She had eaten far too much of the excellent food, she decided.

He smiled while he watched her, then leaned back against the chair. Tossing down the pen, he crossed his arms over the breadth of his chest. "It's after ten in the morning. Time gets screwy when you lose as many hours as we did on the way over."

Chey's mouth made an 'oh' of understanding and surprise. The reason she'd lurched out of bed rose in the back of her mind, however, and she blurted out the question while scraping the tangled mess of her hair away from her face.

"Since she's your wife—pretend wife—won't Valentina be coming here? We're acting like she won't have any interest in visiting Kallaster Castle." It made Chey uncomfortable to think Valentina might suddenly decide to come over.

"I knew I would be bringing you here, so I fed her a whole '*I'm redoing parts of the castle to suit you, my love, you're not allowed to set foot on the island until my surprises are finished'* line. Even if she were to come against my command, we would know in advance because plans have to be made ahead of time for the helicopter. She can't move about easily now that she's my 'wife' without someone knowing. In turn, *we'll* know." He studied her across the desk.

"I see. That's a relief, then. I think it was on my mind before I went to sleep, so I woke up half panicked," she admitted. "Valentina's never been here before?"

"No. She's never set foot on the island. As far as I'm concerned, she never will."

"I can't say I'm sorry. I enjoy knowing I'm sharing something with you that she hasn't—and won't." Chey curled her arms around her middle and returned his searching gaze. "Why are you looking at me like that?"

"Because I like that content expression on your face, and how rumpled you look." He lifted a hand, smile on his mouth, to rub fingers along his freshly shaven jaw.

"You would," she retorted with teasing accusation in her voice.

He laughed. "That doesn't mean I don't appreciate you decked out in some elegant dress, draped in diamonds. I happen to like this Chey, too."

"Which is good. Now and then I like to just laze around. Do you ever do that? Besides back at my apartment?" she asked.

"Sometimes. Right now, things are too precarious, as you may imagine. I'm going to fly back to the mainland shortly to meet up with Mattias. You'll be safe here. Explore at your leisure. I should be back before two or three, at the latest." He uncrossed his arms and closed the folder he'd been working on.

"All right," she said, agreeing easily to exploration. "You're going to finalize plans to put into motion, then?"

"Or try to. We're close, but like I mentioned before—the timing has to be perfect. There needs to be a specific outcome, or it will all be for naught." He glanced away from her to the array of windows through the arches. The day beyond was overcast, the threat of more snow on the way.

"What might happen if your plans go awry? Will you be able to divorce Valentina without backlash?" she asked, twisting a look over her shoulder to get a glimpse of the sky. Then she glanced back at Sander. He was still studying the clouds.

"That will happen no matter what. I'm shooting for an annulment. She can suffer the indignity of our country and her country thinking she abstained from our bed while being pregnant with another man's baby." He grunted, returning his steely gaze to Chey.

"I really hope it works out like you want it to. Is there any chance the King will wrest this away from you?" Chey made a gesture to the castle.

"I hope not. Everyone has considered it mine, as I mentioned, for a long time." He paused, then reached over to tap the telephone sitting on his desk. "By the way, there are phones like this all over the castle. Press the zero for security, one for the head of housekeeping. And this red tabbed button is the panic button. If you perceive any threat at all, get to a phone and push it. The entire island will lock down and when the security finds you, they'll secure you into one of several safe rooms in the castle."

Chey leaned forward to see where the red button was. "All right, I got it." She wouldn't forget.

"The head housekeeper is Mira. She'll see to most everything you might need, unless it's the middle of the night and her relief is on duty. She can point you in the right direction for exploring." Sander leaned back, hands resting in his lap. "I'm getting us both new phones that only connect to each other. That way no one can tap into my regular line."

"Great. I'd prefer to have direct access to you if I can."

"It'll make things easier. Feel free to organize the other half of the closet as you see fit. And make a list of anything you might need that we didn't think of. We can make a shopping run tomorrow or the next day. I'm sure Wynn won't have time to get a delivery off to you by then." He checked his phone when a message came through. "All right, that's my call. Time to take off."

"Don't be surprised if I actually follow through with that offer," Chey said with a sleepy grin. She stood up out of the chair after that, the robe brushing against her ankles. "I'll be waiting. Have a safe trip."

He snorted as he donned his jacket, picked up the folder, then slid his phone into his pocket. "You're a woman. I expect no less."

She pinched his ribs once he was within reach. Chey offered her cheek for him to kiss since she hadn't hit the bathroom and a toothbrush yet. "Your mouth is going to get you into big trouble."

"I hope so." He dusted her cheek with a kiss, then stepped away. "I'll see you later." Sander strode out of the office with purposeful strides.

Chey leaned against the chair and watched him go, amazed at the turn her life had taken yet again in the last twenty-four hours. Catching a yawn with her palm, she trundled back to bed and indulged the need for more sleep.

Exploring and organizing could wait.

Chapter Twenty

The more Chey investigated Kallaster Castle, the more she fell in love with it. After a shower and a change into jeans topped by a heavy sweatshirt of white, she'd gone in search of Mira for directions to the kitchens. Mira, in her thirties with blonde hair and pretty green eyes, finally allowed Chey to get her own lunch when Chey assured her that she didn't mind making it.

Expansive and running the same gray stone theme as the rest of the castle, the kitchens were enormous and offered everything a person could want in the way of food preparation. Chey found the makings for salad and a tuna sandwich in one of two oversized refrigerators. It didn't take her long to eat and learn the different rooms of the kitchens. There was a section for pastries and baking, another for grilling and cooking. Then a whole other partition for storage, a wine tasting room and separate large refrigeration units big enough to hold food for a party of five hundred people.

Beyond the kitchens, Chey discovered a hideaway patio covered with trellis overlooking a small garden with foliage that was probably lush and green in the spring. The hallways inside, some furnished more than others, led to medieval looking parlors, sitting rooms and a library with a two story ceiling. All sorts of nooks and crannies could be found near stairs, at the end of hallways and attached to a few of the sitting rooms.

On the upper floors, many open areas sported balconies giving different views of the island. Some faced the mountain peak, others faced the ocean and the bay. After three hours of exploring, she still hadn't seen it all.

Back in Sander's room to await his arrival, she started in on the closet organization, taking him at his word that it was all right to do what she wanted with her 'side'. Or sections. There was more than one wall to mess with. Smaller niches broke off the main closet with more space to hang clothes or arrange other articles, such as scarves, coats and sweaters. It was so different and charming than anything she'd ever done that she completely lost track of time.

"I see you didn't let any grass grow while I was gone," Sander said behind her.

Chey fumbled the folded sweater she had in her hands and whipped a look over her shoulder. Grinning, she set the sweater on the stone shelf and turned around.

"Of course not. This was too good of an opportunity to waste." She searched for clues about how his day had gone, but the only difference Chey could define was three buttons on his shirt undone that hadn't been before up near his throat.

He shucked the jacket and walked it to a hanger on his side, then finished undoing the buttons and peeled the shirt from his shoulders. The skin beneath was golden despite the season, muscles rippling whenever he moved. He tossed the shirt into the laundry basket and undid the buckle at his waist.

"Looks like you got most of it organized," he said with a glance over his shoulder. The belt slithered free. He hung it on a rack with no less than twenty other belts.

"Most of it. There is an apartment room full of space left," she said, as if he wasn't aware.

He smiled, though it lacked his usual devilish charm.

That was Chey's first indication that his mind was set toward more serious thoughts. She couldn't really blame him. "How did it go with Mattias?" she asked.

Sander bent over to remove his shoes, socks and then his slacks. A pair of black boxer briefs hugged his hips, leaving nothing to the imagination.

Any other time, Chey might have taken advantage of the situation. Or at least tossed a tease his way. Today she remained quiet.

"Three days," he said. The slacks went the way of the shirt, as well as the socks.

"Three days?" she echoed, frowning. "What's in three days?"

"When we blow this thing wide open." He glanced at her while he took a pair of jeans from a shelf and put them on. Leaving the zipper down and the button undone, he reached up to rake both hands through his hair, pulling the band free of the tail.

Chey watched the transformation from Prince to rugged Sander with no small amount of appreciation and awe. It was a distant appreciation, however, because the news made Chey's stomach clench.

"How are you going to do it?"

"The King informed us today that he will be officially naming me heir to the throne." Sander tugged a ribbed sweater the color of slate and slid it over his head.

"I thought you were already the heir?"

"I am, for all intents and purposes. But there are rituals, things to make it official. He'll make a state address, so that there is no guess work for the citizens of the country." Sander's mouth tightened. He found fresh socks and boots to slide his feet into.

"Why do I have the impression that there's more to the story?" she asked. With each new revelation Sander gave, his demeanor changed, subtly growing darker.

"Because that little bitch went to him and confessed she's pregnant," Sander retorted, anger edging his voice. "She told him it's mine."

. . .

It wasn't often Chey heard Sander curse—at least in a language she understood. This time, she echoed the sentiment in her mind. Valentina was going for broke.

"How could she do that?"

"Easy. She told him it happened on that visit I paid her, when we were set up in Italy." Sander straightened and finally buzzed the zipper up and fastened the button on his jeans.

Chey remembered hearing about that when she'd first arrived in Latvala. The eldest brother had been wooing some woman the Queen wanted him to make his wife. Helina must be gloating for all she was worth.

"Does this change anything?" Chey asked. She couldn't see her way around the complications, wasn't sure how it might affect Sander. Or her.

"It moves the schedule up faster than we wanted, but we'll work with it. The sooner the better, before Valentina pulls something else out of her hat that puts the whole thing in jeopardy." Sander reached for Chey's hand and led her from the closet, snapping the light out along the way.

Chey followed to the side bar, where he released her to pour himself a drink.

"Want something?" he asked.

"No thanks. I had a whole bottle of water with lunch not too long ago." Chey swiveled to sit in a nearby chair and pulled a leg up to tuck beneath her.

"Did you decide how you're going to break the news?" she asked then.

"The announcement will be televised. He'll do it from here, since this holding will officially become mine. Once he makes his statements, I'll be expected to step up and make a few of my own. That's when I'll do it." He knocked back a drink, hissing in the aftermath.

"Oh. On television?" Chey's eyes widened.

"Yes. Mattias is even now coordinating with a producer to play parts of the Valentina tape on cue. It's risky though. Damn. It's very risky." He licked his lips and leaned a hip against the side table.

"Because you're not sure you can trust the producer?"

"That, and Latvala has not seen a scandal like this in a long time. It's not nearly the scandal some monarchies face, but it's more than I care for. It'll have far reaching implications, some of which I worry we haven't thought of, and therefore didn't take into consideration." He finished the drink and set the glass aside.

Chey hadn't thought about the possible international fallout. Deals could be reneged on, countries might cut ally status—any number of things. Although she thought that was more likely to happen to Weithan Isle than Latvala, considering Valentina was the manipulative one. And the King, but it didn't sound as if Sander was going to out him to the public. She could hardly blame him.

"Do you think people will think less of you for taking this route? Announcing her deception on television?" Chey asked, when that idea presented itself.

"It's possible. I'd like to think people will believe I'm doing this in the best interest of Latvala, rather than for myself. We can't have the country ruled by someone else's bastard. It could cause the collapse of the country should that child decide to wreak havoc later in life." Sander tongued his teeth and shook his head.

"It's risky, too, because the King won't know what you're doing. So he'll be on camera, right? His reaction will be broadcast for all to see. I imagine he won't be happy about that," she said.

"Not even a little bit happy," Sander replied. "Valentina will be there as well. She has no idea it's coming. She thinks this whole thing will exalt her into a whole other stratosphere, celebrity wise."

Chey cringed inwardly. She would *not* want to be Valentina when that betrayal came out.

"She should have thought about her manipulations beforehand. Never mind crowing about it in public, how she was using you." Chey paused, then asked, "What excuse are you giving her about not sleeping in her bed?"

"The most obvious one. That I'm angry about the way she trapped me into marriage. I've told her she'll get my attention when I'm good and ready to give it, and not a second before. She knows better than to push me too far." He brought his attention back to Chey. His gaze lingered on her eyes.

"It'll all be okay. I think it'll work out how you want it to. It's just the details and things in the meantime."

Sander looked thoughtful. He pushed away from the side table and approached. Once he stood right in front of her chair, he cupped her jaw in his hand and stroked his thumb over the arch of her cheek. "The details are what will make or break it. I'll make sure we get you somewhere safe while they're here."

Chey stared up at his face and tilted her cheek into his touch. "I was about to ask you if there was somewhere discreet I could watch and still not be seen."

"Yes," he replied with a wry grin. "On television."

Chapter Twenty-One

In the three days before the televised announcement, Chey spent what time she could with Sander when he wasn't hammering out the last minute details. He showed her the dungeons and gave her a brief history on the castle's role in keeping Latvala safe from invasion. They ate lunch on the trellis covered patio, took long, hot soaks in the jacuzzi tub, and wandered the beach hand in hand. Mesmerized by the raw beauty of the bay, Chey promised herself many trips back. Sander was more interested in watching her reactions; every time she glanced aside, his eyes were on her face. He wore a content looking smile and strolled at her side as if he didn't have a care in the world.

They both knew better.

On the morning of the third day, Sander rose early, showered and shaved, and donned a military uniform in navy blue with silver accents. He looked smart and sharp by the time he'd pulled on polished boots, attached his sword to his belt and tied his hair back into a low tail.

Chey chose to wear clothes for comfort, since she was required to stay out of sight. Jeans, a long sleeved white shirt and a mint green cardigan over that. She wore tennis shoes in case she needed to move quickly.

After a warm, lingering kiss with Sander and quiet wishes for a successful outcome, she watched him depart the suite. Mira led Chey to an empty bedroom on the third level with a television hooked up that would give her a firsthand view of what the rest of the public would see. This room also overlooked the entrance gate, giving Chey the ability to watch everyone arrive. As long as she stayed behind the curtain and observed through the crack, no one would see her.

Chey paced the room, agitated and nervous, as the minutes ticked by. At precisely nine-thirty, the security began to arrive. They came by boat, and then overland, flanking the drive and the perimeter of the castle. Valentina arrived first by helicopter and was driven onto the castle grounds much as Chey and Sander had been a few days past. Chey watched

Valentina's car cruise along the drive toward the front doors. She wondered what the Princess thought, and whether Valentina was already deciding on what to change to put her stamp on the structure.

The chop of rotor blades cut through the air, lifting off once more to return to the mainland and pick up the King and Queen.

Everything was ready.

Chey turned the television on. So far, the screen showed news anchors in Kalev discussing the upcoming event, with flashes of Sander growing from child to man, preparing to take on the official honor of heir to the throne. The pictures of Sander as a boy were endearing and charming, and Chey smiled to herself more than once. Even as a child he had a presence about him, a rakish sort of charisma that had carried over into manhood.

She realized then that even at the risk of a broken heart, she wouldn't change a thing. It was worth fighting for, this relationship, especially after spending the last three days with Sander at the castle. They fit together well, alternating between playful banter, serious conversation and intense passion. Chey better understood now why Mattias had pushed for Sander to take this path where he might have a shot at real love rather than a lifetime with someone like Valentina, who obviously cared more about the title than anything else.

What it meant for the long run, Chey wouldn't consider at any great length. She couldn't picture herself as Queen, wouldn't know the first thing about supporting Sander in that role. For now it was enough to be with him and work out these problems before she allowed herself to seriously contemplate the Kingdom at that level.

It was more than a little frightening and intimidating.

Distracted by the television, she perched on the edge of the bed and watched as the news anchors came at the story from a different angle. This one stretched into the future, projecting Sander, one day, as King. The supporters they interviewed on the snowy streets of Kalev were enthusiastic and excited. Sander unequivocally had the backing of Latvala's citizens.

Long minutes later, the sound of the helicopter drew Chey off the bed. At the window, she saw the aircraft land and eventually, a trio of sedans pulled away for the castle. The cars filed in, ferrying the King and Queen to the castle doors.

Nervous, knowing the time was short, Chey turned up the volume on the television and pulled over a plush chair to sink down into. Bringing a foot up into the chair with her, she wrapped her arms around her knee and watched the news team begin to shift the focus to Kallaster Castle. A still photo blended into a live shot, replete with a gray sky and snow clinging to the spires and peaks of the castle itself.

The shot switched abruptly to the great hall where a podium with a microphone had been set up, backed by the soaring, beamed ceiling, giant tapestries and chandeliers. It was an impressive angle. In the background, reporters spoke in a quieter voice while they speculated and filled the silence with idle commentary.

Waiting, like everyone else, for the event to begin.

. . .

"And so, I present my son, official Heir

to the Throne of Latvala, with the key to Kallaster Castle." Aksel, dressed to the nines in his own military uniform, looking distinguished and at ease, presented a royal blue velvet box sideways to Sander who stood waiting to receive the final gift of the official announcement. Already a new sash had been given to drape around Sander's shoulder and chest, this one silver lined with red. The ceremony had gone without a hitch, the rite of passage passed down from King to firstborn son. All that was left was to gift Sander the key to the castle and make room for the official Heir to take the podium and give his acceptance speech. Across the bottom of the television screen, a ticker tape scrolled by with the commentary in English.

Sander, square shouldered and debonaire in his uniform, bowed his head and eased the lid up on the velvet box before taking possession of it to show the cameras and small crowd gathered as official witnesses. The gold key nestled into a bed of royal blue velvet looked old, and was, Chey thought, more of an iconic gesture than a usable artifact.

"Thank you, your Highness. I accept the role of Heir to the Throne as well as my new holdings." Sander let the camera get a close up shot of the carved key, before he handed the box over to Mattias who stood at his side.

Then Sander took the podium when the King stepped away.

Chey held her breath. Sander looked commanding and calm, sweeping a look over the gathered. A camera panned the faces watching quickly, in the interim: the Queen watched on with a secret curve on her mouth, as well as Princess Valentina, who looked a lot like the cat who ate the canary. Paavo, Gunnar and their significant others regarded Sander passively, expressions more neutral than not. Natalia observed with her chin notched arrogantly high, eyes covered by a pair of designer shades. Several other dignified men in uniforms or suits flashed quick smiles when they knew they were on camera.

A moment later, the focus shifted back to Sander. He looked straight into the camera.

This was it. No going back now. Chey's skin tingled with nerves and anticipation.

"As Heir to the Throne of Latvala, it is my duty to protect and serve the people of this country. I believe I have proven beyond a shadow of a doubt my loyalty, honesty and integrity in a time when selfishness, greed and corruptness runs rampant. Recently, as everyone is aware, I took a wife," he said, never breaking eye contact with the camera.

Another angle cut in for a quick shot of Valentina's face. She smiled full and bright and dashed a wink at Sander, though everyone knew he wasn't looking. The angle changed again, and Sander filled the screen.

"Because I am a cautious man, and have my country's safety forefront in my mind, I was forced to view and investigate a piece of information that came to me just after I took my vows. I present a little of the evidence to you as it was presented to me." Sander quieted as a voice, Valentina's voice, took the airwaves. It was the same piece Chey had heard, with Valentina all but admitting the lies used to manipulate Sander to her will. Any mention of the King or Queen had been culled, making it seem as if Valentina alone orchestrated the quick engagement and wedding.

The camera cut back to Valentina, whose cat-and-canary expression had been replaced by horror. One hand was at her throat, eyes wide. Paavo could be seen frowning, as was Gunnar.

Sander picked up speaking as the audio portion of Valentina's faded.

"To make matters much worse," he said, staring straight into the lens. Into the hearts of his people. "I discovered directly after this that Valentina is pregnant. With *another* man's child. It is my belief that she planned to step in as Princess, give birth to an illegitimate child that she claims is mine, and have that child one day become ruler of Latvala." He paused as gasps of shock and outrage filtered through the crowd. "I'm here to tell you now, that I *will not* be a party to this country falling into the hands of a child not born of my blood. In response to these stunning insights, I have refused to consummate my marriage. As more details came to light, I see now that it was the best decision I could have made. I demand princess Valentina have a DNA test to prove the child is not mine, and to relinquish her position as my wife for I have already filed an annulment."

A ripple of discord erupted from the gathered, ranging from another gasp to a growl of warning to what sounded like a plea. Amidst those things, the din of hushed, urgent conversation threatened to over ride the announcement.

Even though she knew it was coming, had prepared herself for the intensity, Chey felt as shocked as some people looked. A few legislators were red faced, Valentina appeared ghost white, as if she might faint, and Aksel...oh, the King was fit to be tied. To the casual observer, it probably seemed the King was furious over the duplicity.

Chey understood it was because he had been upstaged. Beat at his own game.

Sander, steely eyed and calmer than anyone else in the hall, continued. "I urge the people of Latvala to realize I do not take these actions lightly, and will protect the lineage of my bloodline with my life. Princess Valentina has committed an act of treason, punishable by arrest and subject to a full trial and persecution if found guilty. I am willing to forgo her arrest if she agrees to and signs the annulment papers before being deported back to her own country for good. The required paternity test will be performed after her child's birth, to clear up the matter of whose heir it is—or is not—once and for all. Thank you."

No sooner had Sander stepped away

from the podium when he was set upon by a circle of council members, security, his brothers and the King. The camera cut to Valentina, whose guards were helping her to her feet while she wilted and slumped against them, as if Sander had subjected her to a hundred lashes.

As a heated argument broke out, the angle switched back to the anchors in the newsroom. Everyone was scrambling. Papers were thrust onto the desks of the news people while they fit their ear pieces in and bumbled through an initial reaction of stunned disbelief before picking up the loose threads of an event gone to hell in a hurry.

On her feet, Chey paced, watching the television and biting at the short edge of a nail. She didn't want to see the news anchors in the newsroom, she wanted to see what was going on with Sander and the King. She was sure the rest of the country felt the same.

Recalling a few short cuts and back halls in the castle, Chey made a hasty decision.

Why wait here, when she could listen to the confrontation in person? She would have no trouble staying out of sight with everyone's focus on the impending implosion between Sander and Aksel.

Hurrying to the door, she opened it, looked out into the hall, and left the room when she saw the coast was clear.

Chapter Twenty-Two

Chey heard the shouting long before she reached the shadowy alcove at the end of the narrow corridor leading into the back of the great hall. She recognized Sander's voice, and Aksel's, and even Paavo's. Ducking behind the seven foot high potted plant covering half the hidden spot, she pressed close to the wall, obscured by the fronds and gloom. Around the corner, in the immense room, the men raged at each other.

It was only then that she realized the shouting match was in the Latvalan tongue.

Damn.

Sometimes, however, English was spoken as much as the other, so she remained, desperate to catch snippets of conversation. Obviously, Aksel was furious with Sander for outing Valentina in such a blunt manner. The woman's fate would race around the country, then to other countries, and onto international magazines that would slander her up one side and down the other.

Chey wished she could feel sorry for the woman who was supposed to be so cunningly sly and sharp. Valentina should have known better than to crow about her triumph in a crowd of people. She should have thought twice before attempting to pass off the child she carried as someone else's. With a sudden turn, Aksel switched to English, his anger such that his words clipped out one on top of the other.

"No! The damage is done! You have no idea what hell you have just unleashed on the Princess, or her people, or even your *own* people! You would deny your own child simply to--"

"That is not my child!" Sander raged. "You believe her lies over your own son? She carries another man's seed and has used your own gullibility against you. Would you have a stranger from another land take the throne, change all we have worked for, bled for? I will not have it!"

"This is about payback. This...this is incredibly selfish and beneath you. Over a girl! A foreigner who would have wrecked you for this country you seem so bent on protecting. Enough!" Aksel raised his voice to be heard over Sander.

Chey covered a gasp with her fingertips. The King was referring to her. *She* was the foreigner he mentioned.

"What you should have done," Sander said, lowering his voice to a menacing growl. "Was be there for me. Supported me, supported her."

"What I should have done was killed her when I had the chance," the King snarled. The sound of his boots cracked over the stone floor as if he'd taken to pacing.

Chey's stomach tightened. Aksel's intentions for her had never been good, and she wondered if the King would secretly send someone after her, just to make sure Sander could not reconnect now that Valentina was out of the way. Or, conversely, to teach Sander a lesson. The King had hinted at it down in the dungeon.

No wonder Sander has been so bent on bringing her home with him that day.

Silence stretched through the great room. Chey hated that she couldn't see what the men were doing. She dared not leave the niche to peek around the corner, however. Anyone might see.

"Here is what will happen now," Sander

said, a tight edge to his voice. "If you do not back down, call off your dogs, I *will* out you to our people the same way I outed Valentina. They will know you conspired with her, against your own son, all for whatever cheap agenda you plotted between you. I don't care what political achievements you thought this would bring you, or the country, but I'm saying right now that Latvala doesn't need it. We're self sufficient, we have good allies and prosperous citizens. To begin engaging in the skirmishes in nearby countries will only bring heartache and harm to our borders. Until it is absolutely necessary, this country won't be lending military support to anyone else. And *when* I take a wife, she will be one of my own choosing, whom I believe will be an asset rather than someone hell bent on bringing change at the cost of our bloodline."

"I could have you arrested for treason--" Aksel didn't get his entire threat out before Sander cut him off.

"But you won't. Because I've set up a system. If I go to jail, or am suddenly arrested, the tapes will be released to the public via an alternate route. All you have to do is turn your back on this whole thing," Sander said. "Pretend you knew nothing about Valentina's duplicity to the public, I don't care. Perpetrate your lies. Rule your Kingdom as you have been. I will keep the information private and we will all continue on our path until I ascend the throne you have just officially promised me."

Chey exhaled a quiet breath. Sander was putting everything on the line. As he'd said he would. In her defense, in his own defense, and in a bid to protect the public from the likes of scheming Valentina. Minutes later, when Aksel replied, he sounded almost *too* agreeable to Chey's ears.

"If this is the only way, so be it. I have misjudged you, Sander. I knew you had the capacity to be ruthless, but I never dreamed I would see the day you unleashed it on your own family. Mark my words: I will be watching. Waiting. The very second you screw up, I will invoke my right to strip you of the power to ascend in my wake. Mattias, prepare yourself. I never thought I would live to say this, but it appears the second in line may yet be King." Aksel's boots thudded over the stone floor with a crack of finality.

Chey wondered at the switch from giving Paavo the official title back to Mattias. Perhaps the King, in his desperation, decided to fall back on the more apparent heir. Paavo had been a good choice under the former circumstances; Mattias must be the best under these.

She heard the group disperse. The Queen, who had been weirdly silent, began murmuring urgently though Chey could not make out her words. The scuff of boot falls came closer, approaching the narrow corridor harboring the spot Chey hid in. She hunkered deeper into the shadow, fearful they were Aksel's men who could somehow see around corners and into the darkness, and knew she'd been hiding there, listening.

The guards walked right by. Neither checked the alcove, nor so much as glanced her way. Chey saw they were Sander's men anyway, not Aksel's. Releasing a pent up breath, she waited until no more sounds came from the great hall before slipping away from her hidey hole. She wanted to get back up to Sander's suite lest he find her missing from the other room, as well as his, and thought his father had found her.

. . .

On her way back to the suite, Chey
wondered, not for the first time, what her
future would be like in Latvala. She was
in love with Sander, no doubt about it,
and unless she missed her guess, he was
well on the way to being in love with her,
too.

Would they be allowed by the council
to take things further? Once this current
turmoil passed, would Aksel and Helina
turn the other cheek and say nothing
when Sander publicly brought her back
into his life?

Once upon a time, Chey thought she
couldn't handle the strain and tension
surrounding Royalty. The subterfuge,
secrets and deception were difficult to
deal with, never mind the blatant danger.

Now, there was no way she would
willingly leave Sander's side. Even if it
meant years of strife dealing with his
family, or always having to look over her
shoulder. She would find a way to have
happiness amidst the ranks. Perhaps she
would have to make her own ways to

protect herself, obtain knowledge that would keep the hounds at bay.

Now you sound just like them, planning and plotting. Chey pressed her lips together when the thought made itself known. Yes, she did sound like Natalia or Helina. What other choice did she have? This was her life she was talking about, and they obviously had no compunction about taking it. Ending it.

Chey would not roll over and die so easily.

Opening the door to Sander's suite, she stepped inside and closed it behind her.

"I was just about to send a search party," Sander said. "Where were you?"

Chey whirled, surprised he had beat her up here. Sander stood next to Mattias; both men had drinks in their hands.

"Mattias," she said in greeting, stepping away from the door. Lifting her chin, she decided to be up front with Sander. "I couldn't help it. I wanted to know what was happening, so I crept down that one back hallway and listened around the corner in the great hall."

Sander snorted. He looked her over, head to toe, dark amusement gleaming in his eyes. "So you *are* an eavesdropper after all."

Mattias laughed regardless of the tense situation and took a drink. "Chey," he finally said. "Did you glean anything useful?"

She walked across the room, closing the distance, relieved neither one seemed angry about her breech in protocol. A girl had to do what she had to do.

"Yes. Do you think the King will back down, now? Will he relent, go back to ruling like you suggested, Sander, and let this drop?" Chey, momentarily overwhelmed at the picture the two Royals made in their military finery, stopped next to a divan and leaned her hip against it. She had that creeping sensation of being out of her element again and attempted to ignore it. Anyone would feel the same, she argued with herself, faced with such a sight. Both Princes wore a mantle of impenetrable intensity that betrayed their attempt at neutral banter.

Sander glanced down into his glass. Gave it a swirl. "All we can do is wait and see. Time will tell what his motives are, or will be."

"Sander has the upper hand for now," Mattias added. He finished off what was in his tumbler and slid it to a side table.

"Won't this cause a lot of dissension in your family? I mean—you just threatened your father with blackmail. I guess I don't understand. I thought you all worked together, that everyone was on the same page," she said, needing clarification.

"There has been dissension for a long time, Chey. This is the way of it. If it doesn't come from within, it comes from without. The King overstepped, put the people of Latvala in jeopardy. He might be our father, but neither Sander nor I will stand back and be a witness or a party to someone not an Ahtissari taking the throne," Mattias said. He slid his hands into the pockets of his uniform trousers.

"He drew the line in the sand, Chey, not us. I would not turn my back on my own heir simply because I wasn't in love with its mother. He chose to be blind about it, chose to believe Valentina. He'll have time to rethink his situation. His time as ruler nears an end. The next generation is ready to ascend. What kind of leaders would we be if we didn't step up when it mattered?" Sander finished off his drink and slid the glass down next to Mattias's.

Glancing between them, Chey

considered their replies. "I guess. It just seems so drastic. He's your father--"

"Yes, our father. A King. But he's not infallible, Chey. When I take the throne, and if the time comes that I make a poor decision that might put the country in jeopardy, I expect Mattias to rise to the occasion and set things straight. It's how it goes. Sometimes the power goes to their head," Sander said, muttering the last.

Chey wondered if, someday, the power would go to Sander's head. He was so centered, so self-efficient. She couldn't picture him making such an obviously wrong decision.

"I see. I'm glad it appears to have all gone your way for now. How long until the full effect of the fallout shows up?" she asked.

"Could be tomorrow, could be several days," Sander said. "We'll keep a low profile here for the next few weeks, see how it shakes out. I won't feel comfortable bringing you out into the open until some of the media frenzy dies down."

"Yes, it's better to keep a lid on it for now," Mattias agreed, glancing between Sander and Chey.

"I don't mind. My things should be arriving from Seattle soon anyway.

Organizing all that will keep me busy."

"That and the holidays are coming. I would have preferred to take you somewhere—skiing in the Alps perhaps—but again, I don't trust other people to keep their mouths shut this close to a scandal. We'll celebrate here." Sander reached up to begin undoing the buttons of his jacket.

"Here is fine. Here is more than fine," Chey said, stepping forward to help Sander with the buttons. Her fingers were deft on the metal, sliding them through their respective holes. She glanced up to see his eyes. Sander stared down at her, a pensive, thoughtful look on his face.

"While you two make plans, I'm going to head back to the castle, keep an eye on things," Mattias said. He strolled for the door.

"See you later, Mattias," Chey said.

The door opened and closed with a quiet click.

"Are you all right?" Chey asked Sander. She peeled the uniform jacket from his broad shoulders and hung it off the back of a nearby chair for now. It left him in a pull over shirt of white that he tugged off after, revealing a swath of golden skin.

"I will be. Are *you?*" he asked, following

355

her with his eyes.

"It's an adjustment. One I'm willing to make. Like we've said, we knew this wouldn't be easy." Chey approached him from behind and fanned her fingertips over the hard muscles of his back. Every time he moved, the sinew shifted under his skin.

"Good. You'll need a tough exterior to deal with all this."

"I'll do whatever it takes." Chey realized then that truer words had never been spoken. She *would* do whatever it took to make it work. Dealing with threats, family trauma, Royal decrees and manipulative plots be damned.

Chapter Twenty-Three

By five a.m. the next morning, news of Sander's public address had spread worldwide. From a borrowed laptop, sitting in bed, Chey surfed the internet to see what people were saying. She found it incredible that there could be so many articles published in such a short amount of time. Most of the opinion pieces slanted in Sander's favor, stating in general that any woman who would try and trap a man with someone else's child, especially a member of Royalty, got what she deserved.

In this case, the criticism of Valentina was harsh. There were a few photos of the Princess skulking from a helicopter to a waiting sedan, head buried inside the hood of a coat so that her features were obscured by shadow. Weithan Isle itself suffered scathing commentary, and some reporters conjectured whether this incident would put a dent in the status of allies between the two countries.

A handful of reporters came down hard on Sander for choosing such a public delivery to end his marriage. Overall, it appeared most had sympathy in spades for the upcoming King. The attempt for a foreigner to try and seat a bastard on the throne was not looked kindly upon.

Later in the day, Aksel sent a written speech to the television stations where it was read by the anchors on the evening news. As everyone close to the event suspected, Aksel pretended to be shocked that Valentina would stoop to that level, and more, that he had supported her while she betrayed him and lied about her pregnancy. He expressed his pride in his son for ferreting out the truth and preventing someone not of their bloodline to ascend the throne.

All in all, Chey wasn't that surprised. She nibbled toast and fruit for breakfast while Sander flew across to the mainland to attend emergency meetings with legislators and advisers.

After lunch, she shut off all television, closed the laptop, and got to work unpacking the first of three boxes that had arrived from Seattle. Wynn had enclosed a note with Chey's most precious belongings.

C,

I hope you know what you're doing. If you need anything at all, call me. I'm dying to know what's going on, so let me know asap. Okay? Don't worry about your stuff. I know what to send and what to put away in storage. Soon as we can exchange email or phone numbers, contact me.

W.

Chey smiled and folded the note away with her things.

If she had her way, the only time she would be returning to Seattle was for random visits.

Latvala was her home now and this is where she intended to stay.

. . .

The weeks between the announcement and the Christmas Holiday passed in a blur. Chey filled her down time learning every nook and cranny of Kallaster Castle, decorating for the season, and taking pictures as winter gripped the landscape. She thoroughly enjoyed walking the half moon bay in snow boots and a heavy parka, camera around her neck, snapping shots of whitecaps over a slate gray sea with snow laden trees stretching inland from the shore.

While Sander was home, she spent her time with him. They ate late dinners before the fireplace, talked about his day on the mainland, and lost themselves in each other when desire flared bright and hot between them. Sander's affections were as intense as they had ever been, with bursts of possession that left her gasping his name.

Five days before Christmas, during a lull in storms, Sander stole Chey away from the castle and flew them to Estonia for a whirlwind shopping trip. They took only two security members who dressed down like they did, all the better to blend in with the crowds.

From a huge mall to smaller shops, Sander whisked her around a decadent commercial district until, exhausted and loaded with bags, they returned to the island. Sander had encouraged her to stock up on things she might need, from clothes to shoes to dresses and heavier winter clothes than she currently owned.

She did not disappoint. It had been fun, even, to shop with abandon, although she discreetly checked price tags because it was ingrained in her DNA to search out sales. Several items were for Sander for Christmas, one for Mattias and still another for Mira. Something small but useful.

On Christmas Eve, Chey dressed carefully in a red gown that hugged her curves through the torso and flared out around her ankles. Wearing the diamonds Sander had bought what felt like a lifetime ago, she styled her hair into a coif of messy curls, leaving several strands to brush against her shoulders. Make up made her eyes dramatic, accentuated her cheekbones, and highlighted her lips.

She left the suite with a small gift in her hands, the one gift they promised each other they would open after a mysterious dinner Sander had arranged. The halls, banisters, ledges, tables and floors all sported some kind of decoration: ornamental swags, lighted garland strands, twinkle-lights, pine wreaths, figurines, Santas and an enormous tree that Sander brought in and placed in the center of the foyer. Chey had decorated it all, with Mira's help, and the effect was pleasing against the medieval castle backdrop.

Descending the stairs, she veered through the foyer, of which the lights had all been set to dim, and followed the archway into the large dining hall. She stopped when she saw Sander standing next to the elaborately laid table. He wore his military uniform, the navy blue with a silver and red sash, silver metal buttons and the belt with a sword attached.

What was going on? Was he leaving for some tour of duty, and chose tonight to tell her?

Stomach clenching uncomfortably, Chey approached the table, gaining his attention when she cleared her throat.

Sander glanced away from the window and raked her with a bold stare. His eyes lingered on the low cut of the bodice, the narrow nip of her waist, and the swirling hem at her feet.

"You look lovely," he said, stepping away from the table. Two settings of China with gold inlay were positioned over Christmas themed mats of green with gold leafing around the edges. Candles flickered next to crystal glasses and a bucket of wine chilled to the side. The scent of food protected by covered silver platters wafted through the air, vying with pine and that of Sander's masculine cologne.

"Thank you. You're...in your uniform," she pointed out needlessly. Chey set his gift down at the corner of the table, out of the way of the dinner arrangement.

"Yes, I am." He stepped closer, one hand resting on the curve of her hip.

Chey looked up into his eyes, attempting to figure out what he was about to tell her. The hair prickled on the back of her neck when a fit of nerves hit. Did he have bad news? Was it his father? Had Aksel regained the upper hand?

Good grief—was she going back to Seattle?

"Are you being sent off somewhere?" she blurted, unable to keep quiet any longer. If it was bad news, she wanted it now.

Sander only curled a faint half smile for her question, which sent alarm bells clanging in Chey's head. Oh no. Just when she'd come to terms with Royalty, when she'd decided she would do anything and everything to stay. Now that she was in love, had moved across the world in secret, he was about to drop a bomb that would shatter her.

Taking her by the hand, Sander led her away from the dinner table back to the foyer. He walked slow, pacing himself, which just made Chey's heart trip hammer in her chest.

Near the eight foot Christmas tree, he paused. Only the glow from the tree lights and the lighted garland provided illumination, casting the scene into a surreal Holiday setting, reminiscent of a romantic painting.

"You're scaring me," she whispered, staring up at his face.

"You have nothing to be afraid of," he said in a low voice. "I'll be here to protect you, keep you from harm. I have so far, have I not?"

Chey considered it. She was having a hard time concentrating thanks to the fear he was about to depart on some mission in another part of the world. "Yes. Even to the point of tackling me to the ground a time or two."

A rumbling laugh spilled from his lips. "Exactly. So the only other thing," he said, lowering to a knee. He held one of her hands, and produced a box in the other. "Is whether you will do me the honor of becoming my wife. Will you marry me, Chey Sinclair?"

Chey, who had just started to frown when he sank to a knee, suddenly gasped in shock. Her eyes flew from his face to the ornate little box of red and gold. A proposal was the very last thing she expected.

Sander released her fingers and opened the box. Nestled inside, a four carat Princess cut diamond in a platinum setting awaited. Smaller channel set diamonds decorated the band as well as a separate wedding ring to be worn along with it. The stones sparkled and shined in the flickering lights from the tree.

Chey's mind went on the fritz. What a bad time to blank out.

He was asking her to marry him. *Marry* him. Even though she knew it might one day be a possibility, this made everything real. She would sit at his side once he took the throne as his Queen.

It was overwhelming. Awe inspiring. Scary.

Sander knelt there with all the confidence in the world, a Prince on his knees, waiting patiently for her reply.

Chey stuttered, then said, "Yes. *Yes,* I'll marry you, Sander Darrion Ahtissari."

He cut her a roguish grin, took the engagement ring out of the box, and slid it onto her left ring finger. Closing the box, he slid it into his jacket pocket and rose to his feet, wrapping an arm around her waist to bring her against him.

Chey laughed and threw her arms around his neck. "I can't believe we're engaged. How long have you known? When did you plan this?"

He kissed her long and hard, preventing any more questions or answers for several intense minutes. Once he broke the seal of their mouths, he stared down with a gloating kind of expression.

"That's for me to know and you never to find out. A man has to keep *some* secrets," he retorted.

Dazed from the kiss, Chey touched her fingertips to her mouth, then looked at the ring in disbelief. What would the King and Queen say?

"Just how many more secrets do you have?" Chey asked, not above sassing Sander just because he'd proposed on Christmas Eve.

"Probably as many as you," he said with a laugh. He kissed her again, silencing her scoff.

"I don't have any secrets. You know everything about me," she said once she came up for air.

"Oh, I think there is quite a bit more about you I need to learn." He leered playfully.

Chey blushed, getting the hint loud and clear. "You're incorrigible. It's impolite to talk about intimate things right after a proposal."

"Then I guess it's downright inappropriate to do this, too," he said, before swooping down to haul her, in all her finery, into his arms. He carried her like a groom might on his wedding night.

"Sander! What are you—put me down!" A pin fell out of Chey's hair. It landed on the floor. Another fell, and another.

"Afraid you'll lose a glass slipper?" Sander snorted, ignoring her protests. He also ignored the dinner waiting on the table and turned for the stairs instead.

Chey laughed despite herself. "I guess that makes you Prince Charming."

"I guess it does. We have a handful of hours before midnight. Trust that I plan to put them *all* to good use."

. . .

About the Author

Born and raised in Corona California, Danielle now resides in Texas with her husband and two sons. She has been writing for as long as she can remember, penning works in a number of genres. To date, she has published eighteen novels and nine short stories. Her interests vary wildly: reading, traveling, photography, graphic art and baking, among others.

There is a black cat named Sheba involved who thinks Danielle's laptop is her personal grooming station.

Check her website for trading card offers, giveaways and announcements!
www.daniellebourdon.com

More books by Danielle Bourdon:

Newest release(romance):
The Royal Elite: Mattias

Romance:

Heir Untamed (Royals Series 1)
King and Kingdom (Royals Series 2)
Heir in Exile (Royals Series 3)
The King Takes a Bride (Royals Series 4)
The Wrath of the King (Royals Series 5)

Fantasy/Romantic Suspense:
Sin and Sacrifice (Daughters of Eve 1)
Templar's Creed (Daughters of Eve 2)
The Seven Seals (Daughters of Eve 3)

Thriller/Romantic Suspense:
The Society of the Nines (Society Series 1)
Violin Song (Society Series 2)
Vengeance for the Dead (Society Series 3)

Young Adult/Fantasy:

The Fate of Destiny (Fates 1)
The Fate of Chaos (Fates 2)
The Reign of Mayhem (Fates 3)
A Crisis of Fate (Fates 4)

Paranormal Romance:
Bound by Blood

Fantasy:
Dreoteth

Made in the USA
Lexington, KY
26 May 2014